MURDER IN ARLES

BOOK 13 OF THE MAGGIE NEWBERRY MYSTERIES

SUSAN KIERNAN-LEWIS

SAN MARCO PRESS

Books by Susan Kiernan-Lewis

The Maggie Newberry Mysteries

Murder in the South of France
Murder à la Carte
Murder in Provence
Murder in Paris
Murder in Aix
Murder in Nice
Murder in the Latin Quarter
Murder in the Abbey
Murder in the Bistro
Murder in Cannes
Murder in Grenoble
Murder in the Vineyard
Murder in Arles
Murder in Marseille
Murder in St-Rémy
Murder à la Mode
Murder in Avignon
Murder in the Lavender
A Provençal Christmas: A Short Story
A Thanksgiving in Provence
Laurent's Kitchen

An American in Paris Mysteries

Déjà Dead
Death by Cliché
Dying to be French
Ménage à Murder

The Stranded in Provence Mysteries

Parlez-Vous Murder?
Crime and Croissants
Accent on Murder
A Bad Éclair Day
Croak, Monsieur!
Death du Jour
Murder Très Gauche
Wined and Died
A French Country Christmas

The Irish End Games

Free Falling
Going Gone
Heading Home
Blind Sided
Rising Tides
Cold Comfort
Never Never
Wit's End
Dead On
White Out
Black Out
End Game

The Mia Kazmaroff Mysteries

Reckless
Shameless
Breathless
Heartless
Clueless
Ruthless

Ella Out of Time

Swept Away
Carried Away
Stolen Away

The French Women's Diet

1

Maggie surveyed the crimson and bright yellow leaves scattered across the terra cotta pavers of the back terrace of Domaine St-Buvard.

She knew if she opened the French doors that separated her from the terrace and garden she would smell wood smoke and with it the promise of the coming coziness of winter. As long as she had been living at Domaine St-Buvard, winter was always defined by long hours curled up in front of the fire, cashmere throws across her knees, a good book, and a steaming cup of tea at hand.

Even with two children, a thriving Internet business, and an active social schedule, winter always tended to be a time to rest, rebuild, and rejuvenate.

Even Maggie's best friend Grace, who ran a bed and breakfast a few miles away, didn't expect any more bookings for the next five months. Maggie knew Grace would use the time to ramp up renovations on her property. But even for Grace—and Danielle too who Grace now ran the *gîte* with—winter was a time to push the pause button and rest.

Maggie stepped outside, her arms laden with the place

settings for tonight's dinner which they'd eat on the stone table that faced the vineyards. She was sure it would be one of the last meals they'd be able to eat outdoors this year.

A few more leaves scuttled across the tiles of the terrace which was bordered on one side by a walled garden and on the other by their vineyard. The house that Maggie's husband Laurent had inherited ten years earlier, known in the nearby village as Domaine St-Buvard, was a very old stone *mas* situated deep in the heart of Provence.

Originally connected to a small but prime vineyard that Laurent had cultivated for the *vin de pays* he produced, now his land had grown to nearly three hundred hectares.

"You should have Mila do this."

Maggie turned to see her husband standing in the doorway of their *mas*. He was frowning, a wooden spoon held loosely in one hand.

Laurent was six foot five—unusual for a Frenchman—and he used his height alternatingly with moderation and to his advantage.

"I enjoy doing it," Maggie said, feeling a lightness in her limbs as she regarded him. It always surprised her, his effect on her.

In spite of the ten years—and two children—behind them, Laurent could still set her pulse racing with just a glance. What surprised her even more was when she reminded herself that she'd met this mysterious, sexy man when she'd come to France to find the truth about her missing sister while he was in the middle of pulling a con.

On her family.

What Maggie had discovered on that fateful trip eleven years ago was a man who resonated with her on nearly every level and who offered her a life more exciting than she could ever have imagined in her wildest dreams.

"*Chérie*?" Laurent said, a wry smile tugging at his full lips. His hair was brown, thick and he wore it nearly to his shoulders. He was broad shouldered, yet he moved with the grace of a cat.

"I was just thinking," Maggie said, blushing.

He knew his effect on her and she knew enough to know how rare what they had together was.

Not that it had always been easy.

"I sent Mila and Jemmy off to find whatever flowers might be left in the lower garden for the centerpiece," she said.

"Did you remind Mila to feed the goat?"

Two months ago their eight-year old daughter had begged them for the little goat and in a moment of weakness they'd relented on the condition that she take care of it.

Meanwhile Maggie was becoming proficient in feeding and tending to an energetic and very naughty twenty-two-pound goat.

"You are too indulgent with them," Laurent said, joining her on the terrace.

Maggie knew Laurent's own childhood had not been a pleasant one, although in many respects it had been privileged. He'd lost his parents early and had been raised by a wealthy elderly grandmother who had too many ghosts to chase to give much thought to Laurent and his younger brother Gerard.

In Gerard's case, the old woman's ambivalence had triggered the beginning of the end.

"You're only a child once," Maggie said. She wasn't the disciplinarian in the family. That would be Laurent. The kids knew it too. They moved easily around Maggie, manipulating her at will. But they were sweet children, compliant and unspoiled—largely thanks to Laurent.

Laurent slipped an arm around Maggie's waist and drew her to him. She turned on tiptoe to kiss him. He smelled like lemons and rosemary. A tinge of smoke clung to his hair and his lips were cool.

"Will you set the braziers up?" Maggie said. "It's getting colder."

Their dinner guest tonight was Danielle Alexandre, their neighbor and the widow of their beloved Jean-Luc who'd passed away the summer before.

Laurent turned to regard the table as if seeing it for the first time.

Maggie suddenly knew it was already too cold to be eating outdoors.

"Should we move things inside?" she asked.

"*Non*," he said, running a hand down her back and then stepping over to where the braziers sat by the side of the house. "Danielle will prefer to eat on the terrace."

The sounds of childish laughter tumbled down the garden path and Maggie turned toward the vineyard. The light was just fading to a soft dark blue. She saw the dogs first, bounding up the pathway toward the house.

"Mila?" Maggie called.

Both children appeared from the bottom of the garden. Ten year old Jemmy was the eldest. He arrived with his face flushed, his eyes glittering with merriment in the aftermath of their footrace. Clutched in his fist were several stems of bedraggled zinnias. Mila hurried behind him. With her blonde hair, she looked like she was glowing in the dusk.

Mila ran immediately to Laurent and although she was too old for it, he scooped her up and held her in one arm.

Now who's indulgent? Maggie thought with a smile.

But the rules didn't often apply to Mila. At least not where Laurent was concerned. He was much harder on Jemmy but there was little that Maggie could do about that. Laurent was chauvinistic and his expectations for his first-born son were different than for his princess. The fact that Mila was feminine as well as beautiful only underscored her irrefutable role to her father.

"Jemmy," Laurent said, kissing Mila and setting her down. "Position the braziers near the table."

Mila came to Maggie to show her the flowers she held—none

of which had an intact stem to support it in a vase. Maggie took them from her and put a hand on her hair.

"Go wash your hands, sweetie," Maggie said before turning to Jemmy who was attempting to position one of the bulky braziers.

"Laurent, he's too small to do that," she said.

"No, I'm not!" Jemmy said hotly and tugged harder on the brazier. Laurent shot a hand out to keep the tall heater from crashing to the stone pavers of the terrace.

That was my fault, Maggie thought as she bit her lip. *I should have just let him get on with it especially since Laurent was clearly watching out for him.*

"Perhaps your mother is right," Laurent said. "Go to the kitchen and start chopping the garlic."

Jemmy flushed angrily and turned to leave. Laurent's hand came down firmly on his son's shoulder and Jemmy froze. After the briefest of moments, Jemmy nodded.

Laurent released him and watched him go inside.

"Why didn't you give him a second chance with the braziers?" Maggie asked.

"Because this way he'll remember what happened when he let his temper get the better of him."

"I don't want him hiding his emotions, Laurent."

Laurent moved the two braziers into place and said nothing.

"Laurent?"

"I heard you, *chérie*. Don't you think you should dress? Danielle will be here any minute."

Maggie knew Laurent was not going to discuss with her how to handle Jemmy. She'd learned that from long experience.

And as for teaching the boy to hide his emotions, well, she also knew that that was something that Laurent frankly saw great merit in.

2

Dinner was *coq au vin* with individual artichoke soufflés. The meal was mostly quiet amidst the evening sounds of the vineyard and the garden—the far off barking of the neighbors' dogs and the rush of the wind among the trees.

Once the last course was served and eaten the children were excused to clear the table and go do their homework.

Maggie couldn't help but wonder if on her own she would have insisted on such perfect table manners. But for a traditional Frenchman—which in so many ways Laurent was— there was no other way. His children would be obedient, silent and well-behaved especially at the dining table.

"Mila and Jemmy are perfection as usual," Danielle said fondly as she watched the two children scamper into the house. "They will give you great comfort when you are my age."

A spasm of pain throbbed in Maggie's heart. She'd always felt sorry for the fact that Danielle and her first husband Eduard had not had children. By the time Danielle had married Jean-Luc it was too late.

Maggie leaned across the table and touched Danielle's hand. The older woman looked tired tonight, Maggie realized. It had been a hard year for Danielle—not the least of which was trying to learn to live without Jean-Luc.

While Danielle now kept busy working with Grace at *Dormir*, Grace's *gîte*, she obviously had many a lonely night to remember and miss her soulmate.

A chill breeze came down through the dogwoods that bordered the terrace, rattling the branches, the leaves long since gone, and flapped the cotton tablecloth. Maggie shivered as an image of the *mistral* darting through Provence formed in her head.

Laurent had gone to oversee the children's chores and activities and came back now with a tray holding three heavy cut crystal glasses and a decanter of Calvados.

"You will stay the night, Danielle?" he said.

Even though it was phrased as a question, Laurent didn't look at Danielle for her answer. Maggie knew he would insist she stay.

Maggie always marveled at how expertly Laurent was able to size up any given situation. It was probably what had made him such a good con artist, she thought wryly. He would know, of course, that—with the constant hum of children in the background—Danielle would naturally prefer to stay the night at Domaine St-Buvard than go back to her quiet room at Grace's.

"*Oui, Laurent. Merci*," Danielle said.

Maggie leaned back in her chair and surveyed the table—a pleasant *tableau* of glasses showing varying depths of wine or water, and flickering candles. She glanced at Laurent at the end of the table as he poured the drinks. He looked relaxed although Maggie, of all people, knew how deceptive *that* appearance could be.

Laurent had lost a dear friend when he lost Jean-Luc—the closest thing to a father he'd ever known. And like Danielle, going on without Jean-Luc was often a struggle. Just thinking of Jean-Luc with his wool tweed cap set jauntily on the back of his head, his blue eyes twinkling and the delight he took in playing *Papère* to Jemmy and Mila brought tears to Maggie's eyes.

"How are your dear parents, *chérie*?" Danielle asked as she accepted the glass of brandy from Laurent.

Assuming Danielle had mistaken her emotion for worry over her parents, Maggie smiled reassuringly at her.

"They're good," Maggie said. "I talk to my mother nearly every day. And my dad is doing fine."

After six months of living at Domaine St-Buvard with Maggie's increasingly deteriorating father, Elspeth Newberry gave in to Maggie's brother Ben who insisted they return to Atlanta where he could be more involved.

Naturally, Maggie thought, her back stiffening with resentment, Ben had been largely unavailable to her parents once they moved back—as she knew he would be—but her mother wouldn't hear any criticism of her brother. With Ben's marginal help they'd eventually sold the family house in Buckhead—long past time Maggie had to admit—and moved her mother and Maggie's niece Nicole to a condo near Nicole's high school. Maggie's father moved into a nearby memory care facility.

All neat and tidy.

Maggie's heart sank every time she thought of them all.

"I'm sure you miss them very much," Danielle said.

Maggie smiled. "I do, of course."

And that was true. Except for the times when she felt a wave of relief not to have to be the one to try to solve her parents' problems at any time of the day or night.

It had been easier for Maggie when her parents came to live at Domaine St-Buvard last year. Laurent had a good relationship with her father. Foggy-headed or not—her dad tended to respond with more lucidity when Laurent was around directing things.

Maggie smiled as she watched her husband as he frowned at the color of the brandy in his goblet.

Directing things was by and large the very definition of

Laurent. Whether in his kitchen, his vineyard, with his children, or at the nearby monastery *l'Abbaye de Sainte-Trinité* where he had created temporary housing for transient vineyard workers, Laurent was always a leader.

He didn't defer easily or often.

Or ever.

"And *les enfants*?" Danielle said relaxing into her chair with her brandy, her eyes closing contentedly.

Maggie watched Laurent gather up dishes and disappear into the kitchen. It was hard for him to sit still. There was always something to do, something to arrange, people to sort out. When Laurent entered the house, she heard Jemmy's voice in the kitchen as if in protest and she imagined Laurent had come upon the child doing something he shouldn't.

"They're good," Maggie said. "Mila's goat is turning into a pain but I suppose that's all part of raising kids. Hey, I made a joke! Might not translate, though."

"I understood it, *chérie*. Very amusing."

Ever since Danielle had moved to *Dormir* with Grace and Grace's teenage daughter Zouzou, Maggie and Laurent had seen much less of her than when she had lived closer. But the extra work was good for Danielle and kept her occupied. As happy as Danielle had been with Jean-Luc, being productive and feeling useful wasn't something that had been a big part of her life until now.

Danielle had seamlessly integrated into the little family at *Dormir* and provided a level of stability and maturity that Grace desperately needed. Even Grace often remarked that she had no idea how she'd managed before Danielle came to live with them.

Although the door to the house had closed, Jemmy's voice was louder now and more insistent. That was surprising since Laurent rarely brooked disagreement with his various edicts.

"Jemmy is growing up," Danielle noted.

She sees it too.

"I feel like he's a little ahead of schedule," Maggie said, glancing through the French doors. She could see Laurent's shadow—big and imposing—as he stood with his hands on hips looking down at his first-born who just as clearly was standing up to him.

"How so?" Danielle asked.

"He doesn't seem as compliant as he was a few months ago. He argues with me now."

"Ah."

"And Laurent too."

Danielle glanced toward the house and sipped her drink.

"He is his father's son."

Maggie laughed. "I'll tell Laurent you said so. I'm sure that'll make him feel loads better."

"Grace tells me that Jemmy's school wants to advance him an extra grade next year?"

Maggie sighed. It certainly wasn't a secret but she was sorry to be reminded of the issue on an evening when she'd nearly managed to ignore the stress and strains of the week.

"We all knew he was smart," Danielle said.

"Too smart," Maggie said. "I'm not sure putting him in classes with kids a whole year older is a good idea."

"Why not? Zouzou tells me Jemmy only plays with the older children as it is."

"That's just what I'm talking about. I want him playing with kids his own age."

"Jemmy is the best judge of that, surely?"

"He's ten years old, Danielle. He's not the best judge of what socks to put on in the morning. And yesterday he took the dogs to the village—and forgot them there!"

"So what is the answer?"

"I don't know. I want to homeschool him. Laurent wants him advanced."

"What does Jemmy want?"

"Danielle, I'm surprised to hear you even ask! I thought the French thought we Americans were too indulgent with our children. Would *your* parents have asked your vote on how you were schooled?"

"I was not as clever as Jemmy."

"Again, I'm not convinced that's a good thing."

That night as Maggie and Laurent were turning in for the night, Maggie leaned over in bed and touched his shoulder.

"What was all that between you and Jemmy tonight?" she asked.

"It was nothing. The light, *chérie*?"

"It didn't sound like nothing. Was he being disobedient?"

"*Non*. He just had a ...question."

"What was the question?"

Laurent sighed heavily and turned to Maggie and pulled her toward him with one arm while with the other hand he reached over and turned out the bedside lamp.

"It was just a question between fathers and sons," he said enigmatically, kissing her on the forehead.

Maggie knew she wouldn't get anything more definitive out of him. And perhaps that was for the best.

"It was a nice night," Maggie said as she settled in his arms.

Through the brief fluttering of the curtains at the window she could see the moon and imagined how it must be illuminating their vineyard below. She shivered for some reason.

"Danielle seems happy," Laurent said.

"I really think she is."

The fact that Laurent hadn't turned over to settle into sleep told Maggie that he was still thinking about something. She watched the moon and waited, enjoying the security of his arms.

"You are worried about your papa?" he asked quietly.

Maggie smiled in the darkness, feeling her heart fill with love for her husband. He had so much to do, so many people to worry about and care for.

"Him and everyone else," she said.

"That is a lot of worrying," Laurent said giving her a final kiss before turning away and falling almost immediately asleep.

It always amazed Maggie that a man who'd lived so many years on the edge—barely out of the reach of the police at any given moment, hardly able to trust even his own compatriots and partners in crime, who constantly measured and weighed the odds of catastrophe against the risks necessary for possible gain, not to mention the nefarious things he'd done in his life that Maggie *didn't* know about—that he could fall asleep so easily and sleep so soundly.

She continued to watch the moon until a veil of dark clouds stole across its face, easing her and her world into darkness.

3

Grace watched the leaves scuttle across the back patio. She pulled her cashmere scarf tighter around her throat and set her mug of coffee down on the stone wall that separated the patio terrace from the flower garden.

She made a mental note to make sure that Gabriel her handy man had put the manure in the proper places yesterday but decided she had a moment to indulge in a quick moment of peace and reflection.

Danielle had texted the night before to say she would spend the night at Domaine St-Buvard, as Grace had assumed she would. It was the first time in nearly nine months since Danielle had come to live with them that she'd not spent the night at *Dormir*. Grace was surprised to realize how much she missed waking up to the older woman's presence in the kitchen.

Over the months they'd quickly gotten into the habit of enjoying their morning coffee together at the big farmhouse table in the kitchen, going over the things that needed to be done that day—who would run into Aix to pick up Zouzou after school—what groceries needed to be shopped for, what extra-special meals needed to be planned.

Because make no mistake, people coming to a bed and breakfast in France expect amazing food.

Ironically the one thing Grace hadn't taken into account when she deliriously threw her arms around Laurent's neck eighteen months ago when he'd told her about his idea for creating *Dormir* was that cooking sumptuous meals would reasonably be a part of the plan.

Not a cook herself (she'd had maids and cooks her whole life until recently), Grace had simply focused on making *Dormir* the quintessential luxury vacation stay exemplifying the best of the south of France. She filled the *gîte* with original local artwork, six-hundred thread count sheets, fresh flowers in every room, aromatherapy of rosemary, roses, lavender and eucalyptus, and plate after hand-painted plate of fresh pastries from Bedard's Patisserie in Aix.

For the first three months she'd managed by buying takeout in Aix and arranging the meals on colorful faience and casseroles or badgering Laurent to make triple his usual amounts when he cooked at Domaine St-Buvard.

But when Danielle moved in after Jean-Luc's death, *Dormir* became what Grace had always envisioned it to be.

Perfectly French in every perfect way.

Grace left her coffee cup on the stone wall and moved to the end of the terrace walkway to get a better view of the vineyard that surrounded the property.

Dormir had once been a fine *mas* rising among a field of vineyards, the stately home for generations of *vignerons* that only a few in St-Buvard even remembered now. After the last world war the owner of the house never returned from the German prisoner of war camp where he'd spent the war. His wife and two children moved to Paris where she had family. Eventually the son sold the house to Eduard Marceau from Dijon who envisioned becoming a major winegrower in the area.

Thirty years after moving to the *mas* with Danielle, Eduard was childless and bitter about the fact. Never fully accepted by the villagers who viewed him as an outsider, Eduard decided that the answer to his problems might be the expansion of his grape empire. This had been a reasonable assumption since there were two large tracts of vineyard that abutted his own.

One was seventy-five hectares and owned by Jean-Luc Alexandre, a bachelor and brother of the notorious Resistance hero Patrick Alexandre. Jean-Luc's land had been owned by the Alexandre family for generations.

The other piece of land was owned by Nicolas Dernier of Paris. Monsieur Dernier was unmarried and when he died, his land passed to his nephew Laurent Dernier.

Unfortunately it was this event that would be the undoing of Eduard.

Since there were no children from their union, when Eduard died last year his land passed to Danielle who had by then married Jean-Luc. Danielle promptly sold both the house and land to Laurent.

The property was renovated to include two small mini-cottages, updated plumping, a new kitchen and a small swimming pool under the plane trees that at one time shaded the empty terrace of an unhappy woman and her vitriolic husband.

Sometimes when Grace was doing some endlessly tedious chore, like polishing the door knobs or beating bedroom rugs on the clothesline, she would catch sight of Danielle weeding the flower garden or raking the front gravel driveway and she would marvel at the fact that Danielle lived in this very house as its mistress for over thirty years.

There was no doubt that they were thirty miserable years.

Grace sometimes caught Danielle working in the kitchen—a kitchen that had been her own just a decade ago—making *pâte à choux* with Zouzou and Mila, their laughter spiraling up and throughout the house.

During those years when Danielle had been virtually imprisoned in the house by Eduard's pride and spite, had it been beyond imagining that someday she might create a life surrounded by people who loved her?

Grace smiled as she remembered the day Laurent made the offer to her: *Come back to France with Zouzou and work the gîte.* He would own it but she would run it. It would allow her to support herself and Zouzou and to remain in the country where she'd discovered she was happiest.

It was the saving of her. No doubt about it.

Amongst the amalgamated scents of wood smoke and the crisp autumn air, Grace could smell the overripe scent of fallen apples from the two ancient trees in the southern corner of the flower garden. Danielle and Zouzou had collected those apples for weeks at the start of the season and made *tartes Tatin*, apple tarts, apple fritters, and apple chutney. From now on until the day she died, Grace was pretty sure autumn would always smell to her like the kitchen of *Dormir* in October with the scent of baking or caramelizing apples and cinnamon wafting through the house.

More importantly, Grace thought with a smile, she had given the gift of that memory to Zouzou too,

The wind whistled gently overhead and Grace looked up in time to see a squadron of geese making its way south. She watched for a moment and wondered when in her entire life she'd taken so much pleasure just from looking up at the sky.

Her reverie was broken by the approaching purr of a motorbike. She glanced at her watch.

They'd said goodbye to their last guests of the season last week and Grace was looking forward to months to retool, regroup, and refresh. So far, the few bookings Grace had managed were just enough to support the next bookings. Grace hated the fact that she had yet to break even on *Dormir* but Laurent wasn't worried and so she tried not to be.

The motorbike's engine shut off abruptly at the front of the house. Brad was earlier than he'd said he'd come over but he'd been coming earlier and earlier. Grace knew he wanted to move in with her and God knows they had plenty of room, especially in the winter with six hand-curated, artfully designed and fastidiously furnished bedrooms among three cottages and only she, Zouzou and Danielle living there.

She picked up her coffee mug and made her way across the terrace to the gate that led to the front of the house, hurrying to get to the front before he knocked on the door and woke Zouzou. It was Saturday and one of the few days Grace didn't have to drag the child moaning and protesting from her bed to go to school.

Grace shut the gate behind her and walked quickly around the house in time to see Brad pulling off his helmet and running his hands through his hair. He had thick auburn hair and a close-cut ginger beard that served to showcase his cheekbones and full lips.

He was handsome of course. Grace hadn't yet graduated to a point of maturity where she could date a homely man no matter how charming or witty. And as Maggie had once teased her: *you know what you have to put up with to get a good-looking guy, right?*

All joking aside, there was some truth to that. A balding, pudgy man would not be as comfortable nagging her to let him move in. He'd be more inclined to be content.

"Good morning!" Brad called to her, his face crinkling into a smile as she walked toward him.

American, living in Aix at the Hotel Cezanne, he was supposedly writing a murder mystery although Grace had yet to see any evidence of any actual writing. She had not raised the question of *where* he got the money to allow him to live in Aix although Laurent had asked her about it no fewer than three times already.

She knew Laurent was protective of her and he knew her track record—with the possible exception of Windsor—was less than reassuring. She still cringed at the memory of Laurent carrying her screaming over his shoulder out of a Paris bistro three years ago in order to prevent her from making a further fool of herself over a man she never should have trusted in the first place.

She went to give Brad a quick kiss and then turned to let them in through the front door.

"You're early," she said.

"Well, I'm excited to see Arles. I've only been there once on a bus tour."

They were to pick up Maggie and Jemmy later that morning in order to attend a massive *brocante* taking place within the city's famed amphitheater. Danielle would bring Mila home later this morning where they would spend the day baking with Zouzou—something both girls and Danielle loved to do.

"You've probably already seen the best bits," Grace said as they entered the house. She worked to tamp down a flash of annoyance. She'd been hoping to have time to dress and relax before her day began.

"There's coffee in the kitchen," she said.

"Are you cross with me, darling?" Brad asked, stopping in the foyer and affecting a small pout.

Grace turned to him. "No, of course not." She smiled and gave him another kiss. "I can make some eggs if you like?"

He grinned. "That'd be great. I'm starving."

Grace went into the kitchen and pulled out the eggs from the refrigerator.

Zouzou would probably love it if Brad moved in, Grace thought. He always made her laugh. And she was sure Danielle wouldn't care. Ever since Jean-Luc died Danielle pretty much tended toward the philosophy of the more the merrier.

So why was Grace hesitating?

4

Unlike anyone else's family that Maggie had ever heard of, Saturday mornings tended to be even more chaotic than weekdays at Domaine St-Buvard. She wasn't sure why that was, since the kids were usually glued in front of cartoons on the TV set on Saturday mornings.

Now that she thought of it, maybe it was the cartoon soundtrack that seemed to give most Saturdays their feeling of barely controlled frenzy.

Laurent always went to the food markets on Saturday—the one in Aix was a given but he had a few others that were special to him in different ways. This one always had the best asparagus, that one had the best tomatoes, another could always be counted on for the first truffles of the season.

Food was important to Laurent and while Maggie had to admit that that focus had succeeded in adding a ten-pound weight gain to her frame since she'd married him, the joy and satisfaction that cooking gave her husband was well worth the price of a slightly larger pants size.

"How long will you be in Arles today?" Laurent asked as he stood in the kitchen glancing at the front page of the local newspaper. Maggie knew Laurent intended to cook something specific for tonight's meal, but he never went out shopping with a list.

"However long it takes Grace to find the perfect washstand for an antique pitcher and bowl she has."

Laurent frowned.

"I'm joking. Sort of," Maggie said. "I really don't know what she's looking for. Probably she doesn't either until she sees it."

"Good morning, *mes infants*," Danielle said as she stepped into the kitchen. Laurent turned to pour her coffee.

"Did you sleep well, Danielle?" Maggie asked.

Before Danielle could answer Mila ran into the room and hugged Danielle around the waist.

"Good morning, *Mamère*!" she said. "What are we making today?"

Mila loved spending her Saturdays baking with Zouzou and Danielle. Zouzou, who had had a weight problem two years ago was now—with Laurent's counsel—not only at a normal weight for her age but had developed a passion for baking. At fourteen, she was already determined to go to the French culinary academy in Paris after high school.

"I don't know, *chérie*," Danielle said, her eyes dancing with pleasure. "How about *macarons*? They are hard to make but I think we are up to the task."

Mila clapped her hands gleefully.

"Well, we all know how our Mila loves *macarons*," Maggie said, giving her daughter a kiss.

A horn sounded out front. Maggie glanced out the kitchen window to see that Grace and Brad had arrived.

Laurent kissed Maggie. "No candy for Jemmy. Or Cokes."

Maggie snorted. "Of course not. I am his mother after all."

"Which is why you spoil him," Laurent said as he gathered up his cloth grocery bags for his day of shopping.

The horn honked again and Jemmy appeared in the doorway of the kitchen.

"Mom, let's go," he said.

"Behave," Laurent said to him, raising an eyebrow to underscore to his son that he meant it.

Maggie kissed Mila and Danielle goodbye.

"Everyone have a fun day," she said as she grabbed her purse from the foyer sideboard.

Jemmy hurried out the front door to the waiting car.

The drive to Arles from St-Buvard was less than an hour and on a beautiful fall day like today felt even shorter. Since Laurent had set Grace up at *Dormir* Maggie and Grace had spent many Saturdays combing the roadside *brocantes* and village flea markets for just the right fabrics, pillow cushions, bed linens, artwork and *faience* to give any visitor to the *gîte* the most iconic South of France experience possible.

Maggie had never been much interested in second-hand items or antiques, but Grace had managed to arouse in her a passion for the hunt. Every afternoon that they'd spent looking for something unique or beautiful to enhance one of the *Dormir* cottages had been one that had aided in further bonding the two of them after their rough patch a few years earlier.

It helped that the scenes of the village *brocantes* were usually beautiful in themselves, typically medieval villages or cobblestone towns, often on the verge of golden sunflower or lavender fields.

Since Brad was driving Grace's car this morning, Maggie let Jemmy sit up front with him. Maggie had only seen Brad a few times since Grace had met him at an ex-pat party a few weeks back but she'd liked him instantly. He was easy going—something Maggie was convinced Grace needed. And he was American—again, something Maggie thought suited Grace better than a French lover, although she couldn't put her finger on why.

Laurent on the other hand was reserving judgment on the man.

As they entered Arles from the north, Maggie noticed there seemed to be more pay lots for parking than she remembered before. She was sure that half the lots they'd passed had previously been free parking.

"Just goes to show you how popular Arles is as a tourist destination," she said as she directed Brad in his second circling of the main square in their search to find an available spot.

"There must be a reason people love Arles so much," Brad said cheerfully. He turned to Jemmy. "Right, Sport?"

Jemmy was too interested in the scenery outside his window to answer and just as Maggie was about to reprimand him for not responding, Jemmy shouted and pointed.

"Look! There it is!"

The amphitheater rose around them like an ancient alien spaceship, its two-tiered stone walls a dramatic and pronounced hallmark of the ancient Roman city.

Maggie shivered as she always did when she saw the amphitheater. The fact that it could last so long and be the site of so much misery and death always took her breath away every time she saw it.

"Can we go in, Mom?" Jemmy turned in his seat to look excitedly at Maggie.

"We're meeting some people for lunch first," Maggie reminded him. "Be patient. The amphitheater has been here a long time. It isn't going anywhere."

"Wow," Brad said as he drove toward the imposing structure. "It's really something."

"Oh, there's one!" Grace called out. "Grab it, Brad!"

As Brad maneuvered the car into the spot, Grace and Maggie gathered up their shopping bags and baskets, optimistic that they would find treasures at the amphitheater *brocante* for *Dormir* and Domaine St-Buvard alike.

After paying for the parking spot, the four of them hurried through the narrow stone streets in the general direction of the amphitheater. Grace had arranged for them to meet the event planner for today's *brocante* at a restaurant across the street from the arena.

For a special mention in Maggie's popular Provençal newsletter, the event organizer had agreed to allow them into the *brocante* a full half hour before the rest of the public. It wasn't an unusual arrangement—not since Maggie's newsletter and blog had risen so high in subscription numbers to rate the kind of attention it now commanded.

"Who is this guy we're meeting?" Maggie asked Grace as they walked toward the restaurant.

"His name is Claude Bouquille," Grace said. "He does the organizing for all the main attractions and promotions not just in Arles but Aix and even some in Marseille. He's really excited about being in your newsletter."

Maggie's newsletter had been steadily growing from a simple blog about the ex-pat life in Provence to something that now had its own Etsy store and connections to vendors that covered the entire south of France with products from soaps and candles to handmade linens and faience. Her twenty thousand subscribers, although largely British, were growing to include a growing US audience too.

"Oh, did I tell you, that Fiona Bellemont-Surrey agreed to an interview in my next newsletter?" Maggie said to Grace.

Fiona Bellemont-Surrey was a British ex-pat who'd moved to Provence twenty years earlier and written a string of romance books that catapulted her to fame and prominence in the UK. She lived in the village of Saint-Rémy, about two hours from St-

Buvard and Maggie had been trying to get her to talk to her for nearly a year.

Unfortunately, Belmont-Surrey had a reputation for being a bit of a bitch.

"I never heard of her," Brad said over his shoulder. "Should I?"

Maggie felt a sliver of annoyance.

"Well, you're probably not my audience, Brad," she said. "Fiona Bellemont-Surrey is kind of a big deal for ex-pat Brits living the Provençal lifestyle. I figure her name alone will boost my subscribers by a thousand or more. Plus, she's got her own blog of nearly seventy thousand subscribers she's agreed to let me send my newsletter to."

"How much does that translate to money-wise?" Grace asked.

"It could be a game changer."

"Like you need the money, darling."

"Well, everyone likes money," Maggie said. "But money isn't the point."

"What is?"

"Never mind, Grace. You sound like Laurent. This is what I *do*. I want to create a newsletter that's relevant. One that grows and evolves."

"Well, if it's important to you, it's important."

"Do you have any idea how condescending that sounds?"

Grace laughed. "And I wasn't even trying!"

Maggie watched Jemmy step in front of Brad where she could no longer see him.

"Jemmy, slow down," Maggie said. "I told you, we're going to the restaurant first."

"I heard you," he called back, a hint of petulance in his voice.

"He's fine," Brad said. "I've got him in sight."

Grace slipped her arm through Maggie's.

"Come on, darling," she said cajolingly. "It's going to be a fun day. Relax!"

5

After Danielle and Mila left for *Dormir* to spend the day with Zouzou, Laurent drove to the *l'Abbaye de Sainte-Trinité* and parked in the gravel parking lot.

He'd been working at the monastery with Frère Jean for over three years to help find local work and housing for the area's transients and assorted refugees.

Between *l'Abbaye de Sainte-Trinité* dormitories and the mini-houses Laurent had constructed on his vineyard property, all the harvest workers had comfortable housing for the duration of the work.

Laurent had a dozen people working his harvest this year. Most of them had moved on after the grapes were picked. It was as yet too early for the pruning and general field maintenance that would keep Laurent and his crew of young people busy in the spring.

Three of Laurent's houses had issues that currently made them uninhabitable. The other three workers who had yet to move on. A young couple with a baby had decided to stay and help with the garden at the monastery and do any work Laurent might have for them.

There were also three teenage boys still living at the monastery after the harvest although Frère Jean had confided to Laurent that without work to engage them they were becoming a problem.

As Laurent strode toward the main building of the monastery, an ancient stone structure, the wind blew in sharp angry gusts and the late morning sun already seemed to be fading with the steadily falling temperatures.

He entered the main hall and nodded at an elderly couple seated at one of the back tables, mugs of hot soup in their hands. Frère Jean was standing at the front of the room before an audience of around thirty people.

Laurent frowned as he watched the ex-monk—defrocked but still respected in every manner that mattered—attempt to get the attention and silence of the younger members of the audience. Laurent spotted several people who'd worked on his recent harvest including the three boys who'd together tended to cause more problems than any of the other workers combined.

André Charpentier, eighteen years old, was the son of an out-of-work car mechanic who'd worked in St-Buvard through last winter and then left, leaving André at the monastery saying he would return.

Jabal Berger sat next to André, his face slack but his eyes focused on André as if to emulate his friend's banter, sarcasm, and insolence.

Laurent knew the type—inclined toward trouble but without the originality to do it on his own—Jabal latched onto a leader and followed in his footsteps.

Usually all the way to prison.

Luc Thayer was the third boy. An orphan and a loner, he was rarely with the other boys and was surprised to see him with them now. His arms crossed and a mulish look on his handsome but scowling face, Luc was trouble in all the ways a wrongheaded sixteen-year-old kid could be trouble.

Unlike the other two who seemed to act up for accolades from the girls in the group or for their own amusement, Luc's behavior didn't appear motivated by praise or money or by the idea of doing the right thing.

Laurent moved deeper into the audience and saw Frère Jean look up and give him a look of relief. Laurent moved a narrow metal table holding a tray of dirty dishes out of his way. The sound of its legs scraping loudly on the stone floor echoed throughout the bare-walled dining hall. All the heads of the audience members turned to look at him.

Laurent caught André's eye first and detected—seconds before the mask of arrogance and contempt was donned—a moment of doubt and insecurity.

That would do. He'd made his point.

André elbowed Jabar in the ribs and snickered something to him which made the boy giggle but that was the extent of André's rebellion. Laurent was sure Frère Jean would have no more trouble out of them.

Luc did not turn around.

6

Maggie had been at Café Terrace before. Situated directly across from the Arles amphitheater, it was really more of a tourist café than a proper bistro, but the food was good and the service not too rude. And *that*, she figured, was about the best one could hope for in any French restaurant.

When they arrived at the café, lunch service had just begun. Before they'd even taken their seats Maggie had already had to have two heart-to-heart talks with Jemmy to keep him from dashing across the street and attempting to vault the stone parking stanchions put there to prevent people from parking or driving too close to the amphitheater.

"Lunch *first*, Jemmy," Maggie had said firmly to him. "I know you can be patient and I need you to do that now. How about a Coke with lunch?"

Already she could hear Laurent's admonishment in her ear. He didn't like either of the children to have too many sweets and he downright forbade snacking between meals.

But Maggie rationalized that since she was from Atlanta, the home of Coca-Cola, having a Coke now and then was practically Jemmy's birthright.

Still, she knew bribing him to behave was not good.

As soon as they entered the café, Grace led the way to a table where two men sat. The taller of the two, Claude Bouquille, jumped up and immediately exchanged kisses with Grace and introductions were made all around.

Claude's companion was a small ferret-looking man named Jacky. He had an odor to him and an ugly look in his eye. Maggie made a point to sit as far away from him as possible and parked Jemmy beside her.

"I am delighted to meet you, Madame Dernier," Claude said enthusiastically. "And even more delighted to be a part of your newsletter. My wife loves your interviews with area artisans. She harbors hopes of being interviewed herself."

"Oh? What does your wife make?"

Maggie had had hundreds of conversations like this over the last few years. It was seriously astonishing to her that there could be so many artists and creative vendors in Provence.

"Lavender infused soaps," Claude said. "I see you already have many advertisers for those kinds of products."

"Yes, well. This is Provence, right? One thing we have is lavender—but my newsletter subscribers love it."

"Of course. It is *la belle France, non*?"

The waiter, dour but at least sufficiently attentive, came and they ordered. Maggie was very aware that Jemmy was fidgety. She was sorry she hadn't brought him an electronic tablet to distract him but, again, Laurent wasn't a fan of using artificial devices to make the children behave and so she hadn't.

She was tempted to hand Jemmy her phone like she would if he were five but the very image of it prevented her. Jemmy had always been such an easy-going boy. What had changed? Why did he seem so impatient with everything now?

"Maggie?"

Maggie looked up just as the waiter handed her the glass of rosé she'd ordered.

"*Merci,*" she said to the waiter who made eye contact with her. In fact, now that she thought of it, the man seemed fascinated by their conversation. She glanced at her group and had to admit they stood out a bit.

First there was Grace who was nothing short of gorgeous. Blonde with classic features, perfect alabaster complexion and crystal blue eyes, Grace would always turn heads no matter where she went. She was a goddess in human form. Normally, she alone would be enough to distract even the most cynical French waiter.

But then there was Brad who was movie-star handsome in his own right.

What a strange grouping we must appear!

Claude was tall and balding with an infectious grin. And his friend, Jacky...well, with his unshaven jawline and rumpled clothes he just looked homeless.

Maggie stole a quick look at Jacky and was startled to find him staring at her. She quickly turned her attention back to Claude who was speaking with the waiter.

"Thomas, you must have seen every manner of tourist over the years," Claude said. "They are all fascinated with the amphitheater, are they not?"

The waiter, a tall Ichabod Crane sort of fellow with straight, very white teeth, smiled and nodded at the looming wall of the Roman ruin.

"It is as beautiful as it is fascinating to all who see it," he murmured. "Especially the first time." Then he blushed as if he'd said too much and retreated back to the kitchen.

Claude grinned. "I know everyone in this town on a first-name basis. From the mayor to the waiters. In my business, it is essential. You'd be surprised how helpful even the little men can be."

"So tell me how you got involved in all these special events you put on," Maggie said.

"Well, my background is music and theatrical promotions. And honestly it was my wife that made me become more interested in doing events." He waved a hand to encompass the amphitheater.

"Have you been doing it awhile?"

"About five years. It's fairly lucrative and I get to meet a wide variety of people."

Maggie couldn't help but wonder if Jacky was who Claude was referring to when he said *a wide variety of people.* She wondered what possible function Jacky served for Claude.

"Claude said we can flag any item we like to be held back for later," Grace said, looking up from a small spiral notebook which Maggie guessed was her wish list for *Dormir*. "He said there is an antique water basin and some vintage bed linens that I'm thinking will look perfect in Plum cottage."

Grace had named the three guest cottages after fruit to keep them straight—and to help her handy man—who tended to struggle with understanding her French—to better sort out which cottage she needed him to work on.

"It is of course no problem," Claude said glancing at his watch. "Shall we go in a quarter of an hour?"

Already Maggie could see a line begin to form at the entrance to the amphitheater directly across from the café.

"That's impressive," she said, nodding at the growing crowd of people. "How did you advertise this?"

As Maggie watched the crowd her eye was caught by the sight of a young man dressed all in black. He wore a dark slouch hat and a half cape around his shoulders. His odd clothing wasn't what drew her eye however.

It was the unmistakable hate-filled glare that he was shooting at her table

"My advertising was not nearly as effective as it would have been," Claude said, "if I had been able to make the announcement in your newsletter." Although he was still smiling for some reason Maggie felt it was somehow less authentic than before.

"Well, my newsletter doesn't go out to the locals," she said. "You'd only have told people living in the UK."

"People in the UK have much disposable income," Claude said. "I would be happy to advertise my events to them."

"Well, next time you will," Maggie said, watching Jemmy push his French fries around on his plate, his eyes glued to the amphitheater entrance. She turned her attention back to Claude. "Did you have a display ad you wanted me to publish or…?"

"*Mais non*," Claude said, looking from Maggie to Grace and back again. "Grace said you might write about today's event. Is that not possible? Jacky is here to photograph anything you need."

Maggie was surprised. Most people opted for an ad. But she knew a small article—penned by her—would carry more clout to her subscribers.

Except what if the brocante is lame? Or worse, a rip-off?

She'd built up a bank of trust with her subscribers. If she told them the October Amphitheater *Brocante* was an annual sales experience not to be missed, they'd believe her. Not to mention the fact that her subscribers were mostly offshore. If they booked their flights for their next trip to Provence based on an event that Maggie said was worth experiencing—and it turned out not to be —then where would she be?

"Instead of a piece," she said, "since I already have one for next month's newsletter…" And that was true now that she had the Bellemont-Surrey interview nearly lined up. "…how would you feel about a display ad for your wife's lavender soaps? I can place it right up front so nobody misses it."

"You would do that?" Claude asked happily, his authentic smile back with a little something extra. "That would be *superbe*!"

Maggie and Claude shook hands and Maggie couldn't help but think that the best part of the deal—aside from not having to write copy she potentially didn't believe in—was not having to spend the afternoon with Jacky dogging her every step.

7

The impressive two-tiered amphitheater could seat over twenty thousand people and featured more than one hundred and twenty dramatic arches, several sets of viewing galleries and staircases, and a warren of catacomb subterranean tunnels and pathways.

As Maggie stared up at the amphitheater the thought came to her as it always did that this imposing structure—still such a vibrant, integral part of life in Arles—was built only ninety years after the birth of Christ.

Even more astonishing was the fact that this benign tourist attraction had also been the scene of countless bloody gladiatorial battles.

Maggie shivered at the thought of the brave and terrified men who were thrown to hungry bears and lions for the amusement of people who sat in these stone seats cheering them on before heading off to lunch somewhere in Arles.

"Darling?" Grace said turning to Maggie. "Are you all right? You look positively pale."

"This place always creeps me out a little," Maggie said with a weak smile.

Grace laughed her little bell of a laugh and slipped her arm into Maggie's.

"Okay, so let's stay focused. We're looking for antique lace and possibly an antique washstand today. Not heads on spikes. *D'accord*?"

Cued by thoughts of blood and mayhem Maggie turned to look for Jemmy. She spotted him walking next to Brad who was pointing out something at the top tier of the stadium seating.

Maggie turned back to Grace and the job at hand.

Even though today's event was supposed to be only antiques there were still the ubiquitous tables of *socca, pissaladier*, and pizza slices along with homemade jams from the nearby nunnery and table after table of spices, the scent of which could be detected the moment one emerged from any of the several tunnels that spilled out onto the arena's interior arena.

Maggie looked in amazement at the kiosk presentations of the colorful spices—most of which she'd never heard of before—as well as the mountains of dried rosebuds and sacks of semolina that looked like sandbags waiting for a storm.

Since October was fully into mushroom season in this part of France, Maggie wasn't surprised to see one table groaning under mounds of every possible variety of mushroom.

Grace charged ahead to the tables that appeared to be loaded down with linens as Maggie wandered over to the tables groaning with vintage dinnerware and crystal. She touched a finger to the rim of a delicate Spode ewer with rose buds painted on it and her throat felt thick and scratchy.

Instantly she recalled the three weeks she'd spent in Atlanta last summer helping her mother clear out the family home so that Elspeth and Maggie's niece Nicole could move into their new smaller place.

The whole process had been gut-wrenching but Maggie knew she'd had it easier than most people since she wasn't doing the job *and* grieving the loss of a loved one at the same time as so many people were forced to do.

All of the Newberry family china—every piece that had glistened on multiple table settings over the years through holiday after holiday—was as familiar to Maggie as her own face. She remembered all the years of family get-togethers and the happy days when her sister was still alive and her father still remembered who they all were. She remembered the whole family gathered around the family heirloom china for festival Christmas toddies and later singing carols around the baby grand piano.

The thirty-thousand dollar piano was eventually donated to the local women's shelter when Maggie's brother Ben finally gave up trying to find a buyer for it. Nobody wanted their family treasures.

Nobody in the family and nobody outside it.

Ben was divorced and living in a one-bedroom condo. Elise was dead. Maggie lived across the ocean.

That summer Maggie spent downsizing her parents' home marked the official end of family dinners, festive holiday meals, Thanksgiving and football weekends. All of it was gone in the time it took to cart the dishes and linens and crystal out the door where it went for pennies on the dollar to the Buckhead junkman or straight to the curb to be picked up by any vaguely interested neighbor before the garbage truck came.

Blinking tears away, Maggie turned from the vintage dishes before her and hoped very much that whoever had eaten off these dishes and celebrated graduations and weddings and Christmases with these champagne glasses had relinquished them because they were ready to pack up and tour the world with their lover.

But she seriously doubted that was the case.

"Darling! Did you see the Brussels lace?" Grace hurried over to Maggie, her face flushed with excitement. A long swath of

Swiss tatted lace lay in her arms. "It's exquisite. The notecard at the table said it was made in Zurich *by nuns*."

"That's cool," Maggie said, forcing the image out of her head of her family's heirlooms sitting on the street curb.

"And did you see the furniture? There's a Savannah tufted chaise lounge in the most divine blush silk you've ever seen. They're asking six hundred for it. I think I'll offer three."

Maggie followed Grace over to the furniture which sat on wooden platforms in front of a lower section of Roman stone seats. She couldn't help looking up and wondering what the prisoners slated for execution had thought from this very same viewpoint. Were the spectators laughing? Encouraging?

"What do you think, darling?" Grace asked as she stood in front of a stack of quilted padded headboards.

"Is this a chaise lounge?" Maggie asked.

"No, silly. We haven't gotten there yet. What do you think about the headboards?"

"Don't all your beds already have headboards?"

Maggie knew Laurent had given Grace money for this shopping trip. She also knew that Grace had yet to pay a single month's rent on *Dormir*. She certainly didn't have the money to buy headboards she didn't need. But Maggie bit her tongue. This was Laurent's project. One of many.

Grace laughed. "Oh, you're hopeless. Where is Brad? It's often good to get a man's point of view."

It wasn't until that moment that Maggie realized she hadn't seen Jemmy for at least the last quarter of an hour. The moment they walked into the amphitheater she'd reassured herself that there was no mischief or harm he could possibly come to in here.

After all, except for Claude, Jacky, Grace and Brad, and the twenty or so vendors standing at their tables and booths straightening their wares and getting ready for the public to be let in there was nobody else in the place.

"I'm going to tell Claude to hold this back for me," Grace said, waving to Claude where he stood with Jacky by a long table of incense and North African spices.

"Where's Jemmy?" Maggie said as she turned full circle, scanning the arena interior, looking for the quick movements of a ten-year-old boy.

But Grace only had eyes for the antiques and treasures she'd come to find.

"I'm sure he's here some place," Grace said absently as she knelt to examine the fabric on a floral vanity chair.

Maggie turned and hurried toward the entrance they'd come through. All the other entrances were blocked. She climbed the nearest stairs which took her to the first tier of stone seats but high enough to get a good view of the entire interior of the Roman ruin.

Jemmy was nowhere to be seen.

8

Frère Jean hurried down the long stone corridor, his hand outstretched, reaching for Laurent's.

"Hello, my friend," Frère Jean said, pumping Laurent's hand. "I'm glad you could come."

"Of course," Laurent said, his eyes glancing over the brother's shoulder as he watched André, Jabar and Luc shuffle up the aisle toward them. André and Jabar jostled the other people in their way and laughed derisively. Luc seemed to be memorizing the placement of his footsteps.

Two young girls who'd helped on Laurent's harvest ran up to him, blushing and giggling.

"*Bonjour*, Monsieur Dernier," one of them gushed, her eyes dewy with hero worship.

"Agnes," Laurent said with a smile. "You are staying busy now that there are no more grapes to pick?"

"I'm minding my auntie's two babies," she said. "I just love babies. Don't you?"

Before Laurent could answer, Agnes was edged out of the way by an older woman who stood close to Laurent, her breath redolent of wine and onions.

She had been beautiful once, Laurent thought. It was these women who he felt needed kindness most of all.

"Have you come for dinner?" the woman asked, her hand on Laurent's wrist. "It is my week to work in the kitchen."

"I regret I will miss that," Laurent said, touching her elbow and watching her eyes light up with interest when he did. "Alas, my wife insists on my presence in our dining room."

"*Tant pis*," the woman said naughtily, and Laurent nearly laughed at her boldness.

He had no doubt Maggie would be as spunky when she was in her sixties.

"Laurent, a word?" Frère Jean said, tugging Laurent away from the women.

As they stepped out of the flux of exiting people, Laurent saw that the boys had left the hall.

"There is a rumor," Frère Jean said in a low voice to Laurent.

"Rumors don't trouble me," Laurent said mildly.

"Unless they hint at the truth," the ex-monk said, one eyebrow arching. "You have heard of the saying about where there is smoke?"

"A singularly American adage, I believe," Laurent said.

"Not everything the Americans have is useless," Frère Jean reminded him.

"As I know better than most," Laurent said, a smile playing on his lips.

"It's the boys."

"The three up front?"

"Who else? André was set to leave this week but then he claimed he had word from his father to sit tight because he is returning."

"You don't believe him?"

"I believe the boy doesn't want to be expelled from the dormitory. And I believe he would lie to ensure he stayed."

"Set a timeline for when his father must show himself," Laurent said. "After that, out he goes."

"But where will he go?"

"You cannot take on everyone's problems, *mon frère*. What about Jabar?"

"I have a complaint about him from the father of one of the girls."

"What does the girl say happened?"

"She won't say."

"Is she afraid of her father?"

"I don't know. But I can't throw Jabar out on hearsay and he has a mother living here."

"So you have answered your own question."

Laurent let the silence grow between them as Frère Jean mulled this over. Laurent hadn't asked about Luc yet and as he waited for the brother to offer information on his own, Laurent realized he considered Luc somewhat of a special case. And in fact he had all summer and fall as the boy worked his fields.

Unlike the others, Luc had been careful not to bruise the grapes—not because Laurent had admonished him but because Luc tended to be naturally fastidious—unusual for a teenager. It made him stand out. Even in the mornings where Luc would arrive early and the afternoons when he invariably left the field late.

"I'm thinking of throwing Luc out," Frère Jean said.

"Over a girl?" Laurent asked although as soon as he said it he knew it couldn't be.

"No," Frère Jean said with a sigh. "He's accused of stealing."

"That is serious."

"We can't have it."

"What will you do?"

"Convene a tribunal. For the accuser. And the defendant. Anyone who wants to speak for him." Frère Jean narrowed his eyes at Laurent.

"Me?" Laurent was genuinely surprised. "I don't know him to vouch for him."

"Do you not? He worked for you for two months."

"I would not call him a model employee," Laurent said dryly. "And how he did or did not perform in picking my grapes says nothing about whether or not he is a thief."

"Well, I thought you might want to know."

Frère Jean was quickly hailed by two men with a shovel. He said his goodbyes to Laurent who watched the ex-monk walk away with the men.

His eyes then followed a movement down the gravel path that led toward the monastery's gardens where he spotted the three boys standing and smoking by the stone entrance to the garden.

Laurent watched them for a bit and wondered what it was about Luc that tugged at his consciousness.

It wasn't until he was in his car and on his way to Aix and the food markets that it occurred to him that there was something about the boy that reminded him of someone he knew.

And not in a good way.

9

"Jemmy!"

Maggie felt the panic inch up her throat. She dropped her purse and ran up the steps, higher and higher, until she was midway up the seating tiers. Looking down the only movement she could see was Grace in the arena.

Her jaw clenched painfully.

He isn't here. Jemmy isn't here.

There was only one entrance into the bottom level of the amphitheater but there were more than half a dozen entrances higher up. Maggie turned to the first one she came to and darted through it. She entered a long curving stone hallway with supporting pillars every ten feet.

"Jemmy! Where are you?"

Her voice echoed down the long aisle. The sound of her fear ratcheted up her terror.

Where could he have gone?

For a moment she felt paralyzed by indecision. Should she go back to the café? But why would he go back there? He hadn't been able to wait to get *out* of there.

She turned and ran down the stone hallway. Every few yards there was an arched opening to the arena below. Each time she stepped through the opening and looked out onto the stone seat tiers to see if she could spot him.

Grace waved from the bottom level in the arena. Brad was with her now.

"Do you see him?" Maggie called down.

"No!" Grace shouted back. "But Claude and Jacky are searching for him too!"

Maggie turned and ran smack into Claude. He was red in the face and sweating heavily.

"I'm so sorry," he said. His hands shot out to hold Maggie's arms as if to steady himself. He nodded down the hallway. "You go that way and I'll climb higher."

"I can't imagine he'd go up there," Maggie said, trying to control her mounting fear.

Would Jemmy climb to the top? Is that something he would do?

"I'll go and see."

Maggie felt a blanket of dizziness sweep over her.

Suddenly she thought she could hear the screams of wild animals and the prisoners being flung to them. She could hear the shouts of the audience calling for blood.

A buzzing sound filled her ears and the light began to fade all around her until it was so black she couldn't see Claude or her own hands in front of her face.

"Madame?" Claude said to her, his voice fading in and out. "Are you all right?"

Maggie felt her world shift violently as if she were inside a terrible kaleidoscope, her stomach pitching harshly. And then she was falling. She jerked her hands out to catch herself. As she fell she heard the crowd scream for her blood. The shouts were so loud now it was all she could hear.

"Maggie!" Claude said frantically. "Hello! Help! I need help here! Maggie, open your eyes!"

Maggie's mouth felt dry. She wished Claude would stop shouting because her head was throbbing. The sounds of the horrible spectators still sounded faintly in her brain.

"Maggie, oh, my God, what happened?" Grace's voice came to Maggie, high and hysterical.

Maggie caught the scent of orange blossoms and felt Grace's cool hands as they slipped under her neck.

"Grace," Maggie said, her eyes finally opening. Now she felt the coldness and the hardness of the ground where she lay. She knew where she was. There was no Roman crowd screaming for her blood.

"I *told* her I was just going to have a pee!"

Jemmy's voice came from a long way off. "Why does everyone act like I'm a serial killer because I went to have a pee?"

Maggie closed her eyes and felt the relief flood through her.

"He's safe, darling," Grace said softly.

Maggie nodded but could not bring herself to open her eyes. Not yet. Not just yet.

10

The drive back to Domaine St-Buvard was not a pleasant one.

After it became clear that Jemmy was fine, Grace quickly arranged with the vendors for the items she wanted held for her and then the doors opened and the public flooded into the arena.

After what had happened with Jemmy, all Maggie wanted to do was go home.

She thanked Claude and Jacky for their help in searching for Jemmy, and assured Claude that she would publish his wife's lavender soap display ad as soon as he sent it to her. Then, with Jemmy firmly in hand, she marched out of the amphitheater.

"I don't know why you're so mad at me," Jemmy said indignantly. "I didn't even want to come today!"

"You had to come today," Maggie said, tamping down her annoyance with him. "Your father wasn't able to watch you and—"

"He doesn't have to watch me! I'm not a baby! I'm ten!"

"Lower your voice. You did *not* tell me where you were going—"

"I did too!"

"I won't argue with you, Jemmy! You *didn't* tell me where you were going. You just slipped away!"

"Because you'd have said *no*!"

"So you admit you didn't tell me!" Maggie said, feeling her fury overpower her quickly waning sense of relief.

"Do I need a lawyer?" Jemmy said.

Maggie was astounded at his impudence.

"Don't talk to me like that," she sputtered, not know what else to say.

"But it's okay for *you* to talk to *me* like that?" he said turning and running ahead.

"Don't worry, I've got him," Brad said to her as he lengthened his stride to catch up to Jemmy. "Hey, Sport. Slow down a bit."

Maggie watched Jemmy allow Brad to walk beside him. If she told Laurent what happened today it would be a toss-up as to who would be in more trouble: *her* for letting Jemmy behave like this or Jemmy. Just the thought of that made her mad all over. *She would not defer to Laurent in order to make Jemmy mind her!* She would *not*. Her relationship with Jemmy couldn't be dependent on Laurent making Jemmy respect her.

"Are you okay, darling?" Grace asked. "That was quite a shock today."

Maggie sighed. "You must think I've lost my mind."

"Not at all."

"Liar."

"Well, I guess maybe you did, possibly, overreact just a little? Maybe?"

Maggie laughed and it felt good to laugh. Then she groaned. "What is wrong with me, Grace? I feel like I'm losing my mind. Or my son."

"You are not losing your son." Then they both laughed. "Well, you're not losing your mind either but you're especially not losing your son. He's ten."

"Which means what, exactly? I thought this crap wasn't supposed to happen for another four years?"

"I guess there are no hard and fast rules," Grace said. "Sorry. I'm sure that doesn't help. And look who you're asking. The world's worst mother."

"Don't say that," Maggie said crossly. "Taylor and Zouzou adore you."

"Oh, I love you, darling," Grace said, giving Maggie's arm a squeeze. "Taylor barely tolerates me and Zouzou, well, *adore* may be a bit strong. But she's putting up with me much better these days and as you know *that* was a long time coming."

"Girls are supposed to be way worse."

"Thank you, darling. They are, aren't they? But please don't worry about Jemmy. He's just stretching his wings."

"I thought boys were supposed to push their limits against their fathers? How did *I* get so lucky?"

"Well, have you talked to Laurent? Is Jemmy giving *him* a hard time too?"

"Good question."

By the time she and Grace reached the car, Jemmy was already in the front seat and Maggie was happy to climb in the back and not deal with forcing her son to take responsibility for what he'd done.

She was weary and was sure she had bruises on her hips and knees from where she'd fallen during her faint inside the Amphitheater.

Maybe Grace is right. Maggie thought unhappily. *Talk about over reacting!*

The drive home was filled with Grace's commentary on the items she'd seen and the plans she had for the purchases she intended to make. As the afternoon light began to fade from the sky Maggie saw the ruins in the east of *Montmajour Abbey* backlit against a streaky pale blue pallet.

She flinched in memory of the terrible night she had spent in the ruin, six years ago. Just herself alone with a ghost. She shook the image out of her mind and pulled out her phone to text Laurent the basics of what had happened in the amphitheater.

Laurent didn't respond but the word *Delivered* appeared on the screen under her text so she knew he'd at least read it. That in itself was unusual. Normally Laurent didn't keep his phone with him.

As Maggie closed her eyes to rerun in her mind what had happened today in anticipation of telling Laurent, she remembered the strange young man dressed all in black. It suddenly occurred to her that she'd seen him again when she and Jemmy left the amphitheater.

She'd been so intent on scolding Jemmy that she had only barely registered that the man in black was still there at the entrance.

Was it odd that he had not gone inside when the amphitheater gate was finally opened to the public?

She tried to think if the man had been watching her as he had before when she was at the café but she'd been too focused on Jemmy to register that detail.

It was enough that she'd remembered he was there at all.

An hour later they pulled into the long gravel drive of Domaine St-Buvard. Maggie saw Laurent standing in the front drive waiting for them, a glowing cigarette in one hand.

More importantly, Jemmy saw him.

"Thank you for coming with me today, darling," Grace said, giving Maggie a quick kiss on the cheek. "I wouldn't have gotten the preview if not for you. No trouble on doing Claude's ad for his wife?"

Maggie shook her head. "No, it's all good. Thanks for driving, Brad."

Brad turned in his seat with a jerk. "I'm sorry? Did you say something?"

It was then that Maggie noticed that Brad had been unnaturally quiet for the whole trip. Normally, he was the kind of person who liked to fill any silence with the sound of his own voice.

"I was just thanking you for driving today," Maggie said. As she climbed out of the car and watched Jemmy trudge into the house with Laurent behind him, Maggie wondered if she was imagining things.

Because at that moment, she would have sworn the interior of the car seemed to throb with the unmistakable presence of guilt.

11

That weekend at Domaine-St-Buvard was thick with tension.

After Jemmy had been punished with a week's abstinence from all electronics for his disappearing act at the amphitheater, Laurent seemed to believe that was the end of it.

Maggie was torn between believing she'd overreacted and believing Laurent had dismissed the incident as simply a matter of *what kids do*.

In any case she felt unsettled and anxious going into Sunday. Jemmy stayed home from church with a sore throat which was miraculously cured as soon as church was over. Mila prattled happily about the fun she'd had yesterday at *Dormir* making *macarons* with Danielle and Zouzou.

"Zouzou is going to be a famous *patisserie* chef someday," Mila said from the kitchen counter where she was watching her father make *ratatouille*.

Maggie sat at her desk in her office attempting to work on her newsletter but her mind was flooded with yesterday's events. She kept her office door open to hear the sounds of Laurent's cooking and Mila's happy chatter.

Jemmy was upstairs in his bedroom reading or perhaps secretly watching a show on his iPad, likely confident that Laurent would assume complete compliance with the no-electronics edict and not check up on him.

Maggie didn't usually work on a Sunday but after yesterday she felt she needed the distraction.

She hadn't managed to take any photos of the arena before she'd become derailed by Jemmy's disappearance. She was sorry about that since it really had been a dramatic presentation with the vendors and their tables set up in the center of the amphitheater arena.

Her newsletter for the month had more than enough room to accommodate the display ad she'd promised Claude as well as a few lines of captions under the photos to talk about the event itself.

Unfortunately, since they ended up not staying for the actual event, Maggie would need to reach out to Claude to get his summation of the day. Getting the assessment of the event from the event organizer wasn't ideal, of course. If Claude said it was a blazing success, Maggie only had his word to go on.

But, she reasoned, it was only a few captions and she'd word them such that her judgment of the event was left undetermined.

Next year I'll be there for the entire thing.

She left a placeholder for the Bellemont-Surrey interview—her newsletter centerpiece—and then saved everything and exited the newsletter template.

At the sound of Laurent calling for her and Jemmy to come to the table for Sunday supper, Maggie was feeling much better about the weekend. She was still annoyed that Laurent had downplayed the incident yesterday but as the hours passed, she began to think she'd overreacted after all.

What was the matter with Jemmy? Wasn't ten a little early for rebellion? Was this really normal as Grace seemed to think?

Was Laurent like this when he was young?

And then a vivid, unbidden image of Laurent's brother Gerard jumped into Maggie's head. She quickly forced the image away.

Even though she hadn't known Gerard as a child, she knew Jemmy was nothing like him.

She must be losing her mind to compare the two for even a single solitary second.

Jemmy was a somewhat bratty ten year old with a possible inclination to becoming a difficult teen.

Nothing like Gerard.

The next morning Laurent had business in Aix so he drove both children to the International Bilingual School in town. Danielle would pick up all three children and bring them to *Dormir* where Maggie would pick up her two later in the afternoon. It gave Maggie a rare morning to herself.

Even though Laurent always left his kitchen spotless with every ladle and basting brush in its place, Maggie spent a few minutes wiping down counters and washing up the few breakfast dishes.

Jemmy had seemed like his old self this morning although perhaps a little quieter when Maggie was in the room. She tried to see his mood as respectful contrition and not what she greatly feared it was—annoyed resentment that he'd gotten punished when he didn't feel he deserved it.

She spent an hour looking over her newsletter and proofing it for typos, believing she always had fresher eyes doing this sort of work in the morning. The space where the Bellemont-Surrey story was to go reminded her to send a quick email to Bellemont-Surrey's assistant to see when they could establish a time for the interview.

Then Maggie sent an email to Claude thanking him again for

his help yesterday with her "unfortunate incident" and reminding him she needed the display ad for his wife's lavender.

Satisfied she'd done all she could and with an eye on the clock, Maggie let out the family's two big dogs Buddy and Izzy for one last romp through the garden before tucking them away in their crates for the afternoon.

When Maggie arrived at *Dormir*, Grace was standing in the front drive with her handyman Gabriel. Maggie grinned as Grace looked up and waved to her. Even in jeans and a t-shirt, Grace looked like she'd just stepped out of the pages of *InStyle Magazine*.

Grace strode to the car as Maggie parked and the two women kissed as if they hadn't seen each other in a week instead of just two days before.

"Everything sorted out with your young man?" Grace asked as they walked back to the *gîte* together.

"I guess so. Laurent beat him soundly and then locked him in his room for the week."

Grace arched an eyebrow.

"Or maybe he told him to knock it off and he wasn't allowed to use his iPad for a few days," Maggie said.

"You think Laurent let him off too lightly?"

"Grace, you saw how I reacted. I thought it was a big deal. I mean, I *fainted*!"

They entered the kitchen where Danielle was busy scrubbing the brand-new cooker in the corner. Maggie quickly kissed her and sat down at the kitchen table while Grace poured coffees for them.

"And you still don't think you overreacted?" Grace said gently.

Danielle set down a plate of *palmiers* on the table and turned back to the stove.

"Join us, Danielle?" Grace said but Danielle shook her head.

"I can hear from here," Danielle said, waving a sponge.

"I guess since you put it like that," Maggie said, "you still think I did?"

"It doesn't matter what I think, darling. All's well that ends well, right?"

"You never met Gerard, did you?" Maggie asked abruptly.

"Laurent's scumbag brother? No. But I've heard the stories. Oh, darling, no. You can't be serious."

"I'm not," Maggie said hurriedly. "I'm not. Of course not. Forget I said anything."

"Jemmy is a sweet boy with a good heart," Grace said, putting her hand on Maggie's. "He's just testing his boundaries. That's all. And with a father like Laurent, you can't be surprised."

"What do you mean?"

"Well, look at him. Laurent is bigger than life, isn't he? Not just physically, but he's the commander in chief and there's no mistake about that. It's only natural that Jemmy would push back with him."

"But it's not *Laurent* who Jemmy's pushing back on. It's me."

"Well, you're probably his practice for the big push he sees coming," Grace said laughing. "But don't listen to me. I've made a mess out of nearly every family relationship I've ever had! I'm the last person you should be taking advice from."

Danielle came to the table and patted Grace on the shoulder.

"Don't be silly," she said. "Your children love you. We all love you."

"Oh, Danielle," Grace said, standing up to hug the older woman. "You help me remember not to waste a single day not feeling grateful for all I have."

When Danielle broke from the hug she looked at Maggie and shook the sponge at her. "And as for you, shame on you. Jemmy is just acting out because he is a boy. It means nothing."

"I know," Maggie said. "It's just that before this he was a *perfect* boy. And I guess I got used to it."

Danielle went back to the stove with her sponge. Grace sat down and Maggie sipped her coffee.

"Everything okay with you and Brad?" Maggie asked.

"Of course. Why do you ask?"

"He seemed a little introspective on the drive back from Arles."

"Brad doesn't have an introspective bone in his body," Grace said with a strained smile.

"That's what I thought too. Which is why I ask."

"Everything is fine, darling. Now are you ready to help me with these curtains in Prune Cottage?"

The afternoon went by quickly and Maggie had to admit the best cure for fretting was not sitting at her computer trying to come up with tag lines but fluffing duvets, measuring fabric for curtains and outlining new flower beds in the garden.

After a quick lunch of leftover *blanquette de Veau*, Danielle took the car to pick up the children, and Maggie and Grace focused on trying to match the existing carpet in Strawberry cottage with a set of carpet samples Grace had picked up in Nice a few weeks before.

At one point, Grace and Gabriel walked over to the pool so Grace could show him how he needed to do a better job of fishing the leaves out and Maggie's cellphone rang. A photograph of her mother materialized on the screen. As she always did when her mother called, Maggie made a quick calculation. It was four o'clock in France so it was ten in the evening in Atlanta.

"Hey, Mom. Is everything okay?"

With her father living in a memory care facility, every phone call from her mother was potentially, sickeningly, *The One*.

"Well, not really," her mother said in annoyance.

Maggie had long noticed that at a certain age her mother had become less interested in greeting Maggie and finding out how her life was going and much more focused on complaining about all the things going wrong in her own.

Maggie still hadn't gotten used to the change.

"Your brother was supposed to pick me up at the memory care center an hour ago and he's still not here," Elspeth said with agitation.

"Mom, it's ten o'clock there. Did you call Ben?"

"Yes, of course I called him. He's not answering. He does that sometimes and now what am I supposed to do?"

"You've just been sitting there for the last hour waiting for him?" Maggie said as she stared out across the gardens of *Dormir*. Laurent and Danielle had set out the bones of the garden with a stronger emphasis on flowers than vegetables so Maggie was looking at a wide swath of lavender and rosemary.

"You make it sound like this is my fault! Ben was supposed to be here at nine o'clock to pick me up."

"Yes, okay, Mom," Maggie said, rubbing at the burgeoning headache forming between her eyes. "I'll text him. Meanwhile, call an Uber to—"

"I don't know how to do that!"

"Never mind. I'll call a taxi. Are you inside?"

"Yes, and I can tell you they are not happy about that. They like to close up at a reasonable time."

"I'm calling a taxi right now, Mom. Call me back when it shows up."

After a few more moments of conversation, Maggie hung up, called a taxi for the address and then typed a quick text to her brother.

<Mom is trying to get a hold of you. CALL HER.>

When she finished Grace was standing in front of her.

"Everything okay?" Grace asked.

"Just peachy," Maggie said. She turned toward the sound of

Danielle's approaching car as it made its way up the long winding drive to the house.

As the car became visible, Maggie could see there were only two children in the car. She opened the passenger side door as soon as Danielle brought the car to a stop.

Mila jumped out and gave Maggie a quick hug. "Hey, Mom," she said before hoisting her book bag on her shoulder and hurrying into the house.

Zouzou came around the front of the car. Blonde and curvaceous, she resembled her mother in looks but her temperament was much more serious.

"Hey, Aunt Maggie," Zouzou said. "Jemmy told me to tell you he had to stay after school to work on some project. He said to tell you his dad would pick him up later."

Maggie glanced at her phone although she knew she hadn't received any texts or messages from Laurent. She felt a prickling sensation on her scalp.

"Everything okay, darling?" Grace asked again as she walked over to Maggie.

"Jemmy stayed late to work on a project. Here's when I wish Laurent would relent on his no-cellphones-for-kids rule. I mean just because *he* doesn't like them, it would be so helpful in situations like this."

Maggie punched in Jemmy's teacher's phone number and leaned in to take the bag of groceries that Danielle had picked up at the Aix Monoprix.

Jemmy's teacher answered.

"Hi, Madame Segal. This is Maggie Dernier, Jemmy's mother? I was just calling to find out the specifics of the project Jemmy stayed late to work on."

Maggie noticed Grace frowning when she heard this but Maggie ignored her.

"I mean, if it takes extra time to do the project," Maggie said, "a note from you would have been helpful." She tried to keep the indicting tone out of her voice but feared it was there to be read in any language.

"I do not know what you are talking about," Madame Segal said stiffly. "Jemmy is not still at school working on a project. I watched him leave myself right after the bell rang."

12

Jemmy's face whitened when he heard the front door open and slam shut announcing the arrival home of his father. He watched his mother scurry to the door and if he expected her to throw fuel on the fire, he was even more horrified to hear her attempt to calm his papa instead.

"Laurent, now, stop and take a breath," his mother said. "He knows he's made a mistake—"

"Where is he?" his father growled.

Jemmy felt dizzy. He tried to see the words on the page of homework in front of him but they begin to swirl and dance away as he heard the heavy, angry footsteps advance to where he sat in the dining room.

Tonight Laurent was not willing to let things go with a slap on the wrist.

Late that afternoon when his cellphone had begun to blow up with text messages and voicemails from Maggie, he had already edged way past judicious tolerance and was settling in comfortably in full-on parental fury.

Laurent didn't need Maggie to impress upon him the importance of today's misdemeanor, nor did he need her to remind him that she felt his last response to a transgression on Jemmy's part had been less than adequate.

At some level Laurent was aware that his current displeasure was only partly earned by Jemmy and his latest misstep but even though Laurent was aware of it, that didn't stop him from storming into the dining room where Jemmy was meekly pretending to do his homework and ordering him to follow him outside to the terrace.

"Laurent, *please*," Maggie said at his elbow.

"I would have a word with my son," Laurent said, not looking at her. "Alone."

Jemmy got up and for a moment he looked as if he would gather up his papers for protection and bring them with him. But in the end, he left them and followed Laurent outside.

The two dogs were outside and were now clamoring to be let back in since it was their dinnertime. Laurent ignored them and pointed to the stone table that was now too cold to use until spring.

His shoulders slumping, Jemmy walked to the table and sat down. Laurent followed him and put his foot on the bench to bar any escape route.

"What were you thinking?" Laurent said, forcing himself to stay calm.

"Louis wanted to show me his new video game," Jemmy muttered.

"Oh, yes?" Laurent said. "So is it Louis I should be upset with?"

Jemmy didn't respond.

"Answer me." Laurent's voice was cold and flat.

"No, Papa."

"And so you lied."

Jemmy lifted his head. "I only lied to Zouzou."

"I see. So you do not know the difference between lying directly to your mother and lying to her by using someone else to tell her that lie? I thought you were smarter than that. Then clearly you are not to blame."

Jemmy's neck flushed bright red and he looked down at his hands.

"I knew," he whispered.

"Louder."

"I knew." Jemmy wasn't able to look at his father. "I lied so I could go with Louis."

"Is this who you are now? A liar?"

Laurent could see the effect of his words—like sharp slaps. He could almost see the boy recoil.

"No, Papa."

"What more can I take away from you? Perhaps no more TV until you leave home for college?"

Jemmy looked up fearfully as if imagining the full horror of such a prospect.

"Should I forbid you to walk freely around the vineyard? Or to be allowed to see Louis ever again?"

Jemmy looked at his hands miserably. "I don't know, Papa."

"No, I think instead I will withdraw my faith in you," Laurent said.

Jemmy looked up and for the first time, he looked directly at Laurent. Jemmy's eyes were swimming with tears.

"From now on," Laurent said sternly, "unless I see it with my own eyes, I will ask Mila to verify that what you say is the truth."

Jemmy looked at his father in shock, his face pale. "Until... until how long?" he asked.

But Laurent didn't answer.

"Go help your sister set the table," he said brusquely and strode off down the garden to call the dogs before he said something he knew he would be sorry for.

. . .

Maggie watched Laurent and Jemmy through the French doors. Her son looked the picture of dejection, his shoulders slumped, his head bowed. Even at this distance with a closed door between them Maggie could feel Laurent's fury bristling off him.

Wow, zero to sixty, she couldn't help but think. Last Saturday Laurent had essentially let Jemmy off the hook for disappearing at the amphitheater but now it almost looked like he was disinheriting his own son.

Maggie watched them until Laurent turned to walk away. She turned to go into the kitchen.

Should she speak to him? Surely Laurent would tell her what he said to Jemmy.

But isn't this what she wanted? For Laurent to make an impact on Jemmy? To make him realize his actions had consequences?

"Where's Jemmy?" Mila said as she came down the stairs, a library book in one hand. She automatically looked toward the French doors as they opened and her question was answered.

"Wash your hands, Mila," Maggie said. "Dinner will be ready in a few minutes."

Jemmy went to the kitchen and washed and dried his hands before opening the cutlery drawer to set the table.

Maggie bit her lip and forced herself not to speak. She couldn't say anything to Jemmy until she'd spoken to Laurent to find out what punishment he'd meted out.

"*Maman*?" Mila said from where she still stood at the foot of the stairs facing the foyer. "People just drove up."

Maggie frowned. "People?" She joined Mila in the hall in time to hear a heavy knock at the door.

Visitors were unusual at this hour since most people in France were sitting down to dinner.

"Go help your brother," Maggie said as she went to the door and opened it to reveal two stone-faced men, one young and one middle-aged, whose non-uniform clothing of mismatched suit blazer and slacks practically screamed *police*.

Maggie took a step back and her skin began to tingle uncomfortably.

"Madame Dernier?" the older man said.

Maggie heard the French doors open behind her and the sound of Laurent's footsteps as he joined her at the front door.

The two men immediately transferred their attention to the six-foot-five Frenchman.

"Monsieur Dernier?" the older man said, presenting his police badge. "May we come in?"

"What is this about?" Laurent asked, not budging to allow them in.

The man hesitated but the younger one eagerly filled in the silence.

"There has been a murder in the Arles amphitheater," he said.

13

"And why is that of interest to me?" Laurent said gruffly, still not moving to let the detectives in.

"It happened Saturday afternoon," the older detective said, nodding at Maggie. "While your wife was inside the amphitheater."

Maggie rubbed the back of her neck then crossed and recrossed her arms, nausea forming in her stomach as Laurent led the two men into the living room. Before following them she touched the entranceway column in the foyer to steady herself.

This happened at the amphitheater. While Jemmy was missing?

"Jemmy, Mila," Laurent called. "Upstairs. Both of you."

"Monsieur Dernier," the younger policeman said. "Excuse me. My name is Detective Sergeant Jean-Baptiste Moreau. My colleague is Lieutenant Detective Marc Bettoir. May we ask that the boy remain?"

"The boy?" Laurent said, not sure he'd heard correctly. Then he said, "Mila, go upstairs."

"Yes, Papa."

Mila gave one last apprehensive look over her shoulder at Jemmy before running up the stairs.

"Why do you want to talk to Jemmy?" Maggie said, moving into the living room and reaching for Jemmy to hold him near her.

"I am sorry to interrupt your dinner this evening, Madame Dernier," Detective Bettoir said, "But we have witnesses who have reported that your son might have seen something."

"Jemmy, come here," Laurent said. Jemmy left Maggie and went to stand by his father.

Detective Moreau smiled at him.

"Hello, Jemmy. Thank you for helping us with our inquiries. I need to ask you if you saw anyone that day in the amphitheater other than the group you were with."

Jemmy glanced up at his father and then back at the detective. "I saw no one," he said.

"Can you tell us where you went when you left your mother and the others?" Bettoir said. He had a pencil thin mustache that appeared to itch him since he wiggled his nose quite a bit as he spoke. Maggie could see Jemmy was staring at the mustache.

"I went to find a place to..." He glanced at Maggie and then back at the detective. "I went to find a place to pee," he said.

"And where was that?" Moreau asked. "Where did you find to relieve yourself?"

Jemmy shrugged and looked down at his feet.

"You are not in trouble for peeing against a wall if that is what you did," Laurent said in a low voice. "Answer the detective."

"I peed against a wall," Jemmy said quietly, his cheeks flushing.

"Which wall?" Bettoir asked.

Jemmy shrugged.

"They all look alike, do they not?" Moreau asked. "Can you tell us where you went to find this wall?"

Jemmy shrugged again. "I just walked."

Moreau straightened up and ran a hand through his hair.

Maggie had seen Laurent make this gesture a thousand times—always when he was frustrated.

"Who was murdered?" Laurent asked bluntly. "And where was the body?"

It was clear that the older detective would have opted not to answer Laurent so Maggie was glad when the younger one blurted out a response.

"His name was Jean Barbeau. He was a maintenance worker at the amphitheater."

"Where?" Maggie asked. When she spoke both detectives turned to look at her as though surprised to find her still in the room.

"In one of the hallways, Madame Dernier," Moreau said. He glanced back at Jemmy to see if his words would jog the boy's memory but Jemmy said nothing.

"Go upstairs with your sister," Laurent said to him and Jemmy turned and bolted up the staircase.

Then Laurent turned to the detectives. "How was the man killed?"

Maggie moved closer to Laurent. She could tell that Jemmy had paused at the top of the stairs to listen.

"Strangled, Monsieur."

"How did you know to come to us?" Laurent asked the detectives.

"We spoke with the event organizer, a Monsieur Claude Bouquille," Moreau said. "Monsieur Bouquille told us that he was with a small group inside the amphitheater at the time of the murder and that the child in their party had been missing for some minutes."

"Have you talked with the entire party in the amphitheater?"

"We have yet to talk with Madame Van Sant or Monsieur

Anderson, the other two Americans in your wife's party. And of course we must take a statement from your wife."

Maggie felt a wave of nausea. She still couldn't believe that a man had been strangled while Jemmy was wandering around unsupervised.

"Madame?" the younger detective prompted Maggie and she snapped out of her daze.

"I'm afraid I didn't see anything either," Maggie said, wringing her hands. "We were there less than thirty minutes."

"Can you tell me where you were during that time?"

"I was wandering around the tables in the arena with Grace... my friend Madame Van Sant...until I noticed my son was missing."

Maggie wiped a thin sheen of perspiration from her top lip. Just reliving the day's events knowing now that a man had been murdered made her stomach roil.

"And then you left the arena?" the older detective asked.

"Yes, I went up the steps to the next level. I thought I might be able to see Jemmy from up there."

"And were you alone at this time?"

Maggie glanced at Laurent who was watching her with a deep frown.

"Just for a moment," she said. "Claude Bouquille caught up with me and we were going to split up to look for Jemmy but I...I was feeling unwell."

"Monsieur Bouquille said you fainted. Is that not so?"

Maggie didn't dare look at Laurent now. She had left this bit out of her description to him earlier.

"I felt dizzy and I guess I might have fainted."

"How long do you think you were out?"

Hating that they were making such a big deal in front of Laurent of her fainting, Maggie blushed.

"Well, since I'd blacked out, wouldn't Monsieur Bouquille be a better person to ask that question?" she asked tartly.

"I think my wife has given you your statement," Laurent said.

"How do you know the man was killed while we were in the amphitheater?" Maggie asked.

"The body was found as soon as the crowds were let in and the victim's watch was stopped just minutes before, presumably smashed when he struggled with his assailant," the younger detective said.

"In due time the autopsy will confirm that but until then we are confident we have the exact time of death," the older detective added.

Laurent walked the two men to the front door and then, surprising Maggie, went outside with them, closing the front door behind him.

Laurent walked the detectives to their car. A cold evening breeze ruffled his hair. It wasn't Mistral level, but it was definitely bringing a warning of what was to come.

"Do not worry, Monsieur Dernier," Bettoir said as he opened the door of his car. "We are confident that we will be able to close this case in a matter of a few hours."

Laurent was surprised. "You already have a suspect?"

"The Arles police department doesn't see the point in expending more time or money on this particular case," Moreau said, his face stiff as if the words left a sour taste in his mouth.

"For a murder at a popular tourist attraction?" Laurent said in disbelief.

"Yes, well, considering everything, we don't believe anyone else is in danger from this particular assailant."

"And why is that?"

Before Moreau could answer, Bettoir leaned out of the car window and answered.

"Because the victim," he said with a moue of distaste, "was a registered pedophile."

14

Dinner that night was another tense affair.

Between Jemmy's guilt and subsequent punishment over lying about staying late at school, and the arrival of the two policemen with the shocking news about the murder in the amphitheater, all four of the Derniers sat at the dinner table lost in their own thoughts.

Even Maggie, who normally worked to bring everyone back on track during times of stress, seemed more focused on endlessly re-exploring that day at the Amphitheater than trying to create unity at the family dinner table.

"Papa?" Mila asked meekly at one point. "Is Jemmy in trouble?"

"Shut up, Mila," Jemmy said.

"Jemmy!" Maggie said. "Don't you—"

"Leave the table," Laurent said to his son, his tone brooking no argument.

Jemmy tossed his napkin down before going upstairs to his room.

Laurent turned to Mila whose eyes filled with tears. "It's not your fault, *chérie*," he said. "Jemmy is just upset."

"Did...did the police want to arrest him?"

"No, *chérie*. They were hoping he could help them in their inquiries. That's all. Did you have fun at *Dormir* again today? *Mamère* said you made more *macarons*?"

Mila nodded.

"If you have finished eating," Laurent said, "you may be excused."

Mila stood and took her and Jemmy's plates to the kitchen. After she left the room, he turned to Maggie. He saw the fear in her eyes.

"*Chérie*, Jemmy is fine. He is safe."

He knew exactly what she was thinking. He knew it as well as if she'd shouted it from the tile rooftop of Domaine St-Buvard.

Jemmy had been close to the murder.

But what Maggie *didn't* know was how close Jemmy had been to a child molester.

"I know that," Maggie said softly as she stood with her plate and reached for Laurent's.

"You did not mention to me that you fainted."

Maggie flushed. "I was upset. I was really just a little dizzy."

Laurent arched an eyebrow at her words and Maggie turned to escape into the kitchen.

A few minutes later when Laurent knocked on Jemmy's bedroom door, he found his son lying on his bed holding a *Hardy Boy's* book. Laurent breathed a sigh of relief that it wasn't one of Jemmy's electronics. He'd have had to call him on it and that would have gotten in the way of the message he needed to deliver tonight.

Jemmy swung his legs off the bed, his eyes wide with surprise. He'd clearly not expected Laurent to continue their downstairs discussion.

"I shouldn't have said shut-up to Mila," Jemmy said quickly.

"No, you shouldn't have," Laurent said, sitting on the bed. "Tell her so before lights out tonight."

Jemmy nodded, his eyes wide with curiosity about why his father was still in his room.

"I may have been wrong to tell you I didn't have faith in you," Laurent said, further widening his son's eyes in astonishment.

Have I ever told him I was wrong before?

"I have faith that when I ask you a direct question you will tell me the truth."

"Yes, Papa. I will I promise," Jemmy said. His face relaxed a bit.

"What did you see when you left your mother at the amphitheater on Saturday?"

"I told you, Papa. No one. I swear it."

"I'm not asking *who* you saw," Laurent said.

Jemmy looked away for a moment and then seemed to come to a decision.

"There were some kittens," he said finally. "I saw them when we first came into the amphitheater."

"And you went looking for them?"

"I also had to pee!"

"And that's all you saw? Kittens?"

"They looked hungry."

Laurent glanced around Jemmy's room. A nightstand with a clock radio was set next to the bed which was neatly made. Across the room Jemmy's desk was piled high with books and notebooks. The desktop was not tidy but Jemmy's grades were good.

The rest of the room was typical of a young boy. Clothes were on the floor, a backpack on the bed, music earphones dangled from a dresser knob. It was perplexing to Laurent that the child could already have grown as much as he had. It seemed like yesterday when he'd stood in the hospital room with Maggie and held his firstborn son in his arms.

He'd never felt happier or prouder in his life.

"Do you know," Laurent said evenly, "that nobody is allowed to touch your body without your permission?"

Jemmy screwed up his face in confusion. "What?"

"Not a stranger, not someone you know, not even me. Do you understand?"

Jemmy blushed and picked up his book again. "I guess so."

"Are you not sure?"

"No, I'm sure. I understand. Nobody is allowed to touch me. I know that."

"Good."

Laurent stood but Jemmy didn't look at him. He was staring at his book. Something about the way Jemmy was looking at the book made it clear he wasn't seeing the printed words on the page.

He's just embarrassed, Laurent thought. *Worth it if he got the message.*

"Be sure and apologize to your sister."

"I will."

Laurent left the room but as he stood in the hallway pulling the door closed behind him he couldn't help but think that there was something about how Jemmy had answered him that felt unfinished.

After Maggie washed her face and pulled on her flannel night gown and crawled into bed she was pretty sure it was nothing less than miraculous that she'd made it through dinner and the rest of the evening without imploding.

Jemmy had been right there when a murderer was strangling his victim!

She glanced at Laurent's empty side of the bed. He had taken the dogs outside before locking up the house for the night.

Everything felt so unsettled. When Maggie had gone in to say goodnight to Jemmy, the child was polite but reserved.

She picked up the novel she'd been reading and put it back down when she heard Laurent coming up the stairs. He'd done his best to avoid her for most of the evening.

If he thinks for one moment that I'm going to just fall asleep without him telling me exactly what happened in his talk with Jemmy, well, he is either drunk or crazy.

"You are still awake?" Laurent said as he came into the room.

"We need to talk," she said, patting his side of the bed.

"*Chérie*, it's late." He pulled off his t-shirt, undershirt and pullover sweater all in one movement.

"Shut the door, Laurent. It's not that late."

Laurent closed the bedroom door and stripped down to his boxers before slipping into bed next to Maggie and pulling her close.

She'd been down this road before. If he thought he was going to distract her into not asking her questions, she was ready for him.

"I need to *know*, Laurent," she said as he kissed her neck.

"You need sleep, *chérie*," he said. "Aren't you going to Saint-Rémy tomorrow?"

She was surprised he remembered her interview with Belle-mont-Surrey and then reminded herself that this was Laurent. He always heard more than anyone thought he did.

"No, we haven't set a time yet," she said, pulling away from him to look him in the eye. "What did you say to Jemmy?"

"The light, *chérie*?" Laurent said with a yawn.

Maggie clicked the light off. "I need to know, Laurent."

"I handled it. That is all you need to know."

Maggie clicked the light back on and Laurent groaned.

"No, it is not all I need to know. If you told him no TV for a month, I need to know not to allow him any TV."

"I did not ban him from TV," Laurent said with a sigh.

"Well, then what did you punish him with?"

"My words. I told him how disappointed I was in him."

"That's it? He deliberately lied to us and that's all you did? Do *I* need to punish him?"

"He's your son too, of course," Laurent said coolly. "You may punish him on top of my talk if you feel it necessary."

Maggie stared at him. There was something going on here. She didn't know what it was but there was definitely something Laurent wasn't telling her. And if she knew anything, she knew that whatever it was she'd never get it out of him if he didn't want to tell her.

"The light, Maggie?"

She could always tell when he was seriously upset with her. He stopped calling her *chérie* and reverted to her name.

"Do you think he really didn't see anyone?" she asked.

"Why would he lie?"

"Maybe he saw something and it was so upsetting to him—"

"Don't make this worse than it is. Jemmy isn't suffering from PTSD. He said he saw no one."

"How could that be true? He was right there where it happened!"

"He insists he saw only a few cats. You are getting yourself upset over nothing."

"Your son nearly getting killed or witnessing a murder is *not* nothing!"

"If you don't turn out the light, I will go sleep in the study."

After everything they'd been through in ten years of marriage, Laurent had never threatened not to sleep in their bed. Her stomach lurching with premonition, Maggie turned and shut off the light.

After a moment she heard the gentle rumble of his snores telling her he'd fallen asleep.

No goodnights, no I love yous.

Just a division between them as deep and wide as she'd ever felt before.

15

The next day, after Laurent left to take the children to school, Maggie sat at the kitchen table and watched the morning sunlight creep across its rough, scarred surface.

She and Laurent had interacted this morning as if they hadn't fallen asleep estranged and distant. Jemmy was quieter than usual which triggered Mila to be chattier.

All in all, it was an artificial morning that made the anxiety in Maggie's stomach throb inside her like a living thing.

As she watched Laurent's car disappear down their drive to the village road, it occurred to her that she hadn't asked—nor had he volunteered—any details about what he was doing at the monastery these days.

The recent harvest had taken so much time and energy—from all of them—that when it was over Maggie had fallen into the mistaken assumption that it was all behind them.

She should know better. Even without supervising the grape-picking, Laurent was still busy in the harvest aftermath.

Not only did he have a dozen transient young people to more or less keep an eye on, but work in the fields was never really done. The details of that work and what it entailed however were hazier than Maggie wanted to admit she was comfortable with.

How can Laurent have a driving passion that directs his actions day in and day out and I know so little about it?

She emptied the dishwasher and wiped down the kitchen counter although it was perfectly clean.

She reminded herself that for the most part, Laurent's reticence was more a part of his nature than anything triggered by current circumstances. She could sit at his knee every evening and pull every single detail of his day out of him and he would still succeed in holding back information he didn't deem prudent she know.

It was so annoying.

But now perhaps it was more than annoying. Perhaps it was actually dangerous to the health of their marriage.

Maggie washed out her coffee mug even though she knew she intended to have at least three more cups before the morning was over. She had work to do on next month's newsletter.

She needed to sort through her notes from the conversation she'd had a few weeks ago at the St-Buvard Women's Guild. She liked to give them at least a small presence in the newsletter each month. None of her subscribers were particularly interested in what six elderly French villagers had in mind to do with St-Buvard's upcoming village *fêtes*. But it wasn't for *them*.

The goodwill Maggie reaped from the Guild by including the village ladies in her newsletter was every bit as important as the sales on her Etsy store or the advertising revenue that came in from her various vendors.

She sat down at her desk and opened up the document on her computer that she'd roughly entitled *My Life as the Ex-Pat Wife of a French Vigneron*. It was a terrible title. Most American readers would have no idea what the word *vigneron* even meant.

But lately it had become clear that Maggie needed to write a memoir of her experience living in France to sell through her newsletter. Her subscribers wanted to know more about her and her family and her life in Provence.

The problem was, Maggie wasn't at all sure how interesting what she had to say was.

How fascinating is it to write about picking up fish heads for stock at the market or nagging children to bring laundry off the line?

Maggie scrolled through the few paragraphs she'd written and then, stalling, picked up her cellphone to call her mother. After a brief conversation where Maggie was relieved to hear her mother was fine and Nicole was fine and her father was as fine as could be expected, Maggie disconnected. Before she'd hung up she had come very close to promising her mother she would bring the children home for Thanksgiving next month and was relieved when she'd hung up without committing to anything.

She got up to make another pot of coffee and stood in the kitchen drumming her fingers on the counter. Her eyes shifted to the scene out the kitchen window over the farmhouse sink that Laurent had installed last year and she re-envisioned his tail-lights again as he'd driven away this morning.

Where did he go every morning?

She rarely spotted him or his group of wayward teens out in the vineyard these days. Was he at the monastery sorting out behavioral problems with *Frère* Jean? The defrocked brother was more fervid than ever working with Laurent on his various projects, specifically the mini-cottages Laurent had built on the edge of land between Domaine St-Buvard and the road to *l'Abbaye de Sainte-Trinité*.

While the coffee percolated, Maggie went back to her office to get her cellphone. Both dogs lifted their heads from where they lay on the hexagonal floor tiles in front of the French doors.

She hesitated about texting Laurent. Normally she reserved daytime communications between them for important matters like *Don't forget the reblochon!* Or, *we're out of aubergines!*

Laurent had a habit of ignoring his phone at the best of times and Maggie didn't want to encourage the tendency any more than necessary.

She called Grace instead.

"Is this a bad time?" she asked when Grace picked up.

"Hold on a sec."

Maggie heard muffled conversation on Grace's end and then she came back on the line.

"I guess the police visited you, too?" Grace said.

"Last night," Maggie said, and sat down at the kitchen table. From this vantage point she could see straight through the dining room, out the French doors and to the terrace beyond. "You?"

"They just left. They said they're heading to Aix to talk to Brad. I just can't believe someone was murdered while we there!"

"It's horrible," Maggie said, getting up to pour her coffee. She noticed her hands were trembling and decided against more coffee.

"And Jemmy wandering around when it was happening? You must be going out of your mind," Grace said.

Maggie suddenly felt too warm.

"Did he ever say *why* he wandered off?" Grace asked.

"He said he saw some kittens or something. I guess he wanted to see where they lived."

"Typical kid."

"The police said they were going to wrap the murder up today. Did they say anything like that to you?"

"No. But now that you mention it, they didn't seem all that keen to find the killer. It felt like they were just going through the motions."

Maggie realized Grace was right. Both detectives last night had acted strangely perfunctory like they were just ticking off the appropriate boxes.

What else could explain why they thought they could resolve the case so quickly?

"Maybe they already have a suspect in mind." Maggie said.

"There were at least twenty vendors in the arena in addition to us."

"Then why talk to us?"

"Probably just dotting their i's. You're right, though. It does sound strange."

"*Gabriel, non*! That goes *outside*!" Grace said firmly.

"Problems this morning?" Maggie asked, as she saw another call coming through. She recognized that the number prefix was from London.

"I need to run, darling," Grace said. "Catch up with you later?"

"Sure," Maggie said, connecting to the incoming call. She wasn't surprised to hear the clipped, high-pitched tones of Fiona Bellemont-Surrey's assistant Zoe.

"Maggie?" Zoe said without preface, "I'm ready to set up your interview with Mrs. Bellemont-Surrey. Do you have your calendar?"

Maggie walked to her office and flipped open her work diary.

"Good morning, Zoe. Is it raining in London today?"

Fiona's assistant worked offsite and had mentioned before that she'd never even been to France, "*except for Paris which of course you can't really count, right?*"

"Isn't it always?" Zoe said. "How does next Tuesday look? Fourteen hundred hours? In Saint-Rémy?"

Maggie didn't even need to look at her diary. She would move any and all appointments out of the way for this one.

"That's fine," she said, crossing out a dentist appointment and inking in 2 *PM FB-S Interview* in the space.

"There's a gate code," Fiona continued. "I'll text it to you on the day, shall I? Fiona's fierce about security."

"Sure," Maggie said. She hated the fact that because of her turmoil over what had happened with Jemmy at the amphitheater all the excitement she would normally have felt over this phone call wasn't there.

"Right-e-o," Zoe said. "I'll notify Mrs. Bellemont-Surrey straightaway." Then without saying goodbye, the young woman disconnected.

Maggie sat in her chair, her cellphone in her hand and let a seeping of discontentment wash over her.

All she could think of was how close her son had been to a man having the life strangled out of him.

As she sat there clutching her phone and staring into space the fact of Jemmy's proximity to the murder seemed to grow in Maggie's mind like a desiccated sponge filling with water.

Before she even knew she was doing it, she punched in the number on her phone for *Information* and asked for the Arles City Police Department.

It took five full minutes to get from the receptionist to the right department. Maggie remembered only one of the detectives' names—Moreau—and then only because she'd connected him with *The Island of Dr. Moreau.*

Finally a young man's voice came on the line.

"Sergeant Detective Moreau," he said, sounding friendly.

"Yes, hello," Maggie said, suddenly not even sure why she was calling or what she wanted from him. "This is Maggie Dernier. You came to my house last night?"

"Yes, Madame Dernier. I remember you of course."

"I was just wondering if you had a suspect or any more information about...you know, about what happened last Saturday at the Amphitheater."

"No, Madame, but we are in the process of wrapping up all loose ends. Your son didn't remember anything new?"

A throb of dread invaded Maggie's gut. *There it was again. This detective thought Jemmy had seen something. Why did he keep coming back to that? And why would Jemmy have been more likely to have seen something than the rest of them?*

"No, nothing except some cats," Maggie said. "He didn't see anything else."

"Oh, well."

"But if you're able to wrap up the case does that mean you know who killed the man?"

The detective hesitated. "We won't actually close the case. Without solving it, we can't."

"I'm confused," Maggie said. Her eyes fell on a framed photo of Jemmy at two years old being held by Laurent who was smiling broadly. It was just before Mila was born. "Is it because you have no hope of solving it?"

I want the man skulking around the arena strangling people found and punished!

The killer could just as easily have found Jemmy that day.

Yet he was still walking around free, possibly ready to kill again!

"It's not that, Madame," Moreau said with a sigh. "I would love nothing more than to find the person who killed Barbeau but the department will not countenance an expenditure of manpower at this time."

"For a *murder*?" Maggie said, her anxiety creeping up her spine. "What's more important than murder?"

The killer was going to be allowed to run free?

When might he show up next? When Jemmy or Mila were walking down the street, ice cream cones in their hands, and trust in their hearts that the world was a safe place and the police worked to make it so?

Maggie forced the agitating images out of her head.

"I agree with you, of course, Madame Dernier," the policeman said. "But because of the victim's background, I'm afraid the unofficial consensus is that the killer did the city of Arles a public service and since we do not believe any normal citizen is in further danger from—"

"Whoa, whoa!" Maggie said, her mind swirling in bewilderment. "What do you mean he did the city a service? By *killing* a man?"

"No, by killing a convicted child molester."

16

Mila threw her arms around Laurent's neck and kissed his cheek before grabbing her satchel and jumping out of the car to run up the stairs of her school. Laurent watched her go in bemusement and felt his heart skip a beat at the sight of her self-confidence and animation.

Jemmy was out of the car with a quick "*Bye, Papa*" thrown over his shoulder as he hurried to catch up with his sister.

His two children were so different, Laurent mused as he watched Jemmy—his back straight and rigid—ascend the wide stone slab steps to his school. As he watched his son, Laurent found himself wondering if the boy really hadn't seen anything last Saturday besides a few cats. As soon as the thought formed in his head he shook it away.

You sound like Maggie.

One thing he knew was that his wife was blowing the event at the amphitheater way out of proportion and if it was allowed to continue, it would soon become something that nobody would be able to control.

He drove down Avenue Victor Hugo, past the entrance to the Cours Mirabeau and into the inner labyrinth of narrow cobblestone streets that led to the *place Richelme* produce market. Maggie never bothered driving into town, preferring instead to use the underground parking facility at *Les Allées*, but Laurent always drove in even if it meant delays and waiting for a parking spot to open up.

He found a curb with no restrictions two streets from the *place de maire* and parked. Within minutes he was picking through the market's broad selection of root vegetables, fish and cheese.

Normally Laurent was so absorbed in the handling and sniffing of produce combined with conversing with the various vendors that he was in his own world. But because of his past—where he never had the luxury of focusing only on one thing without also needing to look all around him—and because someone who is doing something wrong always moves furtively and unnaturally he noticed Luc immediately when the boy was clearly making every effort to be invisible.

Luc stood twenty feet away next to the cheese vendor's booth, his hands by his side. His fingers were twitching in anticipation. His eyes darted nervously at the wheels of soft and hard cheeses.

Laurent felt a sliver of annoyance. First, that the boy would come to *his* favorite market and attempt to steal, and secondly that he would even think to do it when he was clearly so bad at it.

Dropping the squash he'd picked up, Laurent moved silently until he was within a few steps of Luc.

The second Luc lifted his hand, Laurent cleared his throat.

Luc turned to see him, his face immediately whitening. Laurent nodded to the café at the edge of the market and Luc followed him there. Laurent sat down and ordered two cafés.

"I'm not really—" Luc started.

"Sit," Laurent said.

Luc sat.

"I know they feed you at the monastery," Laurent said.

"Not for much longer," Luc said.

What with the murder and Maggie's preoccupation with it

because of Jemmy, Laurent hadn't given Luc much thought in the last couple of days. He wondered if *Frère* Jean had held the tribunal about the theft yet.

"Are you leaving *l'Abbaye de Sainte-Trinité*?" Laurent asked.

"They said I stole twenty euros from someone's sleeping bag," Luc said.

"Twenty euros is a lot of money."

Luc snorted and the waiter brought the two coffees. Laurent noticed that Luc snatched up the sugar cookie that came with the coffee and popped it in his mouth. The action reminded Laurent that Luc was still just a boy.

"If they make you leave," Laurent said, "what will you do? Steal from the Aix market? Is your plan to ensure you get three meals a day from the Aix police department?"

"I don't have a plan," Luc mumbled, picking up his coffee and looking at it as if he'd never drunk coffee before.

Gerard, Laurent thought suddenly. *That's who he reminds me of*.

The realization brought with it a grinding punch to the gut. Laurent had an unbidden image of Gerard as he'd been at sixteen—the same age as Luc—and then of the monster he'd grown into.

Gerard was killed five years ago in Paris and Laurent realized he'd never really marked that fact. Gerard had been every kind of bad news for so long, Laurent had forgotten what it had felt like to be his older brother.

Luc drained his coffee.

"I wasn't really going to take anything," Luc said defensively. "I don't know what you think you saw."

"I know taking responsibility is the first step to being a man," Laurent said.

"Even if you didn't do anything wrong?"

"Especially then."

"Can I go? Or are you making a citizen's arrest?"

Laurent waved a hand, dismissing him, and the boy jumped up and dissolved into the crowd of shoppers.

Laurent watched a group of tourists milling about the market for a moment and then began to calculate the meal he intended to make later—a simple eggplant gratin with a good white fish—when he realized a part of him was imagining Luc at the dinner table in Domaine St-Buvard.

Sometimes just a simple hot meal can do a lot.

He imagined how Maggie might greet this suggestion. He knew they'd left things unresolved between them last night and that was his fault.

He hadn't been up for the endless conversation he knew Maggie was revving up for.

He hated to admit it, as much as he loved her and her blunt American ways, he'd known he'd needed to be merciless in cutting the discussion off or he'd end up spending another unproductive and sleepless night where nobody felt better, no problems were solved, but another day still had to be managed without adequate sleep.

As he tossed down five euros for the coffees and gathered his produce bags another thought crept into his head. This one nearly made him flinch at its visceral impact.

Luc didn't really remind him of Gerard so much.

Or at least no more than he reminded Laurent of himself.

17

That evening, Maggie was ready for Laurent.

The phrase *lying in wait* came unattractively to mind as she went about her day preparing for the evening but she pushed the words aside. After Detective Moreau's bombshell about who the victim had been, he'd then gone on to reveal that this information had been imparted to Laurent *two days ago* when the police had come to the house.

Laurent had known the murder victim was a child molester.

Jemmy had been wandering through the dark hallways of the Arles amphitheater looking for stray kitties *with a convicted pedophile lurking in one of the nearby corners.*

Perhaps the murder victim had followed Jemmy.

Perhaps he'd been watching Jemmy and when he saw him go down to the tunnels, he went down after him.

Maggie walked to the front door to distract herself from the torturous images growing in her head. She'd sent both children to their rooms to do their homework as soon as they got home after she'd picked them up from school.

And she'd rescinded Laurent's edict against electronics, deciding that if things got noisy downstairs between her and

Laurent, the volume of kids' music and TV shows might help drown out any harsh words.

Besides, it felt good to countermand an order of Laurent's. When Maggie told Jemmy he could use his iPad, he frowned and said, "Papa said I couldn't."

"Well, I'm saying you *can* so it's up to you to do what you want."

Shrugging, Jemmy picked up his iPad from the couch and followed Mila upstairs.

Now Maggie stood in the foyer, a glass of Sauternes in her hand—her second and she hadn't had dinner yet—and watched Laurent's Citroen come up the driveway. The light faded fast in Provence in late October and while it wasn't yet six o'clock, the image of his headlights cutting through the gloom was the first thing Maggie saw.

He'd known about the murder victim being a child molester.

Just thinking the words drove a spike of panic up her spine.

And yet it was all she could think of. A part of her knew she was making things worse and that focusing on a *little* something bad—like Laurent keeping this information from her—was better than concentrating on the *big* something bad—the one she was powerless to do anything about—of how close Jemmy had been not only to a killer but a *child molester.*

She watched Laurent park. His thoughts must have been elsewhere because he'd taken several steps to the front door before he seemed to see that Maggie was standing there. That was unusual. Laurent was typically five steps ahead of her.

Not tonight.

"*Bonsoir, chérie,*" Laurent said, his eyes going first to the glass of wine in her hand before leaning in to kiss her on the cheek as he passed through the front door.

"Oh, we're kissing again?" Maggie said and instantly hated that she'd started out that way. Now he'd know the tenor of things and giving Laurent any advance knowledge at all was usually tantamount to giving the entire game away.

Laurent hesitated in the foyer and glanced around the vacant living and dining room.

"*Les enfants*?"

"Upstairs," Maggie said shutting the front door.

He shrugged out of his jacket, hanging it on the hook in the foyer, his back to her so she couldn't see what he was thinking.

She nearly snorted out loud. As if she'd ever known what he was thinking.

"*Poulet en confit*?" he said, moving into the kitchen.

Maggie had started the meal and then become distracted by her thoughts, the wine, and the speech she'd rehearsed for him.

She watched him wash his hands before turning to the pot on the stove and adjusting the flame under it.

"You knew," she said as she came to the kitchen doorway. "You knew and didn't tell me."

Laurent didn't turn around.

"Laurent..."

"I'm not sure I have the patience for this tonight," he said.

Heat flushed through Maggie's body.

"You act like I frequently put you through something you have to muster the patience for!" she said hotly. "Is that what you're saying?"

"Not at all, *chérie*. It's just that today has been a trying one."

Maggie was momentarily thrown. *A trying one?* She'd spent the last two days obsessing about her son being murdered only to find out he was in more danger of being sexually accosted *first*, and Laurent thought *he'd* had a trying day?

She took a long swallow of her wine and tried to put her thoughts together. She knew Laurent was absolutely capable of turning around, car keys in hand, and leaving the field of battle. And if he did she would get nothing—no satisfaction, no relief from this mountain of fury and indignation building inside her, and no solidarity. Because ultimately, as angry as she was with him, she knew what she really wanted was to be on the same page with him about all this.

"What did you do today?" she asked, trying to keep her voice steady.

Laurent turned to glance at her. After a moment he took down a wine glass and poured himself a glass of the Sauternes.

That's a good sign. It means he isn't thinking of bolting.

"You know I have been working with *Frère* Jean about finding work for some of the young men at the monastery?" Laurent said.

She nodded.

"One boy in particular has been a problem," he said.

"Why? What's he done?"

"The usual. Stealing, staying out after curfew, vandalism. He needs something. I'm not sure what."

"You know you can't save all of them, Laurent."

He narrowed his eyes at her.

"What's his name?"

"Luc."

Laurent turned to stir the *sauce vierge* and then brought down four plates from the cupboard overhead. Only he could reach the plates without a stepladder.

Maggie let the silence grow between them. He'd elaborate when he was ready.

Or not.

She could hear the faint sounds of music coming from upstairs. Perhaps it was Mila. So far Laurent didn't seem to have noticed.

Again, that was always a dangerous assumption when it came to Laurent.

"I'd like to bring him home with me," Laurent said as he crumbled thyme sprigs over the pot and then settled the lid back on top.

Maggie was almost positive she hadn't heard correctly. Did he just suggest that the kid that was giving the monastery so much trouble should come home to *their* house?

Laurent turned to look at Maggie as if waiting for her reaction, confirming to her that indeed that was what he'd suggested.

"You can't be serious," she said.

She watched a muscle tighten in his jaw as he regarded her but he said nothing.

"Bring him *here*?" Maggie said. "A troubled kid? To be with our children? Do you mean for a meal or for...I mean, I'm sorry for his bad luck or whatever—"

Laurent held up a hand, and Maggie stopped talking. She knew he could fill in the blanks better than she could speak them.

But no. Just no.

She didn't want his juvenile delinquent sitting at her table, making Jemmy admire his tattoos and wayward ways, making Mila feel uncomfortable or worse, star-struck. *Just no.*

Later Maggie would think that the schism between them—the moment between *before* and *after*—had happened at that moment. *Before*—when Laurent was drinking wine with her and cooking supper and telling her about his day and then *after*—when Maggie saw his personal charity case sitting at their dinner table and pushing Jemmy even further away from his family.

She felt sick about the all-too-accurate assessment she saw reflected in Laurent's eyes. He was disappointed in her.

Worse than that, he didn't act surprised.

Maggie didn't know which one sickened her most.

"Laurent, think about it! Mila's only eight years old!"

"Luc is not a child molester," Laurent said and Maggie watched him flinch as he instantly regretted his choice of words. For him to blurt something out without thinking was one of the most un-Laurent-like things she'd seen him do.

This kid Luc was under Lauren's skin for some reason. Maggie knew if she thought about it, if she'd just push pause for a moment and *think* about it, she'd realize there was something else going on than she could see right now.

But she didn't stop or push pause. She didn't ask herself why this kid meant so much to Laurent. All she could see was that for some reason, when it came to protecting their family, Laurent didn't seem like he was on her team at all.

"A child molester like the man who was just a few feet away from Jemmy at the amphitheater," Maggie said. "I can't believe you *knew* about Barbeau and didn't tell me!"

Laurent leaned against the counter and crossed his arms, his eyes dark and unreadable.

"Because telling you would be so helpful?" he said.

"How dare you! You don't get to decide that! You had no right to keep this information from me."

He appeared cool and unaffected but Maggie knew that raging waters were just beneath the surface. She knew him well enough to know he was furious.

And somehow that helped.

"Knowing the truth would only have upset you," he said.

"Plenty of lies can conveniently reside in that category, Laurent. Anything else you want to tell me?"

She didn't know why she said that. She didn't think he was keeping anything serious from her. But she was angry and she knew her words would strike a chord.

"You should take a breath," he said. "Go outside and collect yourself."

Furious that he would use the same words on her that he used with the children when they were in tantrum mode, Maggie deliberately set her wine glass down on the counter before she gave in to the impulse to throw it at him.

"You knew who that man was and you said nothing to me."

She didn't know why she kept repeating this. Maybe because deep down she knew she had no real reason to be angry but she *felt* so angry she had to keep hammering away at it.

"How could you knowing that information possibly hurt Jemmy?" Laurent said. "The man is dead!"

And there it was. The crux of the problem.

The man was dead and no threat to anyone. So why was Maggie so threatened by him?

"I'll call the children for dinner," she said, biting off the words and attempting to turn away with some semblance of dignity. Her eyes stung with tears.

She didn't know what she'd achieved here tonight except pushing herself further away from Laurent.

Right when she needed him the most.

18

That evening was a quiet, uneventful one marked by no more arguments or dissension. Both Mila and Jemmy, knowing their parents were at odds, were quiet and subdued.

The next morning, grateful to have a reason to leave the house early, Laurent was on the highway to Marseille where he'd arranged to meet with a couple of potential business associates.

The men were investors in vineyards all through Europe but Laurent was more interested in their ideas that they'd seen in action in other vineyards than their money.

The cellphone mounted on his dashboard chimed and he looked to see his main contact for today's meeting was asking to push the appointment back an hour. That suited Laurent. Marseille had the best fish in all of Europe and he had a favorite vendor he'd not been able to visit nearly enough.

If he packed the fillets with crushed ice, the fish he bought this morning would be perfect for tonight's dinner.

Before he had a chance to tell his contact the delay was no problem, his phone chimed again. This time it was a text from *Frère* Jean.

Laurent frowned. The text read simply: <*Call me.*>

Laurent ran over in his mind all the possible reasons why the monk might need him. Their separate projects involving the monastery's residents overlapped in one or two areas. But with the harvest over, there were fewer and fewer reasons Laurent could think of.

Except for Luc.

Laurent had no idea why *Frère* Jean thought Luc was of special interest to him. The kid had done his work on the harvest, had not caused too many problems and that was that. Laurent couldn't help but think of Maggie and her current worry over Jemmy compared with Luc's problems. It was frankly puzzling to comprehend how Maggie could be so worried about Jemmy.

The boy has everything!

He was driven to school, driven to his friends' houses, supervised in his play, monitored in the completion of his homework, guided and praised for his every endeavor regardless of the outcome.

He's been given everything any child could dream of.

A splinter of unease pierced Laurent. He knew that in spite of all of Jemmy's many gifts and luxuries—far more than Luc or even Laurent himself had ever had as a boy—Jemmy still needed Laurent's attention.

And possibly more than Laurent was currently giving him.

Laurent remembered his own cold and uninvolved father. And while Laurent had weathered the lack of a loving father in his life, in the end, his brother Gerard had not.

Shaking off his growing agitation, and with one eye on the road, Laurent typed in his response to his wine contact that the delay was fine.

Five minutes later, studiously forcing away thoughts of Maggie's unhappiness, Jemmy's generally disruptive behavior and Luc's looming homelessness, his phone lit up with a call.

He picked it up without looking to see who it was.

"*Oui*?" he said.

"Can you come to Aix today?" *Frère* Jean said.

"No," Laurent said. "I am going in the opposite direction."

"Then please turn around. Luc has been arrested."

19

Maggie held her fingers over the computer keyboard and tried to concentrate.

She'd already gotten up four times this morning to let the dogs out, check on the basil in the *potager* to see if it needed watering, and gone upstairs twice—once to make sure the children had turned off the bath water and once to make sure the shutters were closed in her bedroom.

Check and check.

With Maggie and Laurent's fight from last night hanging over the whole family like an ominous pall, breakfast had been strained again this morning. The children didn't need to have heard the specifics of the argument to know their parents were at odds with each other.

Maggie hated that. She had no memory of her own parents fighting. Ever. Nor had she ever heard a harsh word between them.

She'd always assumed her own marriage would be the same and while it was by and large relatively turmoil-free, she had to admit that she and Laurent butted heads many more times than her parents had.

Partly that was because in her parents' generation everyone accepted their roles and just plowed ahead. If Laurent had been American, he'd have evolved as Maggie assumed most American men had—accepting that their wives worked and were not automatically the main housekeepers in the marriage.

Although now that she thought of it, that wasn't how her brother Ben's marriage had been. Ben had been the sole breadwinner and his wife Haley content to keep her body in shape with tennis and her skin glowing with facials. Staying in shape and hosting the occasional formal dinner party had been the extent of Haley's marital responsibilities as far as Maggie could tell.

But however it was "back home," Laurent *wasn't* an American husband. Not by a long shot. His default reaction to Maggie had always been to be protective, paternalistic and at times downright chauvinistic.

There were times when that amused and even charmed Maggie.

But there were many more times when it made her dig in her heels to underscore to him that she was not his possession but an equal partner in their marriage. It had taken a long time and many sharp turns along the way, but for the most part Maggie thought she'd managed it.

Laurent was proud of what she'd achieved in her work with the newsletter and even, if you put his Gallic feet to the fire, admitting the help she'd given the local police in solving certain mysteries in the area. Not the least of which was the case last spring when, if not for Maggie's "meddling," Laurent would have gone to prison for a crime he didn't commit.

Maggie stared out the floor-to-ceiling window in her study. Even though it wasn't yet midday, it was grey and forbidding outside.

She worked out a stiffness in her lower back with her fingers and then glanced again at her computer. She was supposed to be outlining a piece she wanted to publish during the holidays about some of the Christmas markets in the area. She had a stack of notes she'd gathered from the last couple of years.

Except somehow she just didn't feel in the Christmas spirit.

Her cellphone buzzed and she snatched it up from her desk.

"Hello?"

"Good morning, *chérie*," Danielle said. "You are right by your phone, I see."

"Oh, good morning, Danielle."

Who was she expecting? Laurent? There was no way he'd have a serious conversation with her by phone. As far as he was concerned, phones were for emergencies or urgently needed grocery items. Which in Laurent's case were usually the same thing.

"I am on my way," Danielle said. "You are still happy to take a break with me?"

Maggie had completely forgotten that Danielle was coming over. She glanced guiltily at her computer and the blinking cursor on the screen.

Ever since Jean-Luc had died in Maggie and Laurent's vineyard the year before, Danielle and Maggie had gotten into the habit of taking walks to the spot and enjoying a thermos of coffee and a quiet moment together. It felt like a visit with Jean-Luc.

"Yes, of course," Maggie said. "I hadn't forgotten."

"Zouzou made *canelés* yesterday," Danielle said. "And I have a thermos filled and ready. I'll be there in five minutes."

"See you then."

Relieved to have an excuse to stop pretending to work, Maggie got up to get her jacket and the dogs' leashes. Laurent was able to walk them off lead but Maggie knew if she tried they'd end up half way to Nîmes before she realized they were gone.

She tucked her cellphone in her jacket pocket and then on

impulse, dialed the number that had reached Detective Moreau the day before.

An irritated receptionist informed her that Detective Moreau wasn't answering his line and before Maggie could respond, she rerouted the call to Moreau's partner.

"Detective Bettoir," he barked into the line.

"*Bonjour*, Detective Bettoir. This is Maggie Dernier. I was hoping you—"

"That case has been closed, Madame. I am sorry we cannot give out any information on it."

Maggie felt a pinch of annoyance in her gut.

"Well, I know it has *not* been closed because your partner told me yesterday that you're just going to sit on it so let's try this conversation again, why don't we?" she said tightly.

A heavy sigh rattled the other end of the line.

"I am sorry my colleague felt the need to confuse you, Madame. But the fact remains that *we* are not on the case any longer."

"He said that *no one* was on the case," Maggie said.

"That is not entirely true. The case will remain open until additional evidence allows us to move forward on it."

"Well, how is *additional evidence* going to crop up if nobody is actively looking for it?"

"I am sorry, Madame. I must go now." And then in a burst of frustration, he said, "Why would you care about justice for someone like him? I would have thought that a mother of all people would not care."

Maggie felt herself recoil at the man's harsh words.

"Good day, Madame Dernier," Bettoir said and hung up.

20

The vineyard rows ambled over the gently sloping hills in perfect precision behind the farmhouse. A burst of breeze snagged at Maggie's long hair, whipping it around her face and she shivered inside her jacket. The midday sun no longer was able to mitigate the morning's brisk entrance. It stayed cold all day now.

Maggie carried two portable stools and a blanket. She managed to hold both dog leads while Danielle carried the thermos and the bag of *canelés*.

"It's getting colder," Danielle remarked as Maggie positioned the chairs at the top of the northeast quadrant of the vineyard.

Someone else might think what they were doing was morbid, Maggie thought as she settled onto one of the chairs and handed Danielle the wool throw for her knees. But she and Danielle both looked at it as a sort of picnic with Jean-Luc. And as Laurent had mentioned to her once before: that was really all that mattered.

Thinking of Laurent caused Maggie's chest to ache with an undefinable sadness. She glanced back at the house. From the vantage point of the vineyard the *mas* looked like how it must have looked a hundred years earlier, when it was constructed after the first World War. The late autumn sun in this part of France seemed to make the *mas* glow from within.

The muted golden radiance of its limestone walls had likely fostered the same impression of heavenly brilliance to generations of owners of Domaine St-Buvard.

Maggie often thought back to the moment when she'd first laid eyes on Domaine St-Buvard. With its golden stone walls and Juliette balconies, she'd been quite impressed at the time.

But it had taken time to love it.

"Is everything okay?" Danielle asked, handing Maggie a cup of coffee. "The children?"

Maggie shook her head. "Laurent and I are fighting."

Danielle's eyebrows rose in surprise but she didn't say anything.

"It turns out that the guy killed at the amphitheater on Saturday was a child molester," Maggie said. "And Laurent knew but didn't tell me."

"Surely that is not such a terrible crime," Danielle said. "I meant Laurent," she said hurriedly.

"I know. And hearing myself say it out loud just made me realize how stupid it sounds."

"Not stupid, *chérie*. You are upset. Of course it is understandable. That such a creature could have been so close to Jemmy..."

"Exactly! Thank you, Danielle. At least someone understands."

"But you must not allow this to come between you and Laurent," Danielle said, gazing back at the house.

Maggie knew that just sitting here gave Danielle a kind of peace she got nowhere else. She didn't have to be talking to Jean-Luc while she was here. Just being near him—or near where he'd left this world—was enough.

Maggie sipped her coffee and felt the tranquility of the moment and the place infuse her. Jean-Luc had often had that effect on her when he was alive.

"What do the police say?" Danielle asked.

"They say they're done with the case."

"*Vraiment*?"

"Yes, and not because they've arrested someone but because they don't feel like the victim deserves justice."

Danielle frowned. "This upsets you."

"Well, yeah," But Maggie blinked because Danielle had a point.

Why does it upset me?

"Is it weird that I can't seem to let it go? The murder victim was a creep and a predator. Why do I care that he's dead?"

"I do not think that is why you are upset, *chérie*," Danielle said.

Maggie looked over the vineyard for a moment, Danielle's words ringing in her head.

She's right. I don't care that Barbeau died. I didn't even know him.

"I think what I care about," Maggie said slowly, testing out the words as she spoke them, "is that the police seem to be deciding which people get justice and which people don't."

They sat quietly for a moment.

"I cannot believe he has been gone for over a year," Danielle said softly.

"I know."

The vineyard always looked so peaceful after the harvest. But also bereft. Maggie let the quiet of their surroundings engulf them and the feeling of Jean-Luc's presence work its magic.

"So what will you do now, *chérie*?" Danielle asked as she poured out the last two cups of coffee for them.

"About the murder? What can I do?"

Danielle gave her a baleful look. "Have I not been with you when you have dug into a question you needed an answer to? *Many* times?"

Maggie grinned and felt another kink release in her shoulders and in her mind.

"Do you know if the police talked with Grace's boyfriend Brad?"

"I believe Grace mentioned that they did."

"Because it just occurred to me that there was about five minutes when Brad was missing at the amphitheater."

"Surely you're not suggesting Brad had anything to do with the murder, *chérie*. Does it not make more sense that one of the *brocantes* vendors killed the man? How would Brad even know the victim?"

"I don't know." Maggie stood up and shook a few leaves out of the wool blanket she'd laid on her knees. "I just know I have no idea where Brad was during the time of the murder. I wonder if Grace knows."

"I am sure it would not be the nicest question you could ask your dearest friend, *chérie*. Can you refrain?"

Maggie gnawed on a nail. "But then how am I going to find out? Do you think I should ask Brad directly?"

"Oh, dear. I'm not sure that would be much better."

The dogs had been content to sit curled up by their chairs but once Maggie stood up they became agitated at the thought of going back to the house. Danielle reached over and took the lead of one of them, allowing Maggie to manage the other as well as both stools.

"It was a lovely visit," Danielle said as they turned to head back to the house. "A little chilly but I know Jean-Luc enjoys the dogs."

"He loved his own dogs so much," Maggie said.

"He did."

They walked the rest of the way to the house in silence. It was nearly lunchtime but Danielle had made plans to meet friends in Aix. After Maggie put the dogs in the house, she walked with her around the side of the house to Danielle's car.

"So do you approve?" Maggie asked. "About my finding out who killed him?"

Maggie and Danielle both knew that Laurent wouldn't be happy about it and right now the two of them had enough problems between them.

Danielle hesitated, choosing her words carefully.

"I think, *chérie*," she said finally, "that everyone in this world, depraved or not, deserves justice."

That night Maggie was determined to reconnect with Laurent. Since she knew the way to her husband's heart almost invariably involved food she spent the afternoon putting together what she knew was one of his favorites: grand *aïoli.*

She also knew it was a summer dish and Laurent wasn't a fan of eating produce out of season. But as she set the potatoes in a pot to boil and began to peel the hardboiled eggs, she knew he'd at least appreciate the effort.

Since Laurent had to be in Aix that afternoon he had picked up the children from school. Once home, Mila and Jemmy grabbed their afternoon snacks and raced outside with the dogs to feed Mila's little goat. Laurent handed Maggie an envelope he'd picked up at the school.

The school needed an answer about whether or not to bump Jemmy a grade. Maggie read the letter with mounting anxiety since she was only too aware that it was yet one more thing she and Laurent were not in agreement about.

After handing her the envelope, Laurent went outside to make his usual circuit of the vineyard. Always before he would walk the perimeter of his property to clear his mind but since his property had grown so much, now he just walked until it was time to turn around.

As Maggie watched him stride away, his back straight but his head down, she felt a stab of dismay that he hadn't said anything about what she was making in the kitchen. For him to be uninterested in food was truly a watershed moment.

And not in a good way.

Maggie reran the tapes in her head of their fight last night and although it had shown a painful lack of connectivity, she didn't think anything either of them had said was really so bad.

Surely, nothing we can't come back from?

Dinner that night was a little better. She did finally see the surprise in Laurent's eyes when she served up the grand *aïoli*, which gave her a modicum of comfort that the world hadn't totally shifted off its axis. The meal itself helped too. The thick garlic mayonnaise was soul-satisfying and paired wonderfully with the steamed cod, steamed potatoes, carrots and boiled eggs.

Towards the end of the meal, Jemmy mentioned there was a field trip to Cassis in the coming weeks and all students needed parental signatures.

"Can I go, Papa?" he asked, knowing that his current doghouse status did not at all make the field trip a sure thing.

"Yes, fine," Laurent said.

"That sounds like fun," Maggie said, then added impulsively, "Laurent, how about if you invite that boy Luc to dinner this weekend?"

"Who's Luc?" Mila asked.

"Yeah," Jemmy said. "Who's Luc?"

"He's someone your papa knows," Maggie said, wondering why Laurent wasn't answering her. "Is that not a good idea, Laurent?"

Laurent wiped his mouth with his napkin and dropped it on the table.

"I need to fix a hole in the fence on the western wall before it gets dark," he said.

Maggie glanced out the French doors to the vineyard. It was pitch dark.

"What's for dessert, *Maman*?" Mila said. "Is it *pots de crème*?"

The little ramekins full of chocolate custard sat on the counter in plain sight.

"Yes," Maggie said, rubbing the space between her eyes as if that might somehow help her understand what was going on with Laurent. "Bring them to the table, please, Mila."

Laurent went to the foyer for his jacket. Both dogs—alerted that a possible walk was in the offing—began jumping around him.

"Papa?" Jemmy said, making Laurent who was patting his jacket pockets for his cigarettes turn in his direction. "Can Mila and I take our custards upstairs while we do our homework?"

She fully expected Laurent to insist the children eat their desserts at their assigned places, napkins in their laps, elbows off the table.

In fact Maggie wasn't sure what shocked her the most. The fact that Jemmy would even ask the question or that Laurent would respond the way he did.

He walked to the French doors and said over his shoulder, "Fine."

Then he left—a blast of cold air invading the room when he opened the door—and both dogs at his heels.

Maggie stared after him, her mouth open while Mila and Jemmy grabbed their plates and scurried upstairs.

21

Brad leaned back on his heels and wiped the sweat off his brow. The new sink sat on the floor beside him in the tiny bathroom and he tried to remember what the YouTube video had said about installing the central spout. Did he remove the thingy with the nut and washer first?

"I can't tell you what a help it is that you know about these things," Grace said from where she stood in the doorway, holding a steaming mug of tea. "Gabriel is clueless when it comes to plumbing."

"No problem," Brad said, flashing back to the image this morning when he'd spent thirty minutes watching the video of how to install a bathroom sink after Grace's call and before racing over to *Dormir*.

As usual he'd enjoyed the forty-minute drive to Grace's *gîte* from Aix. While the scenery was largely colorless it was still somehow dramatic. Plus the drive gave him time to compute how many days left he could afford to stay at his hotel in Aix.

Why won't she invite me to stay at Dormir?

He clenched his jaw in frustration. It would solve so many

problems. Most of them his and all of them having to do with money.

He knew money couldn't be the hold-up on Grace's end. Just last week he was with her in Marseille when she bought a weird looking lamp that looked like it'd been left out in the rain for two hundred euros.

Two hundred euros!

For an old lamp!

He knew Grace's hesitancy to commit to him wasn't about Zouzou either. He got a long great with the girl. And he'd slept over at *Dormir* plenty of times so it wasn't about trying to protect Zouzou from Grace's wanton ways or whatever.

"Do you think you could take a look at the toilet in Plum Cottage too?" Grace asked, moving out of the tiny bathroom as if confident of his answer.

"No problem," Brad said cheerfully, feeling the sweat bead up once more on his forehead as he tried to remember if the video had mentioned when he disconnected the water line if he should be seeing the O-ring doo-dad connected to the mixer thingamabob.

Or if that was just his fevered, desperate mind trying to make connections that weren't there.

Grace put her tea mug in the sink and looked out the window at Prune cottage where Brad was working. She hadn't thought he'd be so handy at plumbing and she had to admit her surprise wasn't a mark in his favor. Up until today, he'd been eager to pitch in but more at the level of a helpful neighbor—someone who wanted to *appear* to be helpful more than actually contribute.

Was that fair? Was that even true?

She rinsed out her mug and turned to the breakfast dishes. Brad had come over in time to have coffee and croissants with

Grace and Danielle before Danielle retired to the garden for the morning. Grace was pretty sure there wasn't much to do in the garden in mid-November except use it as an excuse not to spend any time with Grace's boyfriend.

Danielle doesn't like him.

The thought came to Grace from out of left field and while she was surprised to realize it, she knew it was true.

Danielle doesn't like him, and Laurent doesn't trust him.

A part of Grace wasn't sure she didn't need Laurent's approval. After all, he *was* her landlord and he had a major stake in the success of *Dormir*.

On the other hand he was extremely untrusting of *any* male Grace brought into her life.

Can I blame him? After my track record?

Grace felt a hollowness form in her chest as she gazed out the kitchen window.

Through it all Brad was helpful and cheerful—when he wasn't dropping hints that he would very much like to be, as he called it, "an integral part of the team," by which he meant, move in.

On the one hand it was tempting. When Laurent first suggested that Grace run Danielle's old *mas* as a bed and breakfast, using her knack for fashion and style, Grace couldn't believe how perfect the situation was for her.

Sixteen months later—with a litany of mixed online reviews, a nearly daily necessity of sucking up to the nastiest, most overbearing guests that ever opted to travel to Provence, compounded by a work day that began before dawn and ended when Grace fell exhausted into her bed—well, Grace wasn't so sure.

She knew it was going to be hard work. She just hadn't realized it was going to be back-breaking, never ending hard work—and *that* was just to keep the place looking pretty or not falling apart around her. It didn't include the hours at her computer trying to snag the attention of American and UK travelers to this part of the world.

And none of that even touched the very hardest part of running a bed and breakfast, which was the absolute impossibility of trying to keep her temporary guests happy.

Her temporary, rude, demanding, belligerent, unreasonable guests.

She watched Brad emerge from the cottage and wipe his hands on the rag he'd stuffed in his pocket and then wipe his face with it.

Another point in Brad's favor, she thought, was that he was good with people. When Grace was too tired to smile at one more complaint, or listen attentively to one more unreasonable demand, she could imagine him happily standing in for her as her calm, compliant and smiling other half.

Her better half.

Just the thought of it made her want to sign Brad up today.

On the other hand.

She knew she wasn't ready for that level of commitment. Not even to make him happy or to lessen her own burden. She wasn't ready.

She poured a mug of coffee for him and doctored it the way she knew he liked it, with cream and sugar, fighting the sudden nonsensical thought that most men she knew and respected—strong, honorable, forthright men—drank it black.

That's ridiculous. What a stupid thing to judge a man on.

Brad came in the door. "Fixed," he said, grinning and clearly very proud of himself.

"Good," Grace said, handing him the coffee. "Take a break before hitting Plum Cottage."

Brad sat down at the kitchen table cupping his mug.

"I guess Maggie was pretty upset about the murder, huh?" he asked.

"Naturally," Grace said as she began to dry the dishes.

"I guess it's understandable," Brad said. "With her kid being so close to that sex maniac and all."

"I think she was more concerned about Jemmy being so close to the murderer," Grace said, although in all honesty she had to admit it was probably a tie.

"My uncle went to prison for sexing with kids," Brad said casually.

Grace turned and looked at him, struck by his word choice.

Not *preying* on them, but *sexing* with them.

"That's terrible," she said.

"Yeah, it ruined Uncle Bob's life."

I wonder how it affected his victims' lives, Grace thought.

"When he got out he couldn't get a job and he had to register as a pervert so everyone knew. Aunt Flo eventually left him."

"You sound like you feel sorry for him," Grace said.

Brad looked uncomfortable. "I do. He was a great guy."

Grace forced herself not to respond. If Brad had a relation who was a child molester of course he would see him from a personal viewpoint. It didn't mean he was condoning what the man had done. Of course not.

Still. She felt an uncomfortable creeping sensation over her skin—just the idea that Brad would feel sympathy for the devil.

22

The next morning Maggie waited for Laurent to leave with the kids before heading out. It had been yet another evening of stilted conversation where it was clear something was on Laurent's mind that he wasn't inclined to share.

And while what she planned to do today would do little to alleviate or solve that particular problem, she figured at least it might help move her closer to a more sane position on the events that happened the day Jemmy had slipped away at the amphitheater.

As she drove toward Arles, Maggie winced in memory of the conversation she'd had with her mother the night before when she'd finally told her about Jemmy's disappearance at the amphitheater and the murder.

"I can't even believe you are tying the two things together," her mother had said. "I vote with Grace. You're overreacting. Little boys wander off. It's what they do. You need to find a healthier outlet for your anxieties, darling."

Almost every part of that sentence was so objectionable and insulting that it was all Maggie could do to seethe quietly and let her mother prattle on. The fact that she was getting absolutely no support for what she considered a very natural reaction to what had happened last Saturday—not from her best friend, her husband or her own mother—was particularly galling.

On the other hand one thing Maggie had learned the hard way over the years was the knowledge that being the odd man out didn't usually mean she was right and everyone else was wrong.

But there's no way I can pretend that Jemmy wandering around a Roman ruin all by himself—except for a child molester and a murderer—isn't my worst nightmare!

Maggie felt angry tears form in her eyes.

I'm a mother. I can't just forget what happened.

As she circled the city square looking for a parking spot she impulsively put in another call to Detective Moreau.

This time he picked up.

"Detective Moreau here," he said.

"*Bonjour*, Detective Moreau. This is Maggie Dernier."

"I am sorry for not calling you back, Madame."

"Not a problem. I'm sure you're very busy. Actually I was hoping for an update on the Barbour murder case."

"Ah, yes, well, there is not much to say really."

"I'm wondering if you've finished talking with all the vendors who were there in the amphitheater that day. Because even if you—"

"We took everyone's statement."

"And nobody looked suspicious? Really?"

"Madame Dernier, there were two CCTV cameras trained on the arena that Saturday," Detective Moreau said. "As well as on the loading dock and the main entrance."

Maggie felt a flair of exhilaration. She hadn't thought there might be cameras!

"And the footage revealed that none of the vendors left the arena during the critical time. They are all accounted for."

Maggie felt a leaden weight settle on her chest. "All of them?"

"Yes, Madame. Only you, and your son, along with Claude Bouquille, Brad Anderson and Jacky Borgue left the arena during the time we believe the murder was being committed."

"Did you talk to Brad Anderson?"

"Yes, of course. My partner and I spoke with Monsieur Anderson two days ago."

"And did he tell you why he was missing during the critical time that day?"

"Yes, he did."

Maggie felt deflated. "He did?"

"Yes, Madame. He said he went in search of a *pissoir*."

Why would Brad be in need of a bathroom? We had just come from a restaurant where there was a perfectly fine men's room.

"Do you believe him?"

The detective sighed heavily. "As you know, Madame, my partner and I are no longer assigned to this case."

Maggie felt her body heat rise. "So that's it? You're *done*?"

"You sound like Adelaide Barbeau. She too is less than pleased."

"Is that the victim's wife?"

"Look, I really need to—"

"Detective Moreau, please. Can you at least give me her address? You said yourself nobody is working the case. What harm would it do?"

"I'm sorry, Madame Dernier, but I must go now," he said firmly before disconnecting.

Maggie spotted a parking lot a good six blocks from the arena but it would have to do. She swung into the lot and parked and then quickly opened up a browser window on her cell phone and typed in *Adelaide Barbeau Arles.*

Within seconds a news report of Jean Barbeau's death came up on her screen.

Along with his address.

Maggie stared at the address for a moment. Did she really want to do this? She'd only planned on visiting the amphitheater today and maybe trying to retrace Jemmy's steps to see if anything jumped out at her as odd. In her experience, the strangest revelations were there to be made if you only looked.

She stared at the address on her screen.

But this.

She opened up Google Maps and typed in the address and watched as her screen drew a line from where she was parked to a street on the other side of the amphitheater.

Quickly paying for four hours in the lot, she glanced again at her phone, locked her car and set out to pay a visit to the newly bereaved Madame Barbeau.

It took her thirty minutes to walk to the address on the map.

Maggie knew from an aerial view of the town she'd once seen that the houses and streets in Arles were all crammed tightly in a near spiral with the amphitheater at its center. The narrow lanes had been built for donkey carts—not SUVs. In some cases they were so narrow a moped could barely fit down them.

As she walked she decided it was clear that Jean and Adelaide Barbeau didn't live in the best part of Arles but that didn't surprise Maggie. Barbeau had been an ex-con and a maintenance worker. Whoever he'd married was probably used to living in squalor.

Maggie picked her way through the garbage-strewn cobblestone lanes with boarded up stores and tattoo shops on either side until she found the address.

Unlike the more grandiose entranceways of apartments in Aix or Paris—unassuming wooden doors that opened up to reveal tidy courtyards or garden entrances of elegant little apartments—Jean and Adelaide Barbeau's front door had peeling paint and profane graffiti scrawled across it.

She'd didn't expect a garden oasis hiding behind this door.

Not knowing who or what she would find, but knowing she needed to at least see the woman who was married to the man who might have been stalking Jemmy, Maggie took in a long steadying breath and knocked on the door.

Immediately a window above her head opened and a woman's head popped out.

"What do you want?"

Maggie stepped back and shaded her eyes. The sun was out brightly this morning.

"I'm looking for Madame Barbeau," Maggie said.

"What for?"

"Are you Madame Barbeau?"

And do you want me screaming your business so your neighbors can hear?

As if she had heard Maggie's unspoken threat, the woman slammed the window shut. A moment later, the front door opened.

Adelaide Barbeau, surprisingly, was not a crone.

While it was true Maggie didn't know what Adelaide Barbeau's husband looked like, she assumed he must be middle-age in order to have committed a crime that he served time for.

Adelaide Barbeau was blonde, late twenties. And pretty.

"Who are you?" Madame Barbeau said, her blue eyes sharp and clear as she examined Maggie's clothing, her purse, her face.

"My name is Maggie Dernier. I was at the amphitheater the day your husband was...killed."

Something flashed across Adelaide Barbeau's face. Something painful but only for a moment.

"Many people go to the amphitheater," she said sullenly. "It is a major tourist attraction in Arles."

"I was there *at the time* your husband was killed. May I ask you a few questions?"

"Why?" The woman crossed her arms and glared at Maggie. "The police don't care."

"Well, it's not good to have a murderer running around Arles, regardless of who your husband...or what he..."

The look on Adelaide Barbeau's face instantly transformed into such vitriol, that Maggie faltered.

"Look," Maggie said. "I'm just trying to help the police find out..."

Adelaide Barbeau took a step off the threshold forcing Maggie back into the street.

"Are you from the paper?" Madame Barbeau hissed. "I know what you want!" She turned and screamed at her own building. "What you all want!"

Then she turned on Maggie and pushed her with both hands.

Maggie lost her footing and came down hard in a sitting position on the cobblestone streets.

"Go away!" Madame Barbeau screamed. "Go away before I set my dogs on you!"

23

Laurent left the St-Buvard *boulangerie* and loaded his purchases into the back seat of his Citreon. He glanced at his watch and saw he had plenty of time to check on Danielle's house before heading to one of his mini-houses on the far side of Domaine St-Buvard to meet with an electrician.

At least a century old, *Domaine Alexandre* was a large farmhouse made of rough fieldstone and wood, draped in verdant cascades of ivy. Jean-Luc and Danielle had lived there happily for nearly a decade.

Laurent drove down the winding driveway toward the house. The memory came to him of the first time he'd driven this way over ten years ago. He and Maggie had just come to St-Buvard to see the house that Laurent's uncle had left him. Laurent had been given Jean-Luc's address as a local *vigneron* who could show him around.

As Laurent had driven up the long driveway, Jean-Luc had suddenly appeared out of the thick line of oleander bushes that bordered the drive—two big hunting dogs by his side—and hopped into Laurent's car ordering him to drive on to the house.

Laurent missed Jean-Luc every day—his wisdom, his balance,

his humor. He had been a trusted partner in the vineyard business with both their operations joined in every way. When Jean-Luc died Laurent bought his fields, but Danielle kept the house which now that she lived at *Dormir* sat vacant and forlorn.

Laurent pulled his car to a stop in front of the *mas*. Not as grand or imposing as Domaine St-Buvard, the Alexandre farmhouse was still stately in its own way.

And now it was no longer vacant.

As Laurent got out of the car, Luc appeared in the doorway of the massive front door, a hand raised in a hesitant greeting.

Luc's right eye was already turning purple from the scuffle he'd somehow managed to provoke during the one night he'd spent incarcerated at the Aix police station.

Luc wouldn't say how he'd gotten the shiner and in the end Laurent hadn't thought it mattered. Either his smart mouth had gotten him corrected according to the parameters of polite society among jail inhabitants, or one of the cops had exercised his God-given right to have a little fun on a quiet night.

Laurent had bailed him out yesterday and ensconced him in Danielle's home until he could give the matter his full attention. If he were totally honest he knew bringing Luc to Danielle's house instead of bringing him home was because of his current issues with Maggie.

"Groceries," Laurent said to Luc by way of greeting.

Luc went to unload the car as Laurent entered the house.

He walked first to the kitchen, which was a rough affair and unlike Laurent's kitchen at Domaine St-Buvard, had never been renovated. The wood floors peeked out underneath the peeling linoleum that Jean-Luc must have installed half a century earlier. The cabinets—handmade and once beautiful and straight—hung askew over an ancient electric stove.

When Danielle lived here she'd kept the place neat and clean. Six months without her touch had left the empty rooms with a scent of age and a thick patina of dust and grime.

Laurent touched the stove. It was cold. An opened and partially eaten tin of *salade Niçoise* that Laurent had brought yesterday sat on the counter and smelled like cat food. Otherwise, the kitchen was spotless. Either the boy had cleaned up after himself or he hadn't tried to cook anything.

Luc set down the basket of groceries that Laurent had brought from his own kitchen and the bakery in St-Buvard.

"You don't cook?" Laurent asked.

"I don't know how," Luc said, pulling a long *baguette* out of the bag.

"You can start by learning how to make coffee," Laurent said gruffly as he turned to the sink and filled the kettle.

Luc sat in one of the chairs in the kitchen. The air vibrated with his expectation and anxiety.

When Laurent had arrived at the Aix police station yesterday to procure the boy's release, nobody had been more surprised than Luc—unless it was possibly Laurent himself.

Luc had been caught damaging a wrought-iron fence that encircled one of Aix's ancient and prized fountains near *place d'Albertas*. No fewer than four citizens had used their cellphones to record Luc as he used a crow bar to pry the wrought-iron railing apart. He was still in the process of destroying the railing when the police arrived.

"Pretty stupid what you did," Laurent said as he placed the kettle on the stovetop and turned on the stove. "Did it have a point?"

Laurent was perfectly willing to believe Luc's crime was just violence for the sake of violence. While he himself had never been drawn to do such things when he was younger, he knew plenty of teenagers who did.

Gerard, for one.

"What difference does it make?" Luc said.

Laurent turned to look at him and narrowed his eyes.

"It makes a difference or I wouldn't have asked," Laurent said coolly.

A beat of silence stretched between them. Laurent turned and pulled out a hand grinder from the cabinet. He set it on the table in front of Luc along with a bag of beans that he pulled out of the grocery bag on the table.

Luc used the measuring cup in the bean bag to fill the grinder. He glanced at Laurent and then turned the crank to grind the beans.

"There was a stupid cat stuck in the sewer drain," Luc said, his voice barely audible over the sound of the grinder.

Laurent watched him for a moment. Then he turned and set a French press on the table in front of Luc.

"Put four spoonful's in the bottom. One for each cup and one for the pot. Then pour not quite boiling water to the line here."

Luc glanced at the kettle on the stove. Laurent turned to pick it up using a folded over dishtowel as mitt. When he turned back to the table, Luc had spooned the ground coffee into the press. Wordlessly, Laurent poured the hot water and put the top on.

"Five minutes if you like it strong," Laurent said.

"I don't know how I like it," Luc said.

Laurent hadn't mentioned to Danielle that he was housing a juvenile delinquent in her house. He was fairly sure she wouldn't mind.

He wasn't exactly sure what he was doing with Luc and he could tell by how the boy behaved around him—unsure and mistrustful—that he had the same question himself. Keeping him here at Danielle's could only be a short-term answer.

What was the question?

One thing Laurent knew if he knew anything was that, like Gerard and himself as boys, being alone was not the answer to any of the problems that plagued Luc.

Laurent glanced at his watch and brought two earthenware mugs down from the counter and set them on the table.

"Learn to drink it black," he said.

24

Maggie got to her feet, the sound of Adelaide Barbeau's slamming front door ringing in her ears. She felt more embarrassed and flustered than hurt, although the prospect of having a dog sicced on her had left her a tad breathless as she hurried away from the Barbeau home.

As she walked she tried to keep what facts she'd just learned straight in her mind—separate from the humiliation of being sent packing.

One thing she now knew was that unless Adelaide had married a way older man, Jean Barbeau had been young man—probably not even thirty. Not that that meant anything specifically to Maggie, but she'd had it in her mind he was older.

The second thing she learned was that Adelaide was attractive *and* she was a strong-willed woman. It made sense that she would be defensive about her husband but she was also angry at the police for not trying harder to solve his murder—all things you'd expect from a normal person.

Both of those observations were a surprise to Maggie. Whether they really meant anything was another thing altogether.

She'd spent so much time thinking and not paying attention to her surroundings that she was surprised when she came to the end of her street and looked up and saw the amphitheater had materialized in front of her. Because of what had happened there Saturday, seeing its ghostly imposing structure gave her a sudden wave of chills.

She knew the Roman amphitheater had originally been built to allow easy access to the seating and sport inside but in the Middle Ages—much like what had been done temporarily for Claude's *brocante* on Saturday—all the easy-access archways had been blocked to make it a defensible fortress.

Rubbing a creepy foreboding from her arms, Maggie hurried across the street to the high wall of the arena in order to follow the only way around to the main entrance from where she could easily find her way back to her parked car. The closer she got to the entrance, the more crowded with tourists her path became.

When she reached the wide and numerous stone steps leading down from the entrance of the amphitheater, she noticed four feral cats sitting on the bottom steps directly across the street from the Café Terrace.

After the afternoon she'd had, she impulsively decided a small glass of rosé would not go amiss.

The café was doing a good business today. Unusual, she would have thought for a Wednesday in early November. She went to the first free table and raised her hand to Thomas, the waiter who'd been there Saturday. He nodded to let her know he'd seen her—which in Maggie's experience could be as far as the interaction went. She leaned back in her chair and waited.

"Madame?" a voice next to her said.

Maggie looked up to see a different waiter standing by her table. He had kind eyes with thick lashes and greying hair. He smiled at her.

"I was expecting Thomas," she said.

"You know my waiters by name, Madame?" the man said with a grin.

Maggie returned his smile, glad for his friendliness. "He waited on me and my friends on Saturday."

A cloud came over his face, making Maggie wonder if the only significance he could attach to that day was the murder that had happened across the street.

"You own this café?"

"I do. For better or worse. Have done for eighty years. I am Jacques Duvall."

They shook hands. "*Enchantez.* I am Maggie Dernier. Wow. Eighty years. I have to say you don't look a day over seventy."

He laughed. "My parents ran it for the sixty years before me. In fact it is the reason I was not here Saturday. I took my mother to see a medical specialist that day. Perhaps you know her too?"

"I'm sorry, I don't," Maggie said. "She's well, I hope?"

It had taken Maggie nearly all of the ten years she'd lived in France but she was finally learning to make small talk. It wasn't easy or natural for her but she'd improved considerably since the early years.

The café owner rocked back on his heels and crossed his arms as though he was ready for a good long chat.

"*Ma mère's* heart is good but she should have gotten the knee replacement many years ago. Now it is too late. *Tant pis*. She once loved to roam every inch of the majestic lady." He waved a hand at the towering façade of the amphitheater. "I myself grew up playing in it like my own play yard, exploring every inch of it. But now my mother cannot manage even two steps up the stairs."

"That's terrible," Maggie said. "I'm so sorry."

He shrugged. "It is what it is. Now she resists even going to the doctor. I think she believes if she doesn't hear bad news, then there is no bad news. If she had her way she would just carry on, no doctors, no medicines, nothing."

"They get set in their ways. It makes it difficult when you are trying to do the right thing by them."

"*Exactement*. And then the child becomes the parent, no?"

"Pretty much."

As soon as Monsieur Duvall took her drink order and left, Maggie was surprised to see Claude Bouquille and Jacky approach her table.

"Maggie!" Claude called to her and kissed her on both cheeks in greeting. "May I?" He pointed to the free chair at her table.

Maggie agreed readily although she thought it strange he didn't include Jacky in his request.

The unpleasant little man stood next to Claude's chair, his eyes scanning the café continuously, his mustache twitching.

"I suppose you have heard?" Claude said, signaling to Duvall to take his order.

"About the murder? The police came to take my statement," Maggie said. "It's horrible."

Claude sucked his teeth and shook his head. "It was such a shock."

"Wait. Did you *know* Barbeau?" Maggie asked.

Duvall approached and took Claude and Jacky's beer orders and retreated before Claude responded.

"I employed him," Claude said.

"I thought he was employed by the city of Arles to do maintenance on the amphitheater."

If Claude employed Barbeau, had he also known his background?

"Yes, well, Barbeau was freelancing for me I guess you could say. A little extra money for him and basically all he had to do was his usual job—perhaps a little more cleanup than usual."

"I see. So did Barbeau come into the amphitheater through the front entrance or by the back loading dock?"

"I have no idea. But the police must know since CCTV cameras were positioned at all entrances."

"Were you aware of Monsieur Barbeau's background?"

Claude made a face. "You mean did I know he was a pervert? Of course not. I left the hiring to Jacky. Didn't I, Jacky?"

Jacky didn't respond except to look indictingly at Maggie.

He's probably an ex-cellmate of Barbeau's, Maggie thought.

"Can I ask you," Maggie said, talking to Jacky now, "how *you* knew Barbeau?"

"Why do you care?" Jacky said with a sneer.

"Jacky!" Claude admonished. "Manners, please. Madame Dernier has a right to know."

Jacky snorted, looked away and spat, clearly not about to answer further.

Claude dug ten euros out of his pocket as Duvall approached with the beers and Maggie's wine.

"Well, it was a terrible thing, to be sure," Claude said. "But what's done is done. I still owe you that ad, Maggie. My wife is delighted she will be in your newsletter!"

He took the beers with a wink at her and then left to find an indoor table with Jacky. It occurred to Maggie that Claude was Jacky's alibi and vice versa since he was by Jacky's side nearly every minute of the time they were in the arena.

Unfortunately that meant Maggie had to rule Jacky out as a suspect for the murder. And that was annoying because Jacky looked like exactly the kind of person who could commit murder.

A nagging and recurring image flitted into her head to remind her that while she was running around hysterically shouting for Jemmy she didn't have eyes on any of the others. At least not for as long as it took for her to recover from her faint.

Was that long enough for one of them to kill Barbeau?

Whoever had entered the amphitheater and strangled poor Monsieur Barbeau—and it took every ounce of her natural beneficence to think of the victim that way—he must have been video taped entering the amphitheater.

A sudden flash of nausea invaded her gut.

Barbeau must have seen Jemmy go inside.

And because Barbeau knew the layout of the arena, he could follow Jemmy, staying in the shadows, and wait for his moment...

Maggie finished her glass of wine and signalled for the bill. The lunch crowd seemed to have morphed into the *apéro* crowd —that time after lunch when a cocktail with nuts or olives got most people through until dinner—and saw that both Duvall and Thomas were unavailable.

Fishing out the correct change, Maggie glanced again at the amphitheater and tried not to see it as a place of death and destruction. As she gazed at it her eye was caught by movement at the base of the arena .

A frail old woman was stabbing the ground with a rubber-tipped walking stick and holding a small margarine tub in her free hand. As she walked, the old woman's hand shook and what looked like pieces of kibble fell out of the bowl.

That must be old Madame Duvall, Maggie thought as she watched the woman and wondered how it must feel to have worked this street corner her entire life—first as a young wife, mother and business owner in one of the busiest tourist cities in France—and now as an old woman whose only job was to feed the feral cats that lived around the amphitheater.

A veil of sadness descended on Maggie as she watched the woman slowly cross the pedestrian walkway toward the Amphitheater.

Did she have other children besides Jacques? Maggie wondered. If so, why hadn't *they* taken her to the doctor? Surely as owner of the popular Café Terrace Jacques was not the most likely person to take his mother if there was someone else who could?

Maggie watched Madame Duvall walk parallel to the wide

stone steps, deliberately navigating around the crowd of milling tourists and bypassing the front stairs. Maggie remembered that Duvall had said his mother couldn't manage the steps any more.

The old woman hobbled along, her head bent and cat kibble dropping out behind her like Hansel and Gretel's breadcrumbs, until she disappeared from view around the back of the wide stone staircase.

Maggie frowned. Did the old lady know another way inside the arena besides the main entrance at the top of the steps?

She glanced at her cellphone to check the time. She needed to start back. Danielle would pick Jemmy and Mila up from school but Maggie still needed to collect them from *Dormir* and get dinner started.

As she picked up her purse, Maggie's eye was drawn to a man coming out of the entrance of the amphitheater at the top of the stairs ahead of a small pod of Asian tourists.

There was something about him that made her look more closely until she realized with a start that she knew him.

25

It was the guy dressed all in black that she'd seen on Saturday.

Not only was he here again at the amphitheater but amazingly, he appeared to be leading a group of tourists.

He's a tour guide?

Maggie watched him point things out to his group and while she couldn't make out his words, she caught the tenor of his voice on the breeze as he moved down the long series of steps.

Unless she was totally losing her marbles, she was sure he'd been watching her last Saturday when she sat in the café with Claude and Grace. He'd acted then like he knew her.

And like he didn't like what he saw.

As he came down the broad steps, it was clear he was leading his group to the café. Maggie was torn between the temptation to slip away unseen and the need to confront him with why he'd looked so angrily at her group on the day of the murder.

Anything suspicious, she told herself. *That's what you look for. Anything out of the norm.*

And this guy with tattoos covering his neck and arms leading a group of foreign tourists around the amphitheater definitely qualified.

Maggie stayed seated at her café table and watched him approach. She could see he was probably still in his twenties. She could also see he wore a circular nametag on his shirt with the name *Bastien* printed on it.

She watched him corral his group of five tourists to two tables and order for them.

Then he walked over to Maggie's table.

"Do I know you?" Maggie asked him.

He sat down in the chair opposite her. "I saw you here with Claude Bouquille on Saturday," he said.

"Is that a problem?"

He snorted. "He cost me six hundred euros last weekend."

Maggie glanced over at Bastien's group of tourists and realized what he was saying.

"Because of the *brocante* you couldn't give any amphitheater tours last Saturday," she said.

"On a *Saturday*!" Bastien said loudly, making several diners turn to look at them. "My biggest day! And it's not the first time that bastard has overridden the arrangements set in place by the city of Arles for his own purposes."

If what Bastien said was true, then closing the amphitheater to tour guides for the day was self-serving and discriminatory.

"I'm sorry. I didn't know. I can see how that would be...annoying."

Behind Bastien's shoulder Maggie saw old Madame Duvall was making her laborious and agonizing way back across the street from the amphitheater. She only had her cane now. Her other hand was empty.

"Look, I'm happy to write you a glowing TripAdvisor review and get all my friends to ask for you by name," Maggie said. "I agree it was unfair what Bouquille did to you."

Bastien sniffed and glanced over at his group to check that they were fine.

"Let me ask you," Maggie said. "Would you say you know everything about the amphitheater?"

"Of course. It is a specialty of mine."

"Are those big archways at the top of the stairs the only way in?"

He twisted around and looked where Maggie was pointing.

"You make it sound like they are not enough," he said. "There are one hundred and twenty arches in the amphitheater and every one leads into the interior."

"Yes but are the front steps the only way inside?"

"Unless you parachute through the top, yes, Madame."

Either Bastien was wrong or the old lady didn't have another way inside. But in that case, how was she leaving the cat bowls inside? And if the cats *weren't* actually inside the amphitheater, then how was it that Jemmy had been distracted by them there?

"You're sure there's no other way inside the amphitheater?" Maggie pressed.

"I know this structure better than the men who built it," Bastien said, puffing out his chest. "There is no other way inside but up the front stairs."

And then another thought came to Maggie.

"After we went inside last Saturday, my son left us briefly to... go exploring. I was wondering if you...from where you were standing at the entrance, if you might have seen him."

Bastien frowned as if in thought and then nodded decisively.

"I did see him. About eleven? Brown hair? I only caught a glimpse of him. Heading to one of the lower level corridors."

"Is that...that corridor anywhere near where...do you know... is it close to...?"

"I'm sorry, Madame," Bastien said more kindly now. "The information as to where the body was found was not released to the public."

"Oh. Sure. Okay."

"And of course there was the other man," Bastien said.

A hard knot developed in Maggie's stomach. "Are you referring to...the murder victim?"

"No, Madame, I mean the other man I saw walking several yards behind your son."

Maggie stared at him. "How...how do you know that wasn't the man who was killed?"

Or the murderer?

"Because I saw this man having lunch with your group not thirty minutes before," Bastien said. "He was the tall man with the red beard."

26

Maggie's hand flew to her throat and she took in a quick, shaky breath.

Brad was walking behind Jemmy? How is it that Jemmy didn't see him?

And how is it that Brad didn't mention this to anyone?

Bastien went to rejoin his tour group when Maggie's phone chimed and she glanced down to see a text from Grace on the screen.

<R U on the way?>

Maggie glanced at the time on her phone. It was nearly five o'clock.

Crap.

She was going to be late picking the kids up.

She texted Grace that she was on her way and left the café. But first, knowing it would cost her time she didn't have, Maggie hurried across the street to the amphitheater. She quickly walked around the side of the steep stone steps and looked for any possible other entrance but there was none. Beside the outer wall she saw a plastic bowl half-filled with cat food.

Maggie frowned. Obviously Madame Duvall couldn't get

inside because she couldn't climb the stairs so she just left the bowl outside for the cats.

Maggie looked up to see the stone wall looming at least sixty feet over her head.

So Bastien is right.

The only way in or out of the amphitheater was via the front stairs.

And of course all the archway entrances had either been barricaded or gated shut on Saturday to ensure that none of the public got to the *brocante* before time.

There goes the idea that there was a secret way in beyond the front entrance

As Maggie walked to her car, her mind reverted to the bombshell that Bastien had hit her with. She tried to imagine why Brad was anywhere near Jemmy that day and why—when he knew they were all searching for the child—he hadn't said anything.

It would explain why he had acted so odd on the drive back the day of the murder.

Maggie's head was swimming by the time she got to her car. As she drove out of town she found herself wondering what any of them really knew about Grace's boyfriend. The fact that Grace has shown epic bad judgment in her choice of men in the past didn't do much to recommend him either.

As Maggie broke free of the rush hour traffic and merged onto the A9, her phone lit up again. She saw the call was coming from London.

"This is Maggie," she said.

"Yeah, sorry, Maggie. Zoe here. Need to change the date of the interview. Fiona wants to try a new dog groomer at the other time. Got a pen?"

Maggie felt a flush of annoyance. Changing the date would almost certainly involve rearranging childcare for Jemmy and Mila. Again.

"Sure," she said, smiling through gritted teeth. "When would be good?"

"Can we say the tenth?"

"Fine," Maggie said. The new date would push the newsletter dangerously close to her deadline. It would likely mean she'd have to write the piece the same night as the interview in order to get it out the next day. Plus Jemmy's soccer game was that afternoon. There was nothing for it. She'd have to miss the game.

Now that she thought of it, she'd missed his last soccer game too. She prayed Laurent had nothing vital going on that afternoon.

After hanging up with Zoe, Maggie accelerated. She'd already gotten one speeding ticket last month that Laurent had been less than pleased about. But she hated taking advantage of Grace's friendship by constantly dumping the kids with her—and then failing to pick them up on time.

Especially since I'll likely have to do it again next week for the interview.

Her phone rang again and she saw it was her brother Ben calling from Atlanta.

A wave of apprehension trembled through her as she answered the call.

Ben never called. Not unless something was wrong.

"Hey, Ben. What's up?"

"Have you talked to Mom yet?"

Instantly Maggie's stomach churned with anxiety.

Was it Dad? Was this the phone call she'd been dreading?

"No. What's going on?"

"I can't believe Mom hasn't told you. Typical. She's just not going to face anything she doesn't have to."

"Ben, just tell me! Is it Dad?"

"What? No. It's Nicole. She's missing."

27

Laurent wasn't surprised to see lights on when he pulled up to Domaine St-Buvard. But he was mildly surprised to see Maggie and the children standing out front.

Has she locked herself out?

He glanced at Luc in the passenger seat next to him. Laurent parked the car. "Stay here."

Suddenly Jemmy materialized at Laurent's car window, peering in at Luc who was studiously looking straight ahead.

"*Maman* dropped her keys in the bushes!" Jemmy said. "Who's that?"

Laurent got out of the car, clamped a hand down on his first-born's shoulder and steered him back toward Maggie where she stood at the front door.

Mila ran to Laurent and he gave her a brief hug, but his eyes were on Maggie.

And *her* eyes were fixed on the passenger in his car.

"Don't even tell me," she said to him. "*No*. Absolutely not. There is already too much going on without this too."

Laurent felt a fissure of anger well up in him. He held out his house key to her.

"Get them inside," he said. "Have they already eaten at Grace's?"

He saw her flush guiltily at his words. He was tempted to ask her where she'd been all day that she couldn't pick up her own children from school and make their dinner. But he bit his tongue.

"*Mamère* made *tartes tatin*," Mila said happily.

Maggie took the keys from Laurent and handed them to Jemmy who ran to the front door with Mila at his heels.

"I'm sorry, Laurent. But this is not a good night for this. You should have called first."

Why? So you could make a daube? Or manage to pick up the children on time?

Laurent couldn't remember the last time he was this furious with Maggie.

Just then he heard the car door slam and he turned in time to see Luc slip off into the bushes that lined the driveway.

Laurent cursed and turned back to the car before realizing his car key was attached to the house key now inside the house.

He strode past Maggie on his way into the house, fury pinging off him in waves.

28

Maggie stood at the kitchen window watching for Laurent's headlights to appear. He'd been gone nearly two hours.

For heaven's sakes, what did he expect? she thought in mounting frustration. *Don't we have enough on our plate without adopting all the world's problems too?* She swallowed hard at the recognition of her lack of sympathy and turned away from the window.

As soon as she'd hung up from Ben on her drive home from Arles, she'd rung her mother as she raced to Grace's to get the kids.

The call had gone to her mother's voice mail. But within seconds a text came from Elspeth saying she was at the memory care facility and couldn't talk right but would call later.

"*Maman*?" Mila said stepping into the kitchen. "May I have dessert? And can I have it in my room?"

"What? Yes, all right. I think there's custard in the fridge."

While Mila got spoons out of the cutlery drawer, Jemmy came downstairs.

"Where did Papa go?" he asked. "And who was that kid?"

Mila handed him a ramekin of custard from the fridge. "*Maman* said we can eat it upstairs."

"I don't know who he is," Maggie said. "A friend of your father's."

Jemmy snorted in an exact copy of his father. "How could that be? He's just a kid."

Maggie's phone began to ring. She picked it up from the kitchen counter and saw a picture of her mother on the screen. At the same time she heard the dogs scratching at the back door.

"Jemmy, let the dogs in and both of you take your custards upstairs. But we can't make a habit of this."

Jemmy ran to the back door and let the dogs in before both children hurried upstairs.

"I mean it!" Maggie called after them, feeling like she'd failed somehow.

"Hey, Mom," she said. "What's going on with Nicole? Ben says she's missing?"

Maggie wedged the phone between her ear and shoulder and began scooping out the dogs' dinner. She carried their bowls to the mat near their crates by the back door.

"I don't know why your brother is being so silly," Elspeth said. Maggie could feel the weariness in her mother's voice. "I'm sure Nicole is fine."

"But you don't know where she is? When was the last time you talked to her?"

"I have a lot going on right now, Maggie. In case you haven't noticed."

"I know, Mom, but Nicole is only seventeen. She's not old enough to be on her own just yet. Ben said—"

"What are you implying? That I'm not taking care of my own granddaughter? Have I not cared for her for the last ten years as any loving mother would? As I did when I raised you and your brother and sister?" Elspeth's voice was shrill.

"No one's saying that, Mom." Maggie ran a hand through her

hair and looked out the kitchen window again.

Where was he? Why was he running after that boy? Did he still intend to bring him back here tonight?

An image popped into her head of the expression on Laurent's face when Maggie said that *now wasn't a good time* to have the boy to dinner.

She tried to remember if she'd ever seen an expression on Laurent's face remotely like it.

None at least that he'd ever directed at *her* before.

"I'm sure Nicole is fine," Elspeth said again, sniffing.

Maggie took in a long breath but felt anxiety welling up in her chest anyway.

Had her mother ever been this apathetic? Was the toll of taking care of Dad—of watching him slowly debilitate—turning her mother into a different person?

"When did you see her last?" Maggie asked between clenched teeth.

"The weekend, I think."

Last weekend was over four days ago.

"And where did she say she was going?"

"To a friend's."

"Which one?" Maggie wanted to scream.

"I forget, honestly. Haley? Taylor? They all sound like last names. Have you noticed that?"

Knowing she'd get no real information from her mother tonight, Maggie asked her to have Nicole call her if her mother heard from her. Then Maggie disconnected.

She stood in the kitchen and, after one last glance out the kitchen window, went to the cupboard where she pulled out an open bottle of *pinot noir* and poured herself a glass. Then she walked to the foot of the stairs and listened. All was quiet.

Maggie realized it had been a while since she'd seen her children play together. Usually one of them would migrate to the other's bedroom and she'd hear laughter or at least voices.

When had that stopped? Was it Jemmy who was no longer interested in playing with his little sister?

She took her glass of wine to the living room. Laurent had already laid the fire so all she had to do was light the match. She felt a stab of guilt. Laurent did so much to take care of his family —to always be one step ahead. To predict and safeguard them.

Why was this boy so important to him?

She realized that was the question she should have done a better job of getting answered before now.

She eased back into the plush couch pillows and tried to relax, tried not to think about where Nicole might be.

Or with whom.

Her phone rang again and she picked it up, hoping it might be Nicole or maybe Laurent.

"Darling?" Grace's voice came out over the line. "Just wanted to double check that you got home safely. You seemed in a bit of a tizzy when you were here."

Later Maggie would wonder why she hadn't been touched by gratitude that her dearest friend in the world had noticed how upset she was and called to see how she was.

Later she would wonder why she hadn't taken a breath to appreciate all the things that were going right in her life.

But just at that moment, neither of those things happened. Instead, the tsunami of emotion that had been building up all day—from the irrational worry about Jemmy and where he'd been that terrible day to Bellemont-Surrey rescheduling the interview to Nicole being missing and finally to that look of disappointment Laurent had given her tonight—all peaked in one big, cataclysmic wave of anxiety and frustration.

Which is why instead of saying any of the other perfectly rational things she might have said, Maggie blurted out the one thing she knew without doubt she should not have said.

"Did you know your boyfriend followed my son last Saturday in the Arles amphitheater?"

29

Needless to say, the conversation had not gone well from there.

"What are you talking about?" Grace sputtered after a few seconds of stunned silence.

"I'm talking about the fact that somebody saw Brad following Jemmy when he left the group last Saturday. I don't supposed he mentioned that to you?"

"So are you suggesting *I'm* in on this too?"

"I'm saying you have a history of covering for some pretty dubious types of men and it wouldn't surprise me if—"

Maggie wasn't exactly sure how much of her sentence Grace heard before she hung up.

Later she would be glad Grace had hung up before Maggie could say more.

Maggie stared at her phone in horror at the realization of what she'd just done.

Should she call back and beg for forgiveness?

Except, if Grace was a semi-normal human being, she would probably not be ready to hear an apology just yet.

Maggie put the phone on the coffee table and looked at it as if it were a live snake.

What is the matter with me?

She ran a hand across her face.

Do I really think Brad was stalking Jemmy? Couldn't there be a perfectly valid explanation for why he was following him? Or maybe Bastien was wrong about what he saw?

She drained her wine, didn't feel one bit better and went to the foot of the stairs, the two big dogs at her heels.

"You two okay?" she called up.

"*Oui, Maman*!" Mila called down.

"Jemmy?"

No answer.

Feeling like she had lead weights tied to her ankles, Maggie began to walk upstairs. She was nearly to the top when he answered.

"I'm okay," he said. "I'm just reading."

"Who's first for baths tonight?" she said as she reversed her steps down the stairs, although she wasn't entirely sure she had the strength to make it all the way back to the couch in the living room.

Both children instantly began arguing with her, their voices rising and falling with the velocity of their arguments.

So it's official, Maggie thought. *I've succeeded in pissing off every person in my life.*

"Fine! Fine!" she called as she went back to the kitchen and poured herelf another glass of wine. "You can skip baths tonight. But make sure you brush your teeth at least."

So there went that Mother of the Year award. What next? Coke with their breakfast in the morning? Captain Crunch instead of vegetables?

She moved back to the living room and picked up her phone again. Grace hadn't called back.

No surprise there. She's probably in the act of deleting my contact information from her phone.

Laurent hadn't called either. Again, no surprise. He rarely carried his phone and never reached out to her when he did.

What in the hell is going on with him?

Both dogs jumped on the couch and curled up next to her. Maggie turned on the television to distract herself and watched an hour of a British home improvement show on cable before going upstairs again to check on the children.

Both of them had taken themselves to bed and fallen asleep. Maggie felt a sliver of disappointment as she gazed at Mila's quiet form.

No goodnights, no prayers said. Just lights out. And gone.

Jemmy had left his desk lamp on. Maggie moved into his room to snap it off, careful not to step on any of the books or CDs on the floor. Neatness wasn't Jemmy's strong suit. Before she turned off the light, she gazed at his face in sleep. His dark eyelashes fluttered against his cheek—as smooth and creamy as a rose petal.

One day not too long from now there would be stubble on that cheek.

One day not too long from now he won't be mine to check on or kiss goodnight.

She bent over him and kissed his cheek. He made a slight noise but didn't wake. Maggie made her way back down the stairs.

She let the dogs out and as she stood on the back terrace watching them sniff and run from bush to rock, she put in yet another call to Nicole's phone and left another voicemail.

Why isn't she calling back? Is she okay?

Suddenly a needle of fear pierced through the haze of two large glasses of wine and Maggie saw an image of Nicole tied up in the trunk of some madman's car. Her heart began to beat in double time.

Just then she heard the unmistakable sound of Laurent's car door slamming shut. She held her breath and listened but there was only the one door slam.

So he didn't find him.

Or he found him but decided not to bring him back.

Maggie called the dogs in and put them in their crates before going to meet Laurent at the front door.

"I'm sorry, Laurent," she said.

Still in his jacket, his collar pulled up against his neck, Laurent immediately drew her in close and held her for a long moment.

"*Ça ne fait rien,*" he said. *It doesn't matter.*

He smelled of lemons and tobacco.

"You didn't find him?"

He gave her a squeeze and turned to hang up his jacket in the foyer.

"Are the children asleep?" he asked.

"About an hour ago."

"They did their homework?" Laurent went to the kitchen and stood in front of the open refrigerator. It occurred to Maggie that he hadn't had dinner.

"They said so," Maggie said as she set her empty wine glass on the counter.

Laurent glanced over at her. "You didn't check?"

Maggie flushed.

"I considered it a special night. What with their father running out and being gone half the night, I didn't feel the need to keep them to strict rules."

He closed the refrigerator door.

"You are too permissive," he said. "Especially with Jemmy. It's not what he needs."

Maggie's nostrils flared indignantly.

"You don't need to tell me what he needs," she sputtered.

"Clearly I do."

"Well, why don't you see to it he gets whatever it is you think he needs instead of running around trying to adopt strays?"

Laurent turned and looked at her.

That look.

The one she thought she'd never seen from him before.

Now twice in one day.

"Jemmy needs firmness, not Cokes and iPods," he said.

Maggie burst into tears and covered her face with her hands. Immediately Laurent was beside her, his arms around her. He led her to the couch. Maggie pressed her face against his broad chest, smelling the wood smoke from outside in his sweater.

"You are a good mother. I couldn't ask for a better mother for my children. I am sorry for my words, *chérie*."

Before she could respond, her phone rang on the coffee table and she pulled away from Laurent to see the screen. It was Ben. Laurent smoothed her hair from her forehead.

"You can call him back."

"I can't," Maggie said and began to cry again. "Nicole is...m-missing."

Laurent's eyes widened. Keeping one arm around her he scooped up her phone.

"Ben," he said. "What is it?"

Maggie watched Laurent's face and felt a surge of comfort as he took the brunt of whatever Ben was telling him. As usual with Laurent it was impossible to tell.

He glanced at her worried expression and gave a slight shake of his head as if to say *nothing terrible*.

Maggie took in a long shaky breath and wiped the tears from her face with the back of her hand.

Then Laurent disconnected and immediately called the Atlanta police.

30

The next day broke cold and wet at Domaine St-Buvard.

Ever since Laurent had taken over handling the Nicole crisis, he had been unfailingly supportive and gentle with Maggie. He brought her coffee in bed and told her to take her time getting up, he would get the children to school.

After the police contacted Nicole's school, it turned out that Nicole was staying at a friend's house. As far as the police were concerned she wasn't really missing.

When Maggie reached her mother in the morning, Elspeth was again maddeningly matter-of-fact. Nicole had finally called her grandmother and attempted to straighten out the whole mess.

After washing the breakfast dishes, Maggie began her day by calling Fiona Bellemont-Surrey's assistant to cancel her interview.

Laurent felt strongly that Maggie needed to go home and sort out the problem with Nicole in person.

He booked her a flight to Atlanta for the next evening. It didn't escape Maggie's notice that her leaving would effectively ease tensions between them.

Laurent would be aware of that too of course.

That afternoon after a long and unproductive day, capped off by Bellemont-Surrey's assistant emailing Maggie that Mrs. Bellemont-Surrey was extremely put out at being "jerked around" and was rethinking the necessity of appearing in Maggie's newsletter altogether.

Her shoulders and spirits drooping Maggie drove to Aix to pick up Mila and Jemmy from school, omitting the best part of the trip by skipping her usual visit to *Bechard's patisserie.*

There's only so much good a creampuff can do.

When she pulled into the carpool she saw Danielle in line to pick up Zouzou. Just as Maggie was about to get out of her car to go talk to her, her phone rang.

Maggie looked down to see a laughing photo on the screen of her wayward niece, all dark curls and alabaster skin.

"This had better be good," Maggie said when she picked up. "How *could* you?"

"Aunt Maggie, it's not my fault!" Nicole said with exasperation. "I told Grandma where I was going!"

"She says you didn't."

"Well, she's losing her memory just like Grandpa!"

Maggie chose to ignore the disrespect. "Why did you need to go in the first place?"

"Because Grandma's at the old folk's home twenty-four-seven! Give me a break! I'm living on Pop-Tarts!"

While Maggie didn't love Nicole's selfish attitude—and she reminded herself that the girl was only seventeen—she had to admit that it sounded as if her mother was spending more and more time at the memory care facility visiting her father.

"We were all so worried," Maggie said tiredly as she watched the line of school children emerge from the school. "And you weren't answering your phone."

"I'm having trouble with my battery," Nicole said. "It runs down a lot."

Said no teenager ever who wasn't trying to hide something.

"You don't need to come back, Aunt Maggie. It'll be a huge waste of time and money. I already told Grandma this."

"Give me the name and number of the people you're staying with."

Maggie talked a few minutes more and then disconnected and called the number Nicole had given her. She spoke with Haley's mother for several minutes before hanging up, confident that Nicole was safe. In fact, staying with her friend Haley was probably the best thing for everyone right now.

As soon as Maggie hung up, she called Delta Airlines and cancelled her flight home and then walked over to Danielle's car.

Danielle rolled down her window. "Everything all right, *chérie*?"

"Yes. But I need you to bring the kids to Grace's if you would. I have an errand I need to run."

"Of course. No problem," Danielle said.

An hour later Maggie was in Arles.

Her decision to go back to the amphitheater came from the sudden realization that her own mother—struggling through what was arguably the most stressful time in her life—had given up on dealing with the challenges of an active teenager. Watching her mother do that made Maggie realize that she was doing the very same thing by not trying to get answers in the Amphitheater murder.

One thing she knew if she knew nothing else: she was never going to be able to face her anxieties or God knows deal with them if she didn't find some answers.

And the Arles police had made it very clear they weren't going to help find those answers.

They had completely stopped investigating this murder. They weren't talking to anyone. They weren't talking to Bastien who saw more than he let on. They weren't talking to Jacques Duvall or even his mother. For sure *she* probably saw plenty that nobody thought to ask her about.

The only parking place she could find was several blocks away from the amphitheater in an unfamiliar neighborhood. As Maggie pulled into a parking spot, she realized she'd worked hard to avoid thinking of the fact that Bastien had pointed the finger at Brad Anderson.

It started to rain as she walked in the direction the amphitheater. Within moments she didn't recognize where she was. She stopped at one point and stood with her back against a window under the awning of a laundromat and tried to get her bearings.

The people who passed glared at her, somehow aware that she didn't belong there. Did she look like a misplaced tourist? She was dressed in a pair of wool slacks with an open-necked blouse and cashmere cardigan. Not exactly tourist garb but neither could Maggie succeed in passing as a French woman. Frankly it was one of the things Laurent always seemed to enjoy about her—her blatant Americanness.

Just the thought of Laurent gave Maggie a sharp jab in the stomach.

Laurent would *not* be pleased if he could see her now—getting wet in a dark street in one of the rougher sections of Arles. And for what? Because she wanted to gain a new perspective? To what end? The police weren't interested in solving this murder.

So why the hell am I?

Tempted to turn around and find her way back to her car but determined not to make the trip a total loss, Maggie stepped back into the street, braving the rain.

She took a few steps and realized the alley to her immediate right had a narrow overhang that would shelter her from the rain. Without thinking of where the alley led, she turned into it.

What late afternoon light was left in the sky seemed to extinguish the moment Maggie entered the alley. A rat was startled from a nearby pile of garbage and scurried out of sight. A dense sour smell seemed to pour off the ancient stone walls of the building.

She was halfway down the alley when she decided that staying dry wasn't worth ending up in the Rhône river or wherever this alley might lead. She turned around. And that's when she saw him.

Twenty yards into the alley. A dark shadow moving purposefully down the alley.

Coming right toward her.

31

Maggie knew if she ran, he would run too.

But she couldn't help herself. Fear catapulted up her throat and she broke into a run, sliding her hands on the rough stone wall of the building beside her to steady herself on the uneven cobblestones.

Her heart pounded in her ears until she couldn't hear the sound of her pursuer over her own gasps. As her terror ricocheted around her brain she tried to swallow the noise of her own panting and strained to hear him behind her.

A slim wedge of light from an open doorway flickered onto the wet pavement in front of her. Maggie darted inside, shocked by the sudden cessation of rain on her face and the wall of loud throbbing music.

She ran into the room, pushing between two men standing at a long wooden bar. The sound of her heart hammering in her ears drowned out the voices of the men beside her.

Her pursuer paused in the doorway—just a dark shadow—and then was gone.

Even though she hadn't seen his face there had been something distinctly familiar about him.

Maggie stared at the open doorway and then with shaking hands dug her cellphone out of her purse.

Thirty minutes later Jean-Baptiste Moreau stood in the doorway of the bar blinking into the darkened interior. He was dressed in jeans with a leather jacket and Maggie realized he was off duty.

She waved to him from where she sat at her table nursing a Kir Royale. He ordered a beer from the waiter and joined her.

"You are sure you don't want to make a formal complaint?" he said as he sat down.

"Whoever it was is long gone by now."

"And you have no idea who it might have been?"

"You think it was just an attempted mugging," Maggie said.

"I have no idea what it was."

"Good because I need you to be open to the possibility that whoever followed me today is connected to Barbeau's murder."

Moreau's eyebrows shot up into the flop of hair that hung nearly in his eyes. The waiter set his beer glass on the table.

"I have a gut instinct about these things," Maggie said. "There are too many questions surrounding what happened for today to be just a coincidence."

Moreau sighed and Maggie wondered how old he was. He looked to be about Nicole's age but that wasn't possible.

"I don't want to get anyone in trouble," she said, "but I talked to someone at the Café Terrace who said he saw someone resembling Brad Anderson cross the entrance of the amphitheater last Saturday."

"So?"

"Don't you care where everyone was during the critical time?"

Moreau sighed again. "I have seen the CCTV footage. I know where everyone was during the critical time. In addition to the fact that Brad Anderson has no motive for killing Jean Barbeau, he was off camera for a total of four minutes. That wouldn't have given him enough time to get to the murder scene, strangle Barbeau and return to the arena."

Maggie bit her lip. So the killer wasn't Brad? She didn't know why she was having trouble accepting that.

"And since we know Claude Bouquille was with *you* during the critical time—" Jean-Baptiste began.

"Yes, but I was unconscious for part of that time."

"And during *that* time Monsieur Bouquille was with his compatriot Jacky. He is alibied for the entire time. In fact they both are."

"What about the truck drivers who unloaded the vendors' stuff? Did you talk to them?"

"It was deemed unnecessary since there is a CCTV camera on the loading dock. Everyone who unloaded items from trucks that morning were either vendors—and therefore accounted for in the arena—or hired workers who never entered the amphitheater, with the exception of Barbeau who was unaccounted for after entering."

"Wait. So you never saw the victim on camera after he entered the amphitheater through the loading dock?" Maggie asked.

"That is correct but since we know he didn't *leave* the amphitheater alive, how is that information helpful?"

"All information is helpful," Maggie muttered as she drummed her fingers on the table. She saw that the detective was watching her closely.

"I'm not crazy," she said.

"Of course not, Madame."

"Okay, except the way you said that makes it sound like you think I am."

"I don't know what to say to that."

Maggie picked up her purse and pulled her jacket back on.

"I need you to take me to the amphitheater," she said.

"What in the world for?"

"I need to see the crime scene. I need you to show me exactly where it happened."

~

At least some things appear to be getting sorted out, Laurent thought as he got out of the car in front of Danielle's *mas*, two bags of groceries in his arms. Maggie would be back in Atlanta, safe and sound and not causing any more ruptures with the Arles police force or with Laurent's own attempts to sort out Luc and his problems.

When Luc ran off last night, Laurent had come straight to Danielle's and waited for two hours but the boy never showed.

Now, he set groceries down on the kitchen counter and could see by the rumpled blanket and pillow on the floor of the salon sitting room that Luc had slept there last night.

"Luc?" he called, hearing his voice echo throughout the unfurnished house. He knew he needed to get the boy's situation settled and soon. He couldn't keep him here. The boy needed a family. Guidance. Not a big empty house.

Laurent turned the oven on and made himself familiar with Danielle's kitchen. Within minutes the house felt friendlier and warmer, more like a home to come back to. He went to the main salon and stuffed the small franklin stove with wood but held back on lighting it.

Then he returned to the kitchen where he removed the marinated chicken pieces he'd brought from his own kitchen. He used one of Danielle's large Le Creuset Dutch ovens to sauté lardons before adding the chicken pieces from the wine marinade.

As the chicken browned, Laurent chopped onions, mushrooms and carrots and added them to the pot.

Once he covered the pot and set it simmering over low heat he made a list of chores for Luc—including finding more kindling in the surrounding woods—and then gave a rough inspection of the rest of the house.

After the *coq au vin* was done, Laurent cleaned the pots he'd used and wiped down the counter, then put foil around the casserole. Without heat on in the house, the food would be fine on the counter even if Luc came home late tonight.

Where did he go? Does he intend to come back?

Again, Laurent wrestled with his own intentions. He continued to put off any permanent resolutions to what he was doing. He hadn't called a social service agency—surely something he should have done days ago.

Frère Jean had said that Luc came to the monastery from Alsace-Lorraine at the start of the summer. The boy's parents had been killed in a car accident and he had no siblings. More than that, nobody knew.

Deciding to leave the foyer light on and the front door unlocked, Laurent left the house at a little after five o'clock. The sunlight was already leaching from the autumn sky as he got into his car.

As he backed out of the driveway, Laurent caught a flash of movement in the woods that separated the driveway from Laurent's vineyards. He didn't need to turn his head to know it was Luc watching him like a starving puppy afraid to get too close.

As he drove away, Laurent saw Luc in his rearview mirror as he slipped into the house. He felt a spasm of regret before reminding himself that the boy would have hot food. He would stay warm and dry tonight. And sooner or later he would talk to Laurent.

Was that what he wanted? To connect with Luc? Why? He'd already spent enough time with him to see he was nothing like Gerard. Gerard was petulant and whiny as a child. Luc tended to be stoic and long suffering. Gerard was sly and conniving as a teen. Even with a few blots on his copybook from the summer,

Laurent thought that for a homeless teen with no parental guidance, Luc was remarkably straightforward.

Laurent wasn't trying to save Gerard—an utter impossibility in any case since Gerard was dead and had been way past saving years before that. And he wasn't trying to resurrect his relationship with his brother. That had been doomed from the start.

Had Gerard been born the way he'd become? Venal and crafty? Or had his damaged childhood turned him into something he'd never been intended to be?

When Laurent got home, he let the dogs out, checked the mail he'd collected yesterday but hadn't yet read, and turned on his Italian coffee maker for an espresso before going into his office and sitting down at the computer.

He rarely used the computer—just for paying bills online or sending business correspondence emails to his investors and colleagues about the vineyard but a nagging thought had come to him on the drive home that seemed reluctant to let go of him.

It is surely nothing, he thought. But as with anything, it would be better to know for sure.

He composed a brief two-sentence email, reread it and, satisfied, sent it off, addressed to Lieutenant Detective Roger Bedard in Nice.

When the espresso machine began hissing loudly in the kitchen, Laurent stood up at the same moment the landline on his desk began to ring.

He frowned. Everyone they knew contacted them on their cellphones. He couldn't remember the last time the landline had rung. Only last week Maggie had made an argument for getting rid of it.

As he reached for the phone, an uncomfortable premonition shivered through his outstretched arm.

32

Maggie and Moreau entered the amphitheater by the main entrance at the top of the stairs.

This late in the afternoon most tourists were gone and the gates would be locked in another quarter of an hour.

Maggie had again turned off her phone. If Laurent was so determined to have her home at a certain hour with dinner on the table than he could bloody well do it himself.

Or have married someone else.

"The body was here," Moreau said pointing to a shadowed alcove.

Maggie walked to the spot. She was surprised it was so close to one of the archways off the main hall. If this had been any other day, it would have been mere steps from half a dozen exit points from the amphitheater.

But it wasn't any other day.

"Can you please walk me through what you think happened," she said.

Moreau looked at the nearest hallway, and went to stand in the archway facing the alcove.

"We believe Monsieur Barbeau was roughly here," he said.

"And his killer?" Maggie prompted.

Moreau walked halfway from the archway to the center of the small area and looked around as if undecided.

Did you not even do this much? Maggie thought in astonishment. *Did you really just wrap it up and forget it as soon as you knew who the victim was?*

"We think the killer was somewhere here."

"Facing Barbeau as he came into the hallway?"

"Possibly."

Yes, well without a CCT video stream all of it was just speculation.

"Why wouldn't it have been the other way around?" Maggie asked.

"What do you mean?"

"I mean, if Barbeau was skulking around looking for a victim or whatever, wouldn't it have been *him* in the hallway? And his killer would have come upon *him*? The way you have it, it looks as if Barbeau was stalking his killer."

Moreau looked at her and blinked as if trying to see in his mind the picture she was presenting. He looked again at the spot where Barbeau ended up but said nothing.

"So then Barbeau was dragged to that alcove?" Maggie asked. "And that's where he was strangled? Or was he there to begin with? Lying in wait maybe?"

"No. That much we do know. The footprints clearly showed the scuffle started here in the middle and moved to the alcove where...where it ended."

Maggie felt a chill in the small room. She rubbed her arms to dispel the goosebumps forming there.

"And you have no suspects at all?"

Moreau said nothing.

"And you've definitely eliminated Brad Anderson as a suspect?"

"Madame Dernier," Moreau said tiredly. "Stop. Please. The case is unsolvable."

"Only because nobody wants to be bothered with trying to solve it."

"As you say."

"What else do you know about the victim?"

"He worked at the amphitheater as a janitor for five years."

"Wait. So he served four years in prison and then worked here for five? How old was he when he went to prison?"

"I'm not sure."

"Well, how old was he when he died?"

"Twenty-six."

"So he was *seventeen* when he went to prison?"

"Child molesters come in all ages, shapes and sizes."

"Five years at one job is a long time," Maggie said. "He must have been dependable."

"I'm sure even pedophiles have their positive points."

There was nothing more to see that Maggie could make sense of. They left the room off the main hall and walked toward a man in green canvas overalls who was standing by the main gate ready to lock up.

"Excuse me," Maggie said when they reached him. "A question, please?"

The man was balding and had a hawk nose. He smiled tiredly at her.

"The amphitheater will open tomorrow promptly at zero eight hundred hours," he said.

Moreau walked up behind Maggie and pulled out his police identification to show the man.

"We aren't tourists," Moreau said.

"What can I help you with?" the man said, frowning now.

"Your name, please?" Moreau asked.

"Michel Drenot."

"Monsieur Drenot," Maggie said, "My name is Maggie

Dernier and this is Detective Jean-Baptiste Moreau. You were Jean Barbeau's employer?"

Drenot glanced furtively at Moreau and then at Maggie. "*Oui*," he said.

"I was surprised to hear that Monsieur Barbeau worked for you for so long. Would you say he was a reliable employee?"

"*Oui*."

"So, no problems with him?"

"*Non*."

"Can I ask how you came to offer him the job in the first place?"

"He attended my church."

Maggie had not expected that.

"What church is that, Monsieur Drenot?" Moreau asked.

"*L'Eglise de Saint-Julien*." Drenot cleared his throat. "Jean taught our children's choir and there are many who miss him. I regret if that is not a popular view. Now if you will excuse me."

Maggie and Moreau stepped outside as Drenot quickly chained the front entrance and then, after giving them a curt nod, walked away, leaving them at the top of the stairs.

"Where are you parked?" Moreau asked her.

"Off of Boulevard Emile Combes," Maggie answered distracted. "Is it weird that Barbeau was a Christian? And please don't give me your *they come in all shapes and sizes* quip again."

Moreau shrugged and they started walking in the direction of Maggie's parking lot.

The light had nearly faded from the sky.

"And he directed a *children's* choir?" Maggie said. "How much sense does that make?"

"That *is* odd."

As they walked by the cafés filling up with tourists and locals along the *rue de la Redoute* Maggie glanced at her watch.

"I'm going to be in trouble getting home so late today," she said.

"Perhaps I can help you with that," Moreau said.

"Really?" Maggie grinned at him. "Do tell."

"You didn't by any chance talk with Monsieur Barbeau's widow, Adelaide Barbeau, yesterday, did you?"

"Maybe," Maggie hedged, wondering how this was possibly going to get her off the hook with Laurent.

"I only ask because my department received a complaint about a civilian badgering the murder victim's wife. Since the description she gave matched you..."

"Yes, okay, it was me. I tried to talk to her and she threatened to sic her dogs on me."

"I thought it might be you so I called you earlier today to ask you about it."

Maggie pulled out her phone but it was still turned off. "What time?" she said, turning her phone back on.

"About sixteen hundred hours?"

As soon as her phone screen lit up she saw Moreau's name in her list of *Missed Calls*.

"Yep," she said. "There you are. But how exactly do you think you can help me by...oh, no."

Maggie looked at him with suddenly mounting consternation. "You didn't."

"Je suis désolé, Madame. But when you didn't answer, I called your home number."

"Oh, God. Tell me you didn't leave a message."

"No, Madame."

"Thank goodness."

"Your husband answered the phone."

33

When Maggie walked through the door at Domaine St-Buvard she didn't need to see Laurent's face to know they would be having a serious discussion about how she had been spending her time these days.

Especially when she knew that *he* knew she hadn't picked up the kids from school in four days, nor had she made dinner, done laundry or run any of the dozen or so family errands she'd promised to.

She dropped her car keys in the ceramic dish by the front door and was instantly greeted by the scent of garlic and onions.

Mila ran to the foyer and threw her arms around Maggie's waist.

"*Maman*! Can I come with you to America? Please say yes! I want to see Nicole and *Grandmère*!"

Maggie hugged the child but before she could respond, Mila was gone, skipping back to the dining room where she was in the process of setting the table for dinner.

Maggie hung up her jacket and went into the kitchen. Laurent had Jemmy at the stove sautéing chicken pieces. And even though Maggie knew she was well and truly in the dog house tonight after Moreau's phone call, it took all her effort not to tell Jemmy to stop standing so close to the gas flame on the stove.

Jemmy glanced over his shoulder at her. "I'm making *coq au vin, Maman*!"

"I see that," Maggie said, wishing he would put his eyes back on what he was doing.

Laurent turned to face her, his hands on his hips, a dish towel slung over one shoulder. As usual, his expression was unreadable.

"Mm-mm," Maggie said brightly. "Smells good in here."

Laurent turned to pour a glass of red wine into a glass and handed it to her.

"You're going to need it," he said.

Dinner was Laurent's usual masterful performance in the kitchen. But all through the meal Maggie knew the other shoe was waiting to be dropped from a very uncomfortable height—say about six foot five—and she knew it wouldn't happen until the dishes were done and the children had gone to their rooms to do their homework.

One thing was for sure: Laurent was better at waiting than she was. Of course it was true he was also holding all the cards in this waiting game. So even if he *hadn't* spent fifteen years biding his time and lying his way through every known con in the south of France, he was still in a better position to negotiate the wait on his terms than Maggie was.

"You had a busy afternoon," Laurent said to her as the children began to clear the table.

Maggie wouldn't be tricked by his mild tone. She knew he was furious with her.

"Doing this and that," she said as he refilled her wine glass.

She made a mental note not to drink it. She was already no match for him when he was like this but the few paltry arguments she could make in her favor would be a jumbled snarl of irrational gibberish if she risked another glass of wine.

"This is good," she said of the wine. "One of ours?"

The *vendange* had been over for weeks and she knew they wouldn't be drinking anything from this year's harvest so soon. If there was anything that might sidetrack Laurent and his mounting ire with her it would be his vineyard.

"It is," he said succinctly and then stood up to let the dogs out.

At least usually, she thought with a sinking heart.

As predicted, Laurent waited until the children had gone upstairs. He went outside a second time with the dogs to smoke and Maggie knew her only hope was to throw off his timing. As soon as he closed the door behind him, she grabbed her jacket from off the hook in the foyer and followed him.

"I need you to hear my side first," she said to him.

He turned around, the end of his cigarette glowing in the night.

"The police aren't interested in finding Barbeau's killer," Maggie said. "The killer was somewhere near Jemmy just before he struck. So no, I can't just let this go. He could have...I don't know...found *Jemmy*. I can't explain it any better but I can't let it go."

"You *can* let it go."

"Nope, I can't."

"Have you spoken to your mother today?"

"My mother?" Maggie hesitated, thrown off-track by this out-of-left-field question.

Which was very likely his intention.

"No. But I talked to Nicole."

"So did I."

Crap. That means he knows I cancelled my flight home.

"Laurent, listen. There is no reason for me to go to Atlanta."

"No reason? Your niece was missing for four days and you—"

"Well, she's your niece too. Why don't *you* go?"

Nicole was Maggie's sister's daughter but her father was Laurent's brother Gerard.

The sound of their bedroom shutters rattling in a sudden burst of wind made Maggie jump. She glanced up nervously as though expecting one of the shutters to come flying off. There had been talk of the mistral—the cold and often violent north-westerly wind that charges in from southern France—possibly making an appearance in their area this week.

Laurent threw his cigarette on the terrace pavers and ground it out with his boot. He called to the dogs.

"Laurent, I'm just trying to sort out what happened that afternoon."

"What happened was a man got what he deserved."

"That's not our call to make."

"Do you need more to do? Is that it? Are Mila's cupcakes for her class party tomorrow already made?"

Maggie had forgotten Mila needed cupcakes tomorrow.

"I was planning on stopping at *Bechard's* on the way to school," she said.

"Incroyable!"

Laurent opened the French doors and stomped inside, followed by both dogs just as Maggie's phone rang.

She glanced at the screen and saw it was Fiona Bellemont-Surrey's assistant. Maggie had called that afternoon and left a voicemail saying she could make the interview after all.

Zoe's voice was laced with disapproval. "Mrs. Bellemont-Surrey's time is very valuable and she does not appreciate being jerked around like this. Either you want to do the piece or you don't. She said for me to tell you she *thought* you were a professional."

"Look, I'm sorry," Maggie said as she shivered on the terrace and peered through the French doors. Mila and Jemmy were downstairs in the kitchen with Laurent. "I had a personal matter to deal with that just recently resolved itself. Please tell Mrs. Bellemont-Surrey that her time and this interview is...are at the top of my priorities list."

Zoe sniffed and then said that Mrs. Bellemont-Surrey could meet with Maggie tomorrow morning at eleven o'clock.

Maggie's heart sank.

Saint-Rémy-de-Provence was at least a two-hour drive away. Counting the time for the interview and coming and going, she was going to be gone most of the day—and she'd still need Danielle or Laurent to pick the kids up after school.

Worst timing ever.

"I'll be there," Maggie promised the assistant.

"My, this looks like fun," Maggie said cheerfully as she entered the house.

"Papa made homemade ice cream," said Mila who was sitting at the kitchen counter.

"And I helped," Jemmy said earnestly.

Laurent watched Maggie with narrowed eyes and Maggie forced herself to smile widely at him.

"Listen," she said brightly. "Something's come up and I have to be in Saint-Rémy tomorrow morning so I was wondering if you could stop at *Bechard's* and pick up the goodies for Mila's school event?"

Laurent stared at her, his hand still holding the ice cream scoop, his mouth agape in disbelief.

34

"Can you just explain to me *why*? Is that too damn much to ask?" Brad said as his voice rose over the telephone line.

Cradling her cellphone against her shoulder, Grace got up from the couch where Danielle and Zouzou were watching television and moved into the mudroom off the kitchen.

"I just need some time to think," Grace said.

The branches of the Linden tree out front scratched at the alcove bay window like fingers trying to pry their way into the warm sanctity of the house. A sound like an eerie moaning slipped under the window jamb as the mistral made its presence known.

"Think? About what? We're either a couple or we're not. Do you need a marriage proposal?"

That is literally the last thing I need.

"I can't explain it."

"Don't you think I deserve more than *that* after two months?"

"I'm not breaking up with you, Brad."

"I'd like to know what you call it then. I feel kicked to the curb."

How could she explain what she didn't understand herself? A niggling feeling? An ominous foreboding? Whatever it was, she couldn't put it into words.

But she knew it wasn't right.

"Brad, I just need some space."

"Which means you're breaking up with me."

Grace sighed in exasperation but willed herself not to react to him. He was insecure and he was hurt. Of course he would try to push her buttons.

Why do men do this? Why do they think getting aggressive will somehow reverse a verdict they don't like?

Or is that just the men I always meet?

"Have dinner with me tomorrow," Brad said. "Just you and me. In Aix. Let's just talk."

Grace hesitated.

Did she want to break up with him? If not, then she should be up for a simple meal with him.

"Sure. That would be nice."

After she'd hung up she continued to stare out the window. Danielle had mentioned at dinner that there were reports that the mistral was on its way. By the way the cypress trees out front looked, their top branches swaying and bending, it appeared that the mistral had definitely arrived.

Grace glanced down at her phone and impulsively dialed Maggie's number.

"Hey," Maggie said. "I am so sorry, Grace."

"Darling, me too. Let's forget it. You have so much on your plate these days I never should have gotten upset."

"Don't you love that even though I know I was a pill and you're mad at me I still had Danielle bring the kids to your place when I needed to run an errand?" Maggie said.

Grace laughed. "Well, that's what good friends are for. Even when you're pissed as hell at them, they don't stop being there for you."

"I wanted to call you back and say I was sorry. I don't know what got into me."

"You're under a lot of stress right now. Give some of the load to Laurent. That's what he's there for."

"He's mad at me right now. The only load he wants to take at the moment is the one he wants to drop on my head."

"Why?"

Maggie sighed. "Well, for starters, he thinks I'm too easy on Jemmy. He thinks I'm obsessed with this amphitheater murder. He thinks I'm not doing enough to cook and keep house for him and the kids. He thinks my job is more trouble than it benefits us. Take your pick."

"Wow. That's a lot."

"What about you? How's Brad?"

"He's good," Grace said, wondering why she wasn't telling Maggie that she was on the verge of breaking up with him.

Because then I make it real.

She switched the subject instead. "Zouzou told me that Nicole was missing or something?"

"She was at a friend's house and didn't bother letting my mother know."

"Is our perfect Nicole becoming a bit of a teenager?"

"Sounds like it. Laurent wants her to come to France immediately. You know Laurent. He thinks she's too much for my mother to handle."

"He could be right."

"There is no way Nicole will agree to leave her friends. She's in high school. Plus she knows Laurent. Once she's here, she'll be under his rather massive thumb."

"How well I know," Grace said with a rueful laugh. "And Jemmy? No aftershocks from the whole amphitheater ordeal?"

"He's fine but I've been chasing down some leads as to who might have killed Barbeau. I've already talked with his widow and I'm in touch with one of the two detectives on the case. Did you know the police essentially dropped the whole case? Their reasoning being that the guy was a child molester so good riddance. Can you believe that?"

"Are you seriously trying to run down leads on this, darling? What in the world for?"

There was a pause on the line and then, "Gosh, Grace, you sound like Laurent."

"Well, if I may remind you, Laurent is usually right. I can't believe you're doing this."

"Grace, the guy was murdered!"

"I know, darling. I read the newspaper report. He was also a lowlife who most people think is doing a better job contributing to society as a corpse."

When Maggie didn't immediately answer, Grace said in frustration, "Was he or was he not prowling the amphitheater for children to abuse?"

"Nobody knows what he was doing," Maggie said icily.

Grace realized by Maggie's tone that things had gotten out of hand. Her purpose had been to bury the hatchet with Maggie—not dig up another reason to disagree with her.

"Look, darling, I'm just surprised you'd want to do it. That's all. Meanwhile, let's get together for coffee as soon as you have a minute."

"Sure, Grace," Maggie said with exaggerated politeness. "That would be nice."

35

The next morning began with a bang at Domaine St-Buvard.

That was the sound of cabinet doors slamming as Jemmy rummaged in the kitchen for the soccer ball he was sure he'd put there—fueled by his fury that Maggie had forgotten about his school soccer match after school.

Which wouldn't have been all that unforgiveable, if it weren't for the fact that Maggie had promised to bring team snacks.

When did we all become so Americanized? she wondered as she ruefully watched her son vent his annoyance with her with every door slam.

"I'm really sorry, Jemmy," Maggie said.

"And Papa can't come either," Jemmy said angrily, "so I don't know why *I'm* bothering to go!"

"You're on the team, Jemmy," Mila said patiently. "That's why."

"Shut up, Mila," Jemmy said.

"Dammit, Jemmy, stop it!" Maggie said, her body tensing. "It's *one* game and this is a good opportunity for you to get a grip on your temper."

"Oh, *Maman*," Mila gasped. "You swore!"

"It appears *Maman* might need to take her own advice," Laurent said, as he entered the kitchen, then leaned down to kiss Mila on the cheek. "Ready, *ma petite*?"

Mila picked up her satchel and ran to the front door.

"Look, Laurent," Maggie started, but he held up a hand and turned his attention to Jemmy.

"What did I say about telling your sister to shut up?" Laurent said.

Jemmy's face fell but he gave an angry look at Maggie that could only be interpreted as blaming her for making him say it.

"In the car," Laurent said and for a moment Maggie thought he was talking to her.

Jemmy tucked his soccer ball under his arm and left the kitchen with his head down.

"Jemmy," Laurent said sternly.

Jemmy stopped, his shoulders rigid as he faced the door.

"Did you forget something?" Laurent said.

Jemmy turned and went to Maggie. He lifted up on tiptoe and kissed Maggie's cheek then turned and joined his sister in the drive outside.

"I'd rather not have the kiss at all than have him be forced to do it," Maggie said.

"It was not for you that I made him do it."

"Oh. Right."

He poured himself a cup of espresso and drank it as he stood by the kitchen window, his back to her.

"Nobody would get this upset if I worked in a law firm," Maggie said. "Nobody would think anything of my having to work at the last minute if I worked in an office job."

"You don't need to work in an office," Laurent said, finally turning to look at her. "We don't need the money. We don't need your job."

She blushed furiously. "Well, *I* need it."

"Just as long as we're clear about why you are working." And with that he turned, kissed her on the cheek and left the house.

Maggie watched him through the kitchen window as he drove away with the kids, her cheek still hot from her second forced kiss of the morning.

~

Maggie was in her office putting together her interview questions for her visit with Fiona Bellemont-Surrey when she heard the distinctive grinding of gravel under car tires in her front drive.

Wondering if perhaps Laurent had forgotten something—although in all the years she'd known him she'd never known him to forget anything ever—she hurried to the front door and opened it to see Danielle climbing out of her vintage Peugeot.

Maggie met her in the driveway and they kissed in greeting.

"I wasn't expecting you this morning," Maggie said. She had about fifteen minutes before she needed to leave for Saint-Rémy.

"I told Laurent I would stop by with the extra *haricot vertes* from the *potager* at *Dormir*," Danielle said. Maggie saw a large basket of green beans in the back seat of the car. Danielle opened the door and pulled the basket out.

"I have to head out to Saint-Rémy in a few minutes. Do you have time for a coffee? Laurent picked up an *orange financier* last night."

"I always have time for cake," Danielle said with a smile.

A few minutes later, Maggie put the basket of green beans on the back terrace table so they would stay cool until Laurent could get to them. She poured two mugs from the fresh pot of coffee and set out wedges of the *orange financier* on a china dish.

"Inside or out?" Maggie asked.

"Inside I think, *chérie*," Danielle said. "It's getting colder now. Can you not feel it?"

"I don't think I'm as sensitive to it as you."

"I would have thought being a Southern Belle, you would have thin blood, no?"

Maggie laughed. "People forget it gets really cold in Atlanta in the winter. We even get an ice storm or two to keep us on our toes."

"I do not think of the American South with ice storms," Danielle admitted.

Maggie fed part of her cake to the dogs.

"How is the goat?" Danielle asked.

"The goat was a mistake. I think even Mila knows that. She never remembers to feed it so I end up having to do it."

"Not like a good dog, eh?"

"No contest. Have you thought about getting one? A dog?"

"I do not lack for company, *chérie*."

"I know. But you can cuddle a dog. They're very comforting. You can kiss his little furry face and play patty-cake with his paws."

Danielle laughed. "Perhaps they do things differently in America with their dogs." She leaned over and put a hand on Maggie's hand. "What's wrong, *chérie*?"

"Oh, nothing. Laurent is mad at me again."

"I have observed that the friction between you and Laurent is usually not a bad thing."

"Well, it's certainly exhausting. I have to make this trip to Saint-Rémy today and he's pissed off about my going."

"That does not sound like Laurent."

"He doesn't think I should work."

"I'm sure that is not what he thinks. Would he have built your desk for you? Or commissioned the hand-carved door for your office if he didn't want you to work?"

"I don't know." Maggie began drumming her fingers on the table and glanced at the kitchen clock. She probably should get going if she didn't want to be late. Just the thought of being late with the prickly Bellemont-Surrey nudged her anxiety up a level.

"Perhaps it is something else that is bothering you, *chérie*?"

Maggie groaned. "It's this stupid murder case."

Danielle gave her a surprised look. "The one where the child molester was murdered at the amphitheater? What does that unfortunate man's death have to do with you?"

"You sound like Grace and Laurent. And my mother for that matter."

"I am just surprised that you care so much."

Maggie stared at Danielle as if hearing the words for the first time.

"I don't know why it matters," Maggie said, feeling hot tears gather in her eyes. "Except the guy was so close to Jemmy when he was killed. I can't help but wonder…or worry that Jemmy saw something."

"But Jemmy said he didn't."

"I know, so then I think that if I can just figure out what happened, I can prevent Jemmy from ever being in a situation like that again, you know?"

"You must know you cannot control these things, *chérie*."

"I refuse to believe that."

Danielle laughed. "I know you do. It's one of your most endearing traits, *chérie*. But whether you believe it or not, does not change the facts."

"I can't help how I feel," Maggie said. "I'm convinced I'll get peace if I can find out what happened that day. If I can find out how close Jemmy was to disaster. If I can find out who the murderer is…"

"Well, then you must do what you must do," Danielle said, standing and patting her pocket for her car keys. "But try to remember one thing, *oui*?"

"What's that?"

"Jemmy is safe." She leaned over and squeezed Maggie's hand. "And that is the only thing that really matters, *non*?"

36

In her heart of hearts Maggie knew Danielle was right.

Of course the fact that Jemmy was safe was all that mattered.

But finding out how everything could so easily have gone the other way was important too.

If she could just find out which bullet they'd dodged that day and *how*, then next time—because it was a dangerous world they lived in and of course there would be a next time—Maggie would know how to warn Jemmy and Mila to prepare.

Forcing herself not to think about the murder for at least the duration of her drive to Saint-Rémy, Maggie focused on the scenery and the charming villages along the way that she hadn't visited in years.

The brighter colors of early November bathed the countryside in a muted glow as she headed north. The silvery-green olive orchards and the vineyards—now plucked of their bounty—were interspersed with glimpses of pine-covered mountains behind the pastures she passed through.

Saint-Rémy was famous in France for many reasons. It annually appeared at the top of *France's Most Charming Villages* list and was chock full of delightful bistros, dress shops, antique boutiques and colorful daily markets.

Fiona Bellemont-Surrey wasn't the only one drawn to the village either. Maggie had read that Hugh Grant and Tom Hardy and their families had moved to the area and could be seen sipping demitasse and munching *pain au chocolat* at any of the village's many cafés.

The real estate prices had of course soon reflected the little village's glory with tumble-down shacks sans electricity or running water going for half a million euros. It was a favorite topic with Laurent. As usual he tended to chalk it up to the Brits and Yanks who were more interested in a fantasized ideal than a real life living situation.

Maggie had to agree with him. Unless you had the kind of money of a Hugh Grant or a Fiona Bellemont-Surrey, living in the most charming village in the world would quickly lose its appeal if you had no hot water for your bath.

As she neared Saint-Rémy, the main road wound toward the Roman ruins of *Les Antiques* and Glanum and past the turn to Saint-Paul-de-Maulsole, Van Gogh's hospital.

Jemmy's class had come here last spring on a field trip and Jemmy had talked of little else for days afterward. Maggie was sorry she'd not visited the place herself. It had long been on her list of things to do but even when friends visited from the States there was always so much to see and do further south in Provence—Cassis with its amazing Calanques, the many vineyards in the area, the lavender fields, the sunflowers, Chateau La Coste, Aix, Avignon and Arles—that venturing two hours north seemed unnecessary.

Not like today, she thought with a burgeoning annoyance.

Of all the times to make this drive, today had to rank right up there as the least convenient time of all. Not just because of all the family activities she'd had to bail on, but Maggie had hoped to connect with Jean-Baptiste today to see if he'd learned anything more about Barbeau's employer Monsieur Drenot.

Thinking of Detective Moreau amidst the vortex of family obligations against the soothing vista of the passing scenery of the village itself—still relatively sleepy at this time of day and in this season with all the tourists gone—made Maggie realize that he had been particularly helpful yesterday.

Not in just coming to see her at the bar after she'd been stalked—when he could easily have insisted she come to the police department to report it—but walking with her to the amphitheater to show her the crime scene.

It's almost like he doesn't agree with his department's determination not to investigate the murder.

An uncomfortable thought came to her.

Or is it something else?

Maggie thought of Roger Bedard who had recently moved from Aix where she'd seen him frequently to Nice four hours away.

Also a police Detective, Roger had come into Maggie's life during a troubling patch in the early days of her marriage. He'd given her flattering attention at the same time he was willing to work with her to solve the murder outside Arles of a friend of hers.

That combustible alchemy had resulted in a relationship—usually uncomfortable for both of them—that had lasted these past ten years. While Maggie eventually sorted out her issues with being newly married, Roger was never able to relinquish his infatuation for her.

During the years that followed, Maggie had often used his affection for her to gain any extra help she required from the police in solving a few local mysteries.

Of course there were times when Roger's fixation on her had resulted in a less than desirable result, like when he'd deliberately blocked her attempts to investigate a case that was important to her.

All in all she missed Roger and his steadfast ways, his general openness and his predictability. But she knew his moving away was for the best—at least for him.

Which was why the thought that Jean-Baptiste might be feeling anything remotely similar to what Roger had felt for her was disconcerting.

Let's just hope he's driven to solve this case for his own reasons. And that those reasons have nothing to do with me.

As she neared Saint-Rémy, Maggie passed a shepherd—looking as if he'd stepped out of the eighteenth century. He wore a loose sweater, a beret and a very big mustache as he supervised with a rambunctious black sheep dog his herd of a dozen sheep.

Passing through the village and through *Place de la République,* its main square, Maggie noted the green metal bistro tables out in front of the Café de la Place. She knew from friends that on market days it was so congested there was no getting through the square in a car.

A few moments later she came upon a towering wall of oleanders that hid the entrance to the driveway of the Belmont-Surrey villa which she'd found using GoogleMaps. Turning into the driveway, Maggie felt a throb of excitement.

She pulled up to an intercom affixed to a metal post and announced her arrival. She was immediately instructed by a man's voice, heavily accented in the *patois* of the area, to follow the drive to the front of the villa.

Maggie used her phone to photograph the verdigris iron gates as they creaked open and then drove through them, following the drive which was tightly bordered by tall Cyprus trees to where the road curved and the mansion came into view.

It was what Maggie would have described as the quintessential Provençal villa. Looking like it belonged on the cover of Marie-Claire, it had to be worth two million euros. At least.

Maggie parked in front and stepped out to photograph the house façade from several different angles.

A stern-faced man stood waiting for her on the broad steps at the front of the house. He wore a dark suit that looked like livery to Maggie.

"You may leave your vehicle there," the man said by way of greeting.

Maggie grabbed her briefcase before following him inside the house.

The foyer—larger than Maggie and Laurent's entire kitchen—was covered in gleaming marble tile, its wallpapered walls featuring a series of six lighted gold sconces with silk shades that led the way to the double-paneled walnut doors opening onto a sitting room.

Maggie managed not to gasp. After all, she came from money herself and the house where she'd grown up in Buckhead wasn't small.

But this was a whole different level of rich.

The sitting room was drenched in burgundy silk—from the wall coverings to the matching upholstered seating arrangement grouped around a massive stone fireplace.

Wide marble columns flanked a large oak table with an arrangement of fresh flowers—hothouse, Maggie thought, from the look of them.

In front of the fireplace sat two giant wingback chairs draped in garnet with a small table between them on which sat a glittering silver tea service.

Fiona Bellemont-Surrey stood by one of the chairs, her arm poised across the top, her chin held high as if expecting someone to photograph her. Her hair was tied back in a severe bun which accentuated the harsh lines in her face.

Maggie strode into the room, smiling broadly.

"Good morning, Fiona. Thank you for seeing me today."

The woman turned and looked in the direction of the tea service without responding.

"Your house is beautiful," Maggie said, feeling her stomach tighten uncomfortably.

"I'll ask you to resist photographing it," Fiona said, finally sitting down, her fists bunched in her lap.

"Okay." Maggie sat down opposite the woman. "It's just that people will want to see how you live. And pictures help fill out the story of who you are."

"That is preposterous," Fiona said, finally looking at Maggie. "Do you flatter yourself to think you're going to write the piece that tells *my* story?"

"I don't understand, Fiona. I thought you wanted me to write this piece."

"Will you kindly stop referring to me by my Christian name?"

Maggie blushed in embarrassment but felt a creeping sense of anger too.

After living in Provence for more than a decade, Maggie had several expat British friends. Most were warm and approachable. She'd always felt that the ex-pats she knew shared a common personality feature with all intrepid souls interested in exploring new cultures and different ways of life.

But that was not what she was seeing in this cold, intensely unhappy woman.

"No problem, Mrs. Bellemont-Surrey," Maggie said. "I value your time as I'm sure you do mine so why don't we get started?"

Fiona brushed away nonexistent lint from her wool skirt.

"This might have been a mistake," she said.

For a moment Maggie thought the woman was talking about her skirt.

"I only agreed to this because my publisher insisted," Fiona said.

"I drove two hours to get here today," Maggie said. "I cancelled other appointments for this."

"That has nothing to do with me. I'm afraid I'm going to have to ask you to leave. Kindly do not think of using any photographs you may have already taken. My attorneys will be prompt in their response. Eugene!" Fiona called. "Please show our visitor out."

Biting back a series of retorts that Maggie knew would only end up making her feel worse, Maggie stood and without a word swept past Eugene as he came into the salon.

It took Maggie nearly an hour of the drive home before she was able to calm down enough to sort out what she was going to do now—with an eight-hundred word hole right in the middle of her newsletter.

She comforted herself with the thought that *whatever* Fiona Bellemont-Surrey's life story was, it was clearly an unhappy one and Maggie doubted she'd have been able to interview the woman without uncovering that.

And then what kind of article would I have? My readers don't want to read about how the romantic Fiona Bellemont-Surrey is really an embittered sociopath with a broomstick up her arse.

She could just imagine the article's headline:

"Come to Provence to live in a gorgeous villa and hate the world."

Maggie tried to remember how she'd gotten the lead on the Bellemont-Surrey story in the first place. She was pretty sure the woman's publisher had reached out to *her*.

Well, however it happened, she thought grimly, *it's finished now.*

37

On the way home from Saint-Rémy Maggie put on Van Morrison and let the music ease the kinks out of her annoyance with how her morning had gone.

It helped that she would get home early enough to start dinner—for a change—and perhaps that would assuage the tensions between her and Laurent. Plus, with no mad-dash article to write for Monday's newsletter to consume her weekend, she could spend some much needed time focusing on the children and their activities too.

Laurent was right about that. She'd given both Mila and Jemmy short shrift the last few weeks—perhaps even longer. Tonight would be a good time to get back on track.

Maybe Mila would like to make some sugar pumpkin cookies. There was nothing like the fragrance of allspice and cinnamon in the air to bring a true sense of the approaching holidays to Domaine St-Buvard.

Just as she was wondering if she should give Laurent a call to see if he needed her to pick up anything, she saw that he was calling her.

"Hey there," she said, cheerfully into her cellphone. "I was just going to call you."

"What for?"

"To see if you needed anything for dinner tonight. I'm nearly at the village."

"Not necessary," he said.

Maggie could hear her children laughing in the background.

"We're still in Aix," Laurent said. "Take your time getting home. We'll eat here tonight."

Maggie's heart sank.

Surely he heard the part where I said I'm nearly to St-Buvard?

"Oh, okay," she said. "That's cool."

Bypassing the turn to the village, she continued on toward home.

"How was Jemmy's soccer game?" she asked.

Maggie tried to remember a single other time when Laurent had opted to eat in Aix over coming home.

"Don't forget to feed the dogs," he said as another wave of laughter erupted in the background on his end. "See you this evening."

Maggie disconnected and stared dispiritedly at the road ahead.

Oh joy. A completely wasted day and a great big empty house to come home to.

Luc put the kettle on and stared through the kitchen window. After another night of no sleep he decided he was overthinking his current situation. What he needed to do was focus on the fact that he had a roof over his head and food delivered to him daily and stop worrying about the rest.

Stop worrying that Dernier was going to put him in a pot and cook him or turn him into his house slave.

What does he want with me?

Luc had heard stories at the monastery from some of the other boys of things that had happened on the road when they were traveling, usually alone, from one city to another. Sometimes the boys admitted to doing it for money—as if that was better because they were the ones calling the shots. But another boy, Omar, cried himself to sleep every night. Because he hadn't done it for money and he hadn't been calling the shots.

Luc flushed angrily. He didn't like thinking of Omar. The kid was an idiot and probably dead by now. Social workers had come for him in the middle of summer and taken him away. Frère Jean said he went to be with his parents but everyone knew that was a lie.

There are no happy endings, Luc told himself bitterly. Parents don't come back to life and there's only enough Angelina Jolies in the world to adopt a handful of poor orphans.

The rest of us just carry on until the cops step in to sort us out for good.

The kettle whistled shrilly and Luc cursed the fact that he was supposed to catch it *before* it boiled. He grabbed the handle but forgot to use a mitt. A sunburst of pain shot up his arm and he dropped the kettle onto the stone floor. Instantly he was splashed by boiling water as he stumbled away from the mess.

"Dammit!" he shouted at the empty rafters of the house. He waved his burned hand to try to cool it but it only hurt worse.

Suddenly there was a pounding at the front door. The sound jackknifed all his other senses into the stratosphere. He suddenly heard the ticking of the kitchen clock and detected the pervasive odors of last night's dinner until he thought he might be sick.

He looked through the kitchen window but didn't see Dernier's car.

Dernier wouldn't knock.

He comes right in like he owns the place.

Like he owns me too.

Still, someone was at the door. Someone who probably knew Luc shouldn't be here.

Luc crouched beneath the kitchen window to avoid anyone seeing him and slowly edged into the foyer. The pounding continued.

Through the sidelights that flanked the massive front door Luc saw the shadowy forms of two people on the doorstep.

Was it the police?

If Luc were arrested again he'd be sent to prison this time for sure.

But the *flic* would come in cars, he reasoned.

"Open up, you bastard!" a familiar voice shouted. "We know you're in there, Thayer!"

"Yeah, open up!" another voice crowed.

Luc's feet were moving before he thought to think first. He hadn't talked to another person in three days.

He wrenched open the door and then yelped because of his burned hand.

On the doorstep stood André and Jabar.

"How did you know I was here?" Luc asked shaking his hand in the air to mitigate the flair of pain radiating through it.

André pushed him aside as he entered.

"Marie-France saw you taking a whiz in the eastern vineyard yesterday," Jabar said. "Only we didn't know you were actually *inside the house*."

André went to the kitchen and glanced at the kettle on the floor.

"Sweet," he said, turning to Luc, his eyes glittering with malicious intent.

Suddenly Luc wasn't happy to see them. Lonely or not, suddenly he felt protective of the big empty house, the kettle on the floor, and the peeling, cheap linoleum.

Suddenly he was very very sorry he had opened the front door.

38

The next morning was a typical Saturday morning in autumn. Laurent chopped firewood at the end of the garden—with Jemmy in attendance watching him closely—and Mila measured out ingredients for the Madeleines she intended to bake that morning, humming happily as she went from pantry to fridge and back again.

The weather was sunny but cool. Buddy and Izzy were sunning themselves on the terrace tiles of the back garden and Maggie stood by the French doors, a steaming cup of coffee in her hands as she watched Jemmy watch his father.

He'll want to use the axe now.

She prayed Laurent would make it clear he was too young.

Just at that moment she saw Laurent straighten up with the axe in his hand as he spoke to his son. Then like something out of a horror movie, Maggie watched as Laurent handed the axe to Jemmy.

Her heart racing, Maggie put a hand to her mouth and wondered if she should find a place to sit down before her legs became any more wobbly.

"*Maman*?" Mila said from the kitchen. "What's wrong?"

"Nothing, sweetie," Maggie said shakily as she watched Laurent tousle Jemmy's hair before taking the axe from him. Jemmy immediately began picking up the firewood pieces his father had already chopped.

I'm never going to survive my son's adolescence, Maggie thought, forcing herself to turn away.

Her family had come home after eight the night before—not late by any means but too late for anything more than to sort the kids out with their baths and settle them in their rooms with books. Laurent retired immediately to his office where Maggie heard him on the phone with various colleagues with his wine business.

Today everyone had plans that would take them away from home. Danielle would be by to pick up Mila to spend the afternoon at *Dormir* where she and Zouzou would be making their first attempts at making a wedding cake.

Laurent had a meeting with a wine contact of some kind and an afternoon engagement at the monastery.

Jemmy had a playdate with his friend Louis.

As for Maggie, an email from Claude Bouquille last night when he sent his wife's display ad also included an invitation to a *Cowboys of the Carmague* exhibition at the amphitheater.

Dating back to the early 16th century, the *gardians* were a professional order of cowboys who worked to protect and care for the herds of horses and black bulls that roamed around La Carmague, a region south of Arles on the Mediterranean.

It wasn't an interview with an internationally famous author, but it would be a suitable substitute. The story and photographs of these famed cowboys—or *gardians* as they were known in France—and their traditional white horses, set off by the backdrop of the Arles amphitheater, would go a long way toward providing an adequate substitute for the Bellemont-Surrey piece.

If, that is, Maggie had the stomach to revisit the amphitheater again so soon after everything that had happened.

Maggie packed her knapsack with a notebook, a snack of nuts and raisins and a water bottle. Any other time she would have taken Jemmy with her. He was fascinated with the flamboyant *gardians* and would have loved to see them perform at the amphitheater.

But there was no way Maggie was ready to bring him back to the amphitheater. Not yet. Maybe not ever.

As it was, she knew that the fact that her newsletter-saving opportunity was happening in Arles was not lost on Laurent. When she'd told him last night where she was going, she also promised she would be home early to help with dinner.

Laurent had only nodded.

I don't know what's worse: arguing with him or seeing him give up on me.

Since the failed attempt to bring Luc to dinner two days ago Maggie hadn't mentioned him again, opting to believe that some time should probably elapse before she brought up the issue. She still felt that there was too much going on at Domaine St-Buvard to comfortably fit in a trouble teen.

But she had to admit to being surprised that Laurent wasn't pushing the issue. She could only assume it meant he had his own reservations about the boy.

Laurent had given what he was about to do considerable thought.

In his old life, having good instincts combined with judgment had been imperative. His very life often depended on it and his livelihood absolutely had.

He'd decided that *when* Luc decided to trust him was irrelevant to what Laurent knew he needed to do for the boy right now —find him a place to live long term. A social services facility equipped to handle troubled youths was an obvious answer and one that *Frère* Jean had mentioned the last time Laurent had spoken with him.

Laurent was very familiar with the benefits of the state's social services. While in the end he and Gerard had not been forced to go that route it had always been debatable whether or not it wouldn't have been preferable. His grandmother had done her best for them. But it had never even come close to being what he and his brother had really needed.

Jemmy was in the passenger's seat, his iPad in his hands.

"I told Louis I'd be there for lunch," Jemmy said with a frown as Laurent turned off the main village road onto Danielle's driveway.

"This won't take long," Laurent said.

"We're going to *Mamère's* old house?" Jemmy asked, suddenly more interested in what was happening than the electronic game he'd been playing. "What for? Is she going to sell it?"

Laurent glanced at his son. The boy always surprised him. That a ten-year-old would see the various ramifications of a situation as clearly as Jemmy usually did made Laurent proud. In fact nearly as proud as it also concerned him. He knew what it was like to grow up without a childhood. For all of Jemmy's electronic toys, the boy had the mind of an old soul.

Not always a good thing.

"A friend of mine is staying here," Laurent said. "I need to drop something off to him."

Laurent's decision to bring Jemmy to meet Luc seemed like a brainstorm. They were both basically good-natured boys—although they were both reacting with prickly stubbornness to their current situations. They were both smart and Laurent believed, in spite of Jemmy's recent rebelliousness, they both wanted to please the authority figures in their lives.

At least to an extent.

It was that grey area that Laurent would have to work with.

And since he had been much the same as a boy, it was an area he knew well.

He was only too aware of Maggie's concern about Luc's possible bad influence on the children, especially given Jemmy's recent insubordinate behavior. Putting the two boys together would give her the ammunition she'd need to insist Luc not come to the house again.

He would just have to risk it.

As he pulled down the driveway to Danielle's house, Laurent reached into the glove box and pulled out a small flip cellphone.

"Cool," Jemmy said. "That's vintage you know. Where did you get it? eBay?"

Laurent set the phone on the dashboard. He'd gotten it from one of his friends in the village. It was old but it worked. And Luc needed a way to contact him.

Jemmy was out of the car before Laurent brought the vehicle to a complete halt. By the time he parked the car and got out, Jemmy was standing frozen on the doorstep to the house.

"What is it?" Laurent called to him, his senses suddenly on full alert.

The front step was covered in broken glass.

39

The foyer was the worst.

Both sidelights had been broken. Brick pavers lying on the steps appeared to be the projectiles that had accomplished the damage. Two more bricks lay in broken pieces inside the stone foyer. Laurent stepped over the mess and made his way into the house.

The floor was strewn with debris, broken drywall and glass. The kitchen garbage bin had been emptied onto the dining room table.

This wasn't a home invasion. This was an act of hatred.

Danielle's wrought-iron mug holder was smashed into uselessness, its stoneware mugs now just shards on the counter where someone had taken a hammer to them, denting and gouging the soapstone counter in the process. The door to the salon hung half on its hinge.

"Whoa! Did your friend do this?" Jemmy asked as he stood in the kitchen doorway.

Laurent didn't answer. He stared at the smudges of mud streaking the flowered wallpaper in Danielle's salon—her sanctuary—and the Franklin stove with its door smashed off and lying on the rag rug in front.

"Why would he do this?" Jemmy asked, stepping into the salon.

Senseless destruction, Laurent thought, stunned by the extent of the damage. *Destruction purely for its own sake.*

Had he seen that tendency in Luc?

No, Laurent thought angrily. *He'd have had help with this. No way Luc would have done this on his own.*

Laurent cracked his knuckles and felt heat flush through his body.

But he had allowed it to happen.

Suddenly Laurent knew that whatever he'd thought he'd seen in Luc had only been wishful thinking.

The truth was in the smashed coffee mugs on the floor of the kitchen, the ripped and strewn books—the smell of urine in the once-cozy little salon.

The boy is wild and troubled. He is not a puppy needing a good home.

I was a fool to think differently.

"*Mamère* will be so sad when she sees this," Jemmy says.

Laurent turned to leave. He couldn't stand to look at it another moment or he might feel inclined to throw something through a window himself.

Jemmy followed him to the car where Laurent tossed the flip phone in the back seat. At that moment his own cellphone began to vibrate.

As Jemmy buckled his seatbelt, Laurent stared at the screen of his phone in momentary confusion before answering it.

"Yes?" he said into the phone in mounting fury and frustration.

~

As soon as Maggie saw the French *rasateurs* darting around the bulls inside the Arles arena, she was glad that she hadn't brought Jemmy.

The *rasateurs* were all young men—fit and full of themselves—dressed in form-fitting white trousers, T-shirts and sneakers, each primed and eager to execute the classic and dangerous *Course Camarguaise*. Maggie had seen it performed several times over the years and it always impressed.

Young bulls festooned with red rosettes on their horns were shown into the Arles arena one by one. The young men—some looked to be only boys—darted around the bulls, teasing and taunting them with the intent of snatching the little ribbons without getting gored.

Maggie looked up at the stands. There wasn't a single empty seat, testimony to how popular this event was in Provence. Even she had to admit it was one of the more exciting entertainment events in southern France.

Unless of course you are imagining your own son down there running around with the bulls.

The media and professional photographers had all taken the prime spots for getting the best shots—near the barriers in order to catch the *rasateurs* making their dramatic leaps to safety as needed.

The *gardians* had herded the agitated bulls into the arena through the narrow streets of Arles earlier in the day. Called the *abrivado*, this was an especially difficult task, one that required skilled horsemanship and while Maggie—who used to ride as a teenager back in Atlanta—would have loved to have seen that part of the show, the traffic getting into Arles today—not to mention the distance she had to park from the arena—had made that impossible.

As the young men in white darted among the bulls, Maggie spotted one of the *gardians* leaning against the viewing bar a few rows back from the arena. He looked to be in his fifties. There were fewer and fewer young people interested in becoming a *gardian*—a profession known for its high rate of injuries, exhausting work and low pay.

The cowboy smiled as Maggie approached. In her experience, these older *gardians* were happy to talk about their horses or the bulls.

And her newsletter readers loved it.

An hour later, Maggie had her photos and several interviews from three different *gardians*. She debated talking to the young *rasateurs* too but decided against it. Most of them were so wired at the moment they probably wouldn't even make sense.

Ready to call it a day, she worked her way down the long rows of the amphitheater toward the front entrance. Everyone else in the packed arena seemed happy to continue watching, bull after bull, at least until lunchtime. Just before Maggie slipped away, she caught Claude's eye where he stood with an attractive, petite blonde whom she assumed was his wife. He grinned broadly at Maggie and gave a thumbs-up signal which she returned.

Maggie's first inclination had been to head home immediately. From the distance she'd had to park—nearly a mile from the amphitheater—she wanted to beat the crowds in getting out of town, something that could easily devolve into a lengthy, nightmarish gridlock.

But as she poised at the top of the stairs outside the amphitheater her eye was caught by movement and she saw old Madame Duvall making her slow, laborious way to the base of the amphitheater, a bowl of cat kibble in one hand.

She could follow the old woman and ask her how she was getting inside! Excited to find out once and for all if there was another, secret way inside the amphitheater, Maggie turned to go walk after Madame Duvall when she noticed Jacques Duvall standing on the café terrace, his gaze solicitous and intent as he watched his mother.

And just past Jacques, Maggie was startled to see someone she recognized sitting at the first café table.

None other than Fiona Bellemont-Surrey.

40

Later Maggie would wonder what made her approach Fiona when the woman had done everything she could to present herself to Maggie as unapproachable and unfriendly. But at that moment as she walked toward her, all Maggie saw was a lonely woman in a café. And her heart reached out to her.

"Fiona?" Maggie said when she reached her table.

Fiona looked up, startled and for a moment she looked as if she couldn't place Maggie.

"I'm surprised to see you here," Maggie said. Arles was a good three-hour drive from Saint-Remy. "May I join you?"

"I'm not interested in being interviewed," Fiona said. But Maggie could tell the fire had gone out of her. She may not be interested in being interviewed, but she was very interested in having someone to talk to.

"Did you see the show in the arena?" Maggie asked.

"I've seen it many times. I only came for the *abrivado*."

"Was it amazing? I hated to miss it."

"It was. As always."

Maggie looked around the café's terrace. It was hard to believe Fiona Bellemont-Surrey was sitting here all by herself.

"I'm not with anyone," Fiona said.

Thomas the waiter raised his eyebrows at Maggie and she mimed a cup of coffee. He turned and disappeared inside.

"I've lived in Provence for more than twenty years," Fiona said, staring at her coffee cup. "Sometimes I can't believe it myself."

"That's a long time," Maggie said, not sure what else to say.

"I came over right after the divorce. Did you know that?" Fiona looked at Maggie.

That fact was something everyone knew. Fiona Bellemont-Surrey had been the original *Eat Pray Love* girl. Newly divorced and heartbroken she'd found a different kind of love when she moved to France. Not romantic love. She'd found Provence.

"I did read that," Maggie said. "And that's when you started writing all the books that set a generation on fire."

Fiona snorted. "Romantic nonsense."

Maggie frowned. The romance books that Fiona had written were set in Provence. The France that she evoked in her books could virtually make you taste the croissants and smell the lavender. *And* feel your heart beating faster for the one-true-love you would always discover in her books.

Thomas set Maggie's coffee cup down and discreetly withdrew.

"My daughter hated France," Fiona said. "She was ten when we came."

"I didn't know you had children."

"I'm not surprised. Claire is not eager to make the fact known. She was only with me briefly and then she...she chose to live with James, my ex-husband."

Ouch.

"Can you imagine loving someone *too* much? To the point of mental illness?" Fiona said.

Maggie didn't know what to say to that. She felt an uncomfortable tremor.

"I made a total dog's dinner of the only two relationships I cared about," Fiona said. "And I've spent my life rewriting my marriage in romance book after romance book."

No wonder she wasn't interested in a blog piece on her life story.

"In the end I think it was the fear that Claire would leave that ended up triggering it in reality. I held on too tightly. She said she couldn't breathe." Fiona snorted derisively. "James of course would *never* hold on too tightly. He allowed her every manner of liberty. The girl basically raised herself."

"How is she today?"

Bellemont-Surrey shook her head. "It doesn't make sense to me but she is a well-adjusted young woman. Happily married with two children. And close to her father."

Maggie felt a surge of pity for Fiona. To imagine that your child's happiness could be a source of pain for you was something she could not fathom.

"It was the only thing I wanted," Fiona said. "And I chased it away." She sniffed and pulled a tissue from her bag. "Well, James helped. He lost no opportunity to malign me to Claire. But I made it easy for him."

"I am so sorry."

"I came to the amphitheater with her when she was seven to see the *gardians* perform. Sometimes, when I see them now, I imagine she is just around the corner, out of sight. Or I think I hear her laughter. She did use to laugh. Even with me. Even in those days."

Maggie felt a sudden and immediate desire to race home and throw her arms around Jemmy, kiss him soundly and tell him to go play with an axe.

"So you can see my publisher is a complete moron," Fiona said briskly as if shaking herself out of her reverie. "My whole life has been a lie. Every story I ever wrote was a lie."

Fiona squinted at Maggie. "Have you ever read any of my books?"

"The first one," Maggie said, although she'd only skimmed it.

"Well, I've written eight and every single one of them is just a slightly different version of the first one. All the reviewers said so and they were right. I started out in France to make a new life for myself but all I've done is try to rewrite my life and rewrite the ending."

Maggie couldn't help but think, *How can you find love with someone new if you're constantly reframing the truth about your last one?*

Fiona laughed hollowly. "Love in the south of France. What a joke."

Fiona's valet Eugene materialized at the edge of the terrace and tapped his wristwatch. Fiona turned to Maggie.

"I'm sorry about the interview."

"That's okay," Maggie said. "But I really don't think you should give up on your daughter."

"Looking for a happy ending for me, Maggie? Trust me, not every story has one. *A bientôt, mon amie.*"

Maggie watched the older woman leave the café, her back straight and rigid under the Provençal sun. Maggie felt a rising surge of pity for her.

Even if she'd had permission to do it there was no way she could write any of Fiona's story.

Because there was no way to spin it into anything other than the singular tragedy it was.

After Fiona left Maggie sat quietly in the café for a few minutes before glancing at her watch. She'd promised Laurent she would be back in time to help with dinner.

She gathered up her purse and put four euros on the table for her coffee.

She glanced across the street noting how the sun played against the ancient stone wall of the amphitheater walls as it had done for centuries. Madame Duvall was nowhere to be found.

She must have come and gone and I didn't see.

As Maggie walked away, she stopped at the corner *of rue de la Bastille* and *rue de la Calade*. She glanced at her watch again although she knew only a few minutes had passed since the last time she'd looked.

She thought back to her coffee yesterday morning with Danielle and it was then that the elusive idea that had buzzed her brain so relentlessly for the last few days burst into her brain.

Of course!

Maggie pulled out her phone and typed in the search window *Église Saint-Julien*, the church that Barbeau had attended.

A known sex offender gets out of prison and is allowed to run a children's choir at the local church? What sense did that make?

Maggie watched her phone screen draw a map with a pin showing where the church was in relation to her location.

It wasn't far. If she hurried, she could get there, maybe find someone who'd known Barbeau, ask her questions and be on the road to Domaine St-Buvard before Laurent returned from his errands.

Her eyes on the phone map, Maggie turned to walk in the other direction.

The church façade was a forbidding stone front with a tall double door placed square in the middle. From her cellphone, Maggie saw the church had been built in 1119.

Catholic, austere and with the sounds of the Rhone near enough to hear its waves lapping at the famous stone bridge of lions, it was a forlorn little church. And yet even from where she sat on the stone bench facing it, Maggie could hear through the open doors the sound of children singing. Their voices lifted up, high and sweet, and drifted out to the small square where she sat.

A man sat smoking at the far end of her bench. His face was severe, his features pushed into a frown, his eyes focused on the church door.

Maggie bit her lip and glanced again at the time on her cellphone. If she waited much longer, Laurent would never believe another word from her. She could *not* be late tonight.

Noting her battery was low, she turned it off and tucked it away in her purse to conserve power and turned her attention to the people beginning to come out of the church.

"Papa!"

A little girl around Mila's age ran across the square to the bench where Maggie was sitting and for a moment she thought the girl was coming to her. But the child went to the man. He leaned over and gave her a kiss. His weather beaten and sunburned face was no longer stern but beaming.

What have I learned about judging on looks alone? Maggie scolded herself.

She turned to watch the other children emerge from the church. Most went to waiting parents who materialized around the little courtyard. Others stood waiting for their parents to come out of the church.

None of the children looked particularly traumatized.

Not that I would know what that looks like.

They laughed and teased each other like normal children—not like children who'd been in the grasp of a registered child molester for the last few years.

Maggie stood, ready to walk up to the first person who looked like they were in some kind of authority position in the church, when she saw Adelaide Barbeau walk out the church door.

She saw her at the exact moment that Adelaide saw her.

Adelaide's face hardened and she marched over to Maggie.

"What are you doing here?" she asked.

Adelaide was dressed in a skirt with low-heeled pumps. Her hair was combed and she had makeup on. She looked much more pulled together than even Maggie, who'd come dressed in jeans and a sweatshirt, the better to climb bleachers and run up and down stairs at the amphitheater to get the photographs she wanted.

"I need to know the truth," Maggie blurted out.

Something flinched in Adelaide's face and she stiffened. "No, you don't."

"I do. I'm literally losing my mind."

Adelaide looked away as the last of the children left the square with their parents.

"How did you know about our church?" Adelaide asked.

"Monsieur Drenot told me."

Adelaide snorted. "Is there anyone you *haven't* talked to? You're worse than the press."

The last of the laughing children faded from the square. Adelaide nodded in the direction that the children had gone.

"Doesn't make sense, does it? That he was allowed to work so closely with the children?"

"Why did the parents allow it?"

"Because they knew it was a lie," Adelaide said bitterly.

Was Adelaide seriously going to deny what a jury of Barbeau's peers, a competent prosecutor and at least one victim had affirmed?

"I can see where you might want to think the jury got it wrong," Maggie said gently, "or that maybe the DA was out to get him. But what about his victim? I wonder if the *victim* thought it was all a lie?"

"Actually, yes. I did."

41

"You were his victim?" Maggie said, her voice cracking.

"That's your word, not mine."

Maggie did a fast calculation in her head and her stomach began to buck. Jean Barbeau when to prison when he was seventeen. He and Adelaide were the same age.

"Jean was sixteen when he was arrested," said Adelaide watching Maggie put the pieces together, "And seventeen when he was sentenced. I was eight days shy of my fifteenth birthday."

Barbeau wasn't a child molester.

Maggie rubbed her forehead to temper the shock of what she'd just learned. Her skin tingled. She rubbed harder.

"You were *fourteen*?" Maggie asked, feeling the anguish of the woman seated next to her on the bench.

"At the time of Jean's arrest, yes. Consent in France is fifteen. I missed it by little over a week. But you see, the law is the law."

"Can you tell me how it happened?"

"As these things always happen. Someone hated seeing us together. Someone was in a position to make sure we were separated."

Maggie gave her a questioning look.

"My mother," Adelaide said. "She took me to a physician and had me examined to prove I was no longer intact. She accused Jean."

Maggie felt a jab of nausea at what the mother had done.

"And you were just days away from being legal?"

Adelaide stared out over the little square. The leaves from the surrounding plane trees drifted gently to the ground.

"What did you do when Jean went to prison?" Maggie asked.

Adelaide shrugged. "I ran away. I decided that dying on the streets was preferable to another evening under my mother's roof."

"Where is she now?"

"I don't know. Nor do I care. Father Remey here at the church took me off the streets and helped me. I lived with a family in the parish until Jean was released from prison. And then we married. As you can imagine, with the brand of sexual offender it was difficult for him to get work. Michel Drenot is a member of our parish and my foster father. He gave Jean a job."

Maggie looked at the church and realized how this place must have been such a sanctuary for Jean Barbeau. As she looked at the church, she saw what she had first thought was a small city park but could now see had a waist-high wrought iron fence around it. It was not a park but a churchyard. Through the fence she could see the tips of gravestones. A shovel leaned against the wrought iron gate.

There had been a recent burial.

"Most of the people here know the truth," Adelaide said as she gazed at the church. "So when Jean showed a gift for music, they thought nothing of letting him work with their children. It was only outsiders who didn't know the truth."

"I am so sorry."

"The police aren't interested in finding justice for my husband. They think the killer did them a favor."

"I know."

Adelaide turned to scrutinize Maggie. "Why do you care?"

"I have children. Sometimes I can't sleep at night for worrying about keeping them safe. I imagine every kind of fear and threat you can think of. But there are some things that help me sleep at night. Like trust in the police. Trust that they will not let someone get away with murder."

Adelaide nodded solemnly and the two of them sat quietly for several moments before Maggie stood up.

"I have to go," Maggie said. "But thank you for sharing Jean's story with me."

Adelaide continued to stare at the church and tears gathered in her eyes.

"Can I ask you," Maggie said, "Did your mother ever tell you *why* she did what she did?"

Adelaide's lip curled in revulsion at the mention of her mother.

"She said she was only trying to protect me."

42

As soon as she was on the A54 and pointed home, Maggie turned her phone back on and put a call in to Jean-Baptiste.

"Hello?" he said warily.

"You're not going to believe this," Maggie said. "But Jean Barbeau was not a child molester."

"Who is this?'

"Very amusing," Maggie said. "I didn't peg you for having a sense of humor."

"You do know this is Saturday, right?"

"I know crime doesn't take the weekend off, Detective."

Moreau laughed and then quickly sobered. "Okay, tell me fast because I am about to play a game of boules with my father and I need all my wits about me."

"I went by the church that Jean Barbeau was a member of—"

"Tell me you didn't."

"Don't worry, I didn't talk to anybody new. Adelaide Barbeau was there."

"You do remember that *she* is the one who made the formal complaint against you?"

"Would you please listen? Adelaide told me that Jean was arrested based on *her* relationship with him, not a child's. And she was only a week shy of being legal."

Jean-Baptiste blew out a long breath. "So technically it was illegal but he wasn't a child molester. Poor bastard."

"I know, right? So doesn't this put a new spin on things as far as you people are concerned?"

"What do you mean?"

"I mean, will the police pick up the case again?"

"Madame Dernier, no. Nothing has changed."

"But the truth—"

"Is irrelevant. Barbeau is still a convicted sex offender. The details don't matter."

"How can the details not matter?" Maggie said in frustration.

"Of course it is good to know he wasn't a pervert after all but the technicality of his so-called innocence would not carry any weight in my department."

There was a pause on the line as Maggie tried to get her thoughts together. She could hear laughter in the background from wherever Moreau was.

"So I guess it's back to being just you and me trying to get justice for Barbeau," Maggie said.

She heard the sigh on the line and a pause before he answered.

"I have to go now," he said. "I'll call you Monday unless you want to meet at church and pass notes across the pews?"

"Monday's good," she said.

After hanging up Maggie realized she felt better about some things and slightly worse about others. She felt better about charging full steam ahead to find justice for Jean Barbeau and closure for Adelaide, but worse thinking that whoever killed him didn't necessarily do it because they thought they were ridding the world of society's vermin.

The murderer now was possibly random and decidedly cold-blooded.

All of which made Maggie feel worse about the idea of letting Jemmy and Mila go out into the world without armed guards and a security detail.

Her phone rang and she saw it was Laurent. Her stomach tightened. She was later getting back than she'd said but it wasn't like him to call her because of that. Most likely he was out of some item and needed her to run by the market on her way home.

"Hey," she said, answering. "Everything okay there?"

"We are all home," Laurent answered. "How far away are you?"

"Maybe twenty minutes," she said. "Need me to stop somewhere?"

"No. See you when you get here."

He disconnected and Maggie frowned at the now silent phone.

Laurent never called just to see how close to home she was.

Barring a surprise birthday party—not likely since her birthday was in August—there was nothing she could think of that might account for the odd phone call.

She spent the rest of the drive trying to fit Jacky into the role of murderer and the reasons he might have for doing so. Even though Jean-Baptiste believed the CCTV footage put him in the clear, the fact remained that of all the people in her group that day, only he and Claude knew Jean Barbeau. And Jacky knew him first and best.

Plus whoever had followed her to the bar two days ago—the shadow she saw whisk past the doorway—could absolutely have been Jacky.

Or Claude.

Or Bastien the tour guide.

Or Brad.

She sighed.

Whoever it was, although she hadn't gotten a good look at him, she was sure that she'd seen him before.

By the time she pulled into her home driveway, Maggie had gone through her interchangeable suspects list of Claude, Jacky, and Brad at least three more times before deciding in frustration that she had nothing concrete on any of them.

The light was fading quickly as it did earlier and earlier at this time of year and she'd had to turn on her high beams for the last ten minutes of the drive.

Which was how she saw Laurent standing out in front of their house, smoking. Waiting for her.

Instantly her heart began to pound.

Her first thought was the children but she quickly rationalized that Laurent wouldn't be standing around smoking if one of the kids was in the hospital or dead.

She brought the car to an abrupt stop and swung open her car door. She watched Laurent toss his cigarette aside and walk toward her. She climbed out of the car.

"What is it?" she asked, swallowing her mounting fear. "What's happened?"

"I'm sorry, *chérie*," Laurent said as he slipped an arm around her waist. "It's your father."

43

That night passed in a whirlwind of activity scented by pan after pan of fried and baked food as people came in and out of Domaine St-Buvard. Because Maggie's parents had lived with them the year before, the village considered them honorary members of their community and reacted by bringing more food than any family could consume in a month.

Grace and Danielle were also there. Maggie blamed her focus on the amphitheater murder for why she'd hadn't seen their car in the driveway when she drove up.

Jemmy and Mila were sitting with Zouzou and both dogs in the living room in front of the fire that Laurent was keeping at roaring levels.

Laurent installed Maggie in his office with a glass of sherry and dialed her mother's number for her. Then he kissed her and closed the door.

Her mother was crying when Maggie called but she could hear her brother's deep bass tones in the background and was beyond grateful he was there for her. Ben almost always got it wrong whatever he tried to do in the way of family or emotion, but he'd loved his father and he was present when it counted.

The fact was none of them, no matter how much they'd known this night was coming, were really prepared.

"When is the funeral?" Maggie asked Ben when she got off the phone from her mother.

"Mom wants a memorial service," Ben said. "Dad wanted to be cremated so we'll have the service in about three weeks. That should give you plenty of time to get here."

"How's Nicole?"

"Frankly, she's doing better than she should be. She told me it was like Dad had been gone for months."

"I hope she didn't say that where Mom could hear," Maggie said.

What is the matter with that girl?

"Mom isn't hearing much of anything at the moment," Ben said. "I'm honestly not sure it's sunk in."

"How are you doing?" Maggie asked.

"I'm fine. So you'll be home in three weeks?"

"Just send me the details. And Ben?"

"Yes?"

"Stay close to Mom, okay?"

"Of course."

Maggie disconnected and sat at Laurent's desk. An antique globe sat on his desk next to a vintage corkscrew that Jean-Luc had given him one Christmas. She pushed past a stack of *Vintner* magazines and saw a framed photo partially hidden by the pile. It was a picture of Laurent and Jemmy with Maggie's father—three generations together—standing in Atlanta Memorial Park when they'd gone home one summer. Her eyes burned with unshed tears.

A small tap on the door made her look up and she saw that Jemmy was standing in the doorway.

"You okay, *Maman*?" he asked tentatively.

Not trusting her voice, Maggie smiled through her tears and nodded and he came into the room and put his arms around her.

"I miss, Grandpa," he said. "The *old* Grandpa."

Maggie knew what he meant. He missed the Grandpa who used to take him fishing and to the Coco-Cola Museum. He missed the Grandpa before Alzheimer's changed him into someone he didn't know.

"Me, too, sweetie," she murmured into his hair, a sharp stab of loss throbbing in her chest.

~

That evening felt endless for Maggie. She welcomed the moment when the children were finally in bed, Grace and Danielle and Zouzou had gone home, and it was just her and Laurent.

She went upstairs and washed her makeup off, brushed her teeth and put on her nightgown while Laurent let the dogs out one last time.

This is the night I lost my father.

She stared into the bathroom mirror and saw the sadness in her eyes before turning away to crawl into bed.

Laurent came into the bedroom and pulled off his sweater.

"You are all right, *chérie*?" he asked.

"I'm okay."

"I'll be there in a minute, yes?"

She nodded and picked up a novel from her bedside table but her mind wouldn't focus on the words. She listened to the sounds of water as Laurent took his shower. After a few minutes, he emerged, toweling his hair with rough movements before climbing into bed next to her. He pulled her to him.

"I'm sorry, *chérie*," he said.

Maggie knew he meant not just that she'd lost her dad today but also the breach between them.

"Me, too," she whispered.

They were silent for a moment as Laurent stroked her hair and kissed her forehead. When she felt his strong arms around her she felt as if he were literally lifting the pain and loss out of her heart by his support and love.

"I'm sorry about how I reacted over Luc," she said.

"Don't worry, *chérie*."

"I want you to bring him here."

"Perhaps."

"Seriously, Laurent. I should have trusted your instinct about him. I want to get to know him."

"*D'accord*," he said, kissing her. "*Je t'aime, chérie*."

"I love you too."

Even the silence seemed to surround her like a comforting blanket holding her separate from the pain hovering just outside the penumbra of love that Laurent had created.

"I remember the first time I met your father at Brimsley," Laurent said.

Brimsley was the Newberry family estate situated on two acres in the heart of Buckhead.

The one that had been sold the summer before.

"He said he was going to have to get all the doorways enlarged, remember?" Maggie said. Her father was not a tall man and he always enjoyed teasing Laurent about his height.

"Do you remember when he brought the stray dog home at Thanksgiving that one year?" Laurent said. "And how angry your mother was?"

Maggie laughed at the memory of the Lab mix—leaves tangled in its tail and mud on its coat—and her father's face beaming at having rescued him.

"He was forever doing that sort of thing," Maggie said. "All my friends had Jack Russells and Goldens. We had mutts."

"I think Jemmy gets it from your father," Laurent said.

"Gets what?"

"His love of orphans. He too is also bringing home strays."

Something about his words made a chord hum in Maggie's brain but she couldn't get it to form into a coherent thought.

It was true. Jemmy was a lot like his grandfather in so many ways.

She yawned and Laurent kissed her again.

"Can you sleep, *chérie*?"

"I think so."

Laurent snapped off the bedside light and held her. Maggie heard the thumping of his heart, strong and true as she lay against him. Just before she drifted off she realized that the *something* that had been humming around the perimeter of her weary brain was still there.

And still elusive.

Finally she gave herself up to the much needed healing oblivion of sleep.

44

Maggie spent a good part of the rest of the weekend on the phone with her mother while, in spite of all the food the villagers had brought, Laurent cooked nonstop. Both children alternately helped their father in the kitchen, or went for long walks with the dogs searching for kindling.

Maggie worked at her desk putting together a photo and video montage of her father for the memorial service the next month in Atlanta.

At lunch time Jemmy reported that Mila's goat was not in her pen and a fruitless search of the grounds ensued before it got dark and a tearful Mila went to bed. Laurent assured her the goat was likely fine and just off discovering clover in one of the far pastures.

Still, to Maggie it felt like compounded losses in a sad weekend.

The next morning, Maggie insisted on taking the kids to school so she could do some shopping and allow Laurent to do whatever it was he did all day—probably check in with Frère Jean or monitor the status of the mini-cottages he'd built.

Maggie knew Laurent paid his transient tenants to clean and paint the cottages before they left so they'd be ready for the next group of seasonal workers.

She also knew that for whatever reasons at least three people still lived in the cottages. Again she chided herself for not knowing more about what Laurent was doing.

Was Luc in one of the cottages?

From the brief glance she'd gotten of him, the boy hadn't looked old enough to live by himself and from the few things Laurent had said, not mature enough either.

She made a point to ask Laurent about it tonight.

After dropping the children off at school and promising them she would be the one to pick them up, Maggie parked at the underground parking at *Les Allées* and went up the escalator to the large outdoor square fronted by the famous Dolphin fountain.

She sat on a bench facing the fountain and remembered the first time her parents had visited her in France. It was Thanksgiving—right around this time of the year. They'd come with Nicole—just seven years old at the time—happy to be a part of the Newberry family and blessedly unaware of the murky situation surrounding her birth. With each passing year, Nicole thankfully became less and less able to remember all the terrible things—now more like dreams than real events—that she'd endured as a small child.

Maggie had brought her parents to Aix several times on that first visit and every time her father was drawn to the famous Rotunda fountain. During his college years he'd spent a summer in Aix and while he'd never bothered to learn the language, the Provençal university town had been an indelible experience for him.

Three statues representing Law, Agriculture and Fine Arts sculpted above the fountain were regally guarded by three pairs of bronze lions at the fountain's base.

My father was a young man when he lived here. He had his whole life ahead of him, all the dreams and hopes of youth. He probably sat right here on this bench in front of this fountain many times...

...and now his time was over.

Maggie wiped away a tear. She knew her dad would want her to remember how much he'd loved life and his family. He'd want her to remember how he'd come to Aix as a young man and come back again and again to enjoy it with his family, laughing at holiday feasts, shopping for friends back home, walking the leafy, broad promenade of the Cours Mirabeau—always happy to return.

After a few minutes, Maggie left the bench and walked the famed avenue herself. She picked out one of her favorite cafés—avoiding *Les Deux Garçons* and its rude waiters—and settled in for a pleasant hour of coffee and people watching. She debated calling her mother to tell her where she was, but Elspeth was in the thick of planning the upcoming memorial service and doing her best to stay as distracted as possible.

After a while, Maggie left the café and walked to *Bechards* across the street. The *patisserie* had been voted the best in France a few years earlier and while Laurent had recently decided its *canelés* were no better than the ones at *Jacob's* or even *Paul's*, Maggie still liked to stand in front of its expansive display case and marvel at all the colorful, mouthwatering delicacies.

She bought a sack of *chouquettes*—a snack time favorite of the children's. The fragile puffed-up bursts of egg and flour dotted with its trademark sugar pearl drops wouldn't last much past the moment when she picked the kids up from school, but they would be a nice treat on the drive home.

She also bought a *jambon* sandwich and a *chocolatine*. She found a bench on the Cours Mirabeau and ate her lunch, watching the leaves fall from the majestic plane trees and carpet the rough pavers of the famous promenade.

The market at *place Richelme* had just closed but Maggie

hadn't planned on shopping there anyway. Laurent would have that covered. Instead, she crossed the square to where the flower market was still open. She'd gotten there in time to buy an armful of blue hydrangeas—surely the last of the season—and spent a moment looking at the door to the apartment where her parents had lived the year before.

The experience had been a miserable one for them.

If only you'd come sooner, Maggie thought sadly as she walked past the lacquered blue door to the apartment building.

After that, she made her way down *rue Matheron* to a clothing shop she liked and bought two vintage Hermès silk scarves. One was for her mother because she was so much on her mind. And one was for Danielle who had been so helpful picking up the children and keeping Mila during what had evolved into a very hard month.

Maggie thought Danielle was happy. Or as happy as one might expect after losing Jean-Luc.

She thought of her own mother and wondered how life would change for her now that Maggie's father was gone. He'd been living in the memory care facility for nearly a year so, except for Elspeth's habit of her frequent visits there, it was likely she had already gotten used to being without him.

Maggie felt a spasm of sadness at the thought of her mother in the two-bedroom condo in Buckhead all alone except for a seventeen year old girl who did not want to be there.

Bootstraps, me girl, Maggie scolded herself. *Indulge in a little more retail therapy and then go forward. The problem of Nicole will just have to get in line with all the other problems that need solving right now.*

She went to two more shops after that and came away with a pretty silk night gown that was so light and flimsy she wouldn't be able to wear it for another six months at least now that the nights were cold—*unless Laurent talks me into it, he can be very persuasive*—and a pair of bronze candlesticks.

Weighed down with her purchases and feeling a little better, Maggie glanced at her watch to see she had just enough time to hit the local Monoprix before she needed to pick the children up outside the International School on *rue de Bouc Belair.*

She walked back through town, down the *rue Espariat* under the looming stone spire of the *Église du Saint-Esprit*, across the Cours Mirabeau and back to where she'd parked the car. She put her purchases in the trunk and laid the flowers on the back seat before turning and going up the escalator which opened directly into the largest Monoprix in the area.

While she wasn't sure exactly what Laurent had planned for meals this week, she knew he believed that food—and lots of it—was the key to soothing any hurt—especially grief.

She walked the wide, bright aisles of the grocery store and filled her cart with the basics: milk, juice, cheese, fresh pasta, butter, and yoghurt. She left the produce section of the megastore and added school supplies to her basket in the form of colorful spiral notepads, pens, erasures and bottles of ink—Laurent still liked to use fountain pens, bless him—and *cahiers*. She was looking at a packet of heavy-bottomed juice glasses—they were always getting broken at home—when she saw a face she recognized across the sundries aisle.

Brad Anderson stood staring at a selection of shaving cream, a wire basket on one arm and a frown on his face as if trying to make up his mind.

Maggie marched over to him.

"Someone said they saw you following Jemmy that day at the amphitheater," she said.

Brad stiffened and nearly dropped the aerosol can he'd picked up.

"What? No!"

"You're kind of hard to mistake, Brad. With the red beard and all. He said he saw you."

"Who did?" Sweat popped out on his forehead.

"Someone who has no reason to lie. Unlike you."

"I…I didn't lie!"

"You didn't tell the truth."

He ran a hand through his hair in exasperation and looked around the store as if looking for someone who might rescue him.

"Look, Maggie. It's true. I did see Jemmy down there. I told him to—"

"You *spoke* to him?" Maggie's mouth fell open. If this was true it meant Jemmy had lied. To the police. And worse, to his parents.

"Just briefly. He was peeing against a wall and I wanted to get rid of him since that looked like my only recourse too. I told him you were looking for him. But that was before I knew he was missing!"

"You weren't following him?"

"God, no! Why would I? I had no idea he was even down there."

"And you didn't see anyone else?"

"No. But if I'd told the cops about me and Jemmy's little pee talk, they'd have never let go of it. Especially with the murder victim being a child molester. You see that, right?"

Maggie stared at him and tried to process what he was saying.

Brad lied to the police.

And so did Jemmy.

What did any of it mean? Was Brad just in the wrong place at the wrong time?

"I'm sorry, Maggie. I know I handled this badly but I'm not used to being around kids and I'm still trying to impress Grace and I was almost positive taking a whiz against a wall wouldn't qualify."

Maggie turned and walked away, feeling less enlightened than she had before she'd spoken to him. With the news about Jemmy's lying, she certainly felt significantly less happy.

Fifteen minutes later as she was standing in line at the cash register her phone chimed and she looked to see she'd received a text from Brad. She glanced around the store to see if she could see him but he was nowhere in sight.

She opened up the text.

<Don't know if it's important but I did see someone. It's probably nothing.>

Maggie pulse sped up. *<WHO?>* she texted back.

She watched the dots form and blink repeatedly as he formulated his reply. Finally the text came through.

<An old woman with a cane>

45

Maggie was breathless with excitement as she hurriedly texted Brad back.

<*WHERE exactly*? R *U talking about INSIDE the amphith*??>

<*Yes. Inside. In one of the outer halls. Is important*?>

Maggie stared at his text response in stunned silence.

It didn't matter that the old woman was nowhere near where the murder happened. That was irrelevant.

What mattered was that she'd been inside the amphitheater.

Which meant that there *was* another way in the amphitheater other than the main stairs. And other than the entrances monitored by CCTV cameras.

And *that* just blew the doors wide open off the list of suspects.

As Maggie paid for her groceries and loaded them up into her car, she realized that the one person she'd never questioned—and neither had the police—about what she might have seen at the amphitheater that day was someone who not only watched the amphitheater all day long but had actually gone inside: *Jacques Duvall's mother.*

Maggie didn't for a second believe the old lady could've killed Barbeau.

But she might have seen who did.

And then a thought hit her, searing into her mind like a comet.

If Madame Duvall knew of a secret way in, wouldn't that mean her son Jacques did, too?

Maggie sat in her car in the parking garage tapping her fingers against the steering wheel and looked at her watch again.

She had to go to Arles and she couldn't do it with Jemmy and Mila. She didn't have time to take the kids home, find someone to watch them and then drive to Arles. With the late November light, it would be dark by then. Not to mention if Laurent was home she'd have no excuse for why she was going back out.

Knowing that the old *ask for forgiveness later* rule had always worked better for her in cases like these, she drove to the carpool line and tried to think of what to do.

She needed to go to Arles to talk to Madame Duvall. *Today*.

She couldn't do it tomorrow—half the village was coming to Domaine St-Buvard for a memorial wake and Maggie needed to be there. There was no way she could miss that. Not if she wanted to continue to be Mrs. Laurent Dernier. Laurent's patience was finite and where it bumped up against his limit was almost always when food and the villagers were involved.

He might be annoyed if she were late getting home today.

But he would apoplectic if she was gone tomorrow.

It has to be today.

She pulled into the carpool line and looked around for Grace or Danielle's car when her phone rang. It was Grace.

"Hey," Maggie said, answering. "Where are you?"

"Are you already in carpool?" Grace asked.

"I am."

"Danielle isn't feeling tip-top and I'm stuck here with the plumber. Can you collect Zouzou for me?"

In a flash, Maggie saw the prayed-for miracle fall into her lap.

"Absolutely. Can I leave Jem and Mila with you when I drop off Zouzou? I've got an errand to run."

"No problem. Mila can help Zouzou with the *gateau* she's making. You're a lifesaver, darling."

And so are you, Maggie thought as she disconnected and spotted Zouzou searching the carpool line for her mother's vehicle.

Laurent spent most of the morning cleaning up the damage at Danielle's house but the work only served to make him angrier.

By rights it should be Luc doing this.

Except Luc was clearly beyond any help that a little enforced housecleaning might provide to his character.

Consumed by his angry thoughts, the morning went by swiftly for Laurent. After he was satisfied he'd done all he could until the carpenters could come and repair the windows and the gouges in the woodwork, he drove to the village bar, *Le Canard*, in St-Buvard. The temperatures had been dropping steadily all morning and it was clear that winter had officially arrived.

Just a week from Thanksgiving, he thought, wondering how, with Maggie's father's passing and his own quandary about Luc there was all that much to be thankful for. He shook these pessimistic thoughts out of his mind as he parked and walked across the leaf-strewn courtyard to the bar terrace.

Frère Jean had gotten there ahead of him and sat waiting outside, bundled deep in his heavy wool pea coat, a steaming cup of coffee in front of him. The two men exchanged hurried greetings and Laurent signaled to the café's proprietor that he would have his usual.

A few moments later Laurent picked up his glass of *pastis* and eyed the monk as he sipped his espresso.

"Well?" Laurent said. "I didn't report the vandalism. So how did the boys get picked up?"

He'd heard from an early-morning phone call from Frère Jean that André Charpentier and Jabar Berger were sitting in the Aix lock-up with charges pending.

Luc was still on the run.

"Unrelated to the vandalism," Frère Jean said. "They were caught trying to steal a money bag from one of the chestnut sellers in Aix."

"Idiots."

"Unfortunately, yes."

"Had you ejected them from the monastery yet?"

Frère Jean sighed. "You were right about that. André's father never showed. I told him he needed to go. Jabar volunteered to go with him." The monk shrugged.

"Well, they certainly have a place now," Laurent said.

"And Luc?" Frère Jean asked.

"What about him?"

"Nobody has seen him. He wasn't with the other two."

"It's none of my business."

"He's just a boy."

"As André and Jabar are just boys."

"It's not the same. I think you know that."

"If Luc is so special why kick him out of the monastery?"

"I had to. He stole. The rules are clear. How can I keep order if I make an exception for Luc?"

Laurent drank his *pastis* and ordered another.

An hour later, after saying goodbye to the ex-monk, Laurent drove to the edge of his property and parked.

Over the years during times of trial or tribulation, he often found it helpful to walk his property. It reminded him of the things that remained, that mattered. In each of the four seasons with the land's varying and distinctive features, Laurent found strength and purpose. And today, succor.

The bitterness of his failure with Luc was tart and reverberated throughout his body. He'd been wrong about the boy. His instincts, usually so accurate—unfailingly so—had let him down.

Normally he would walk the vineyards by way of the back garden at *Domaine St-Buvard* but he intended to make a run to Aix later to pick up some rockfish so he left his car on the verge of the road and strode out into the interior of his acreage.

This part of what now belonged to him had once been a part of Jean-Luc's land. It had been in Jean-Luc's family for four generations.

Until one brother went to prison, one descendant to an insane asylum and the remaining brother died without bothering to have children.

Laurent's cellphone vibrated in his pocket and he pulled it out to see it was from Roger Bedard.

Three minutes later Laurent hung up and now stared unseeingly across the horizon. Roger's news was not really a surprise at this point. A part of Laurent had known. Maybe from the beginning.

As he walked he thought of Jean-Luc as he often did when he was out in the vineyards. This morning he remembered the man he'd loved but he also remembered the man Jean-Luc had been when he'd first met him.

Jean-Luc had betrayed him in a manner so brutal it had resulted in the destruction of two thirds of Laurent's vineyards.

A bit worse than a few smashed windows, Laurent thought.

He walked deeper into the vineyard. Divided into quadrants by two tractor roads that carved rutted tire tracks out of the dirt, the property was easily accessible by the necessary harvesting tractors that hauled out the loads of picked grapes each year.

One tractor road stretched a kilometer from the side of Laurent and Maggie's huge stone farmhouse and spanned the width of what had been Laurent's inherited vineyard, all the way to the ancient and crumbling stone wall that separated his land from what had once been Eduard Marceau's property. That was now his too.

Eduard and Jean-Luc had been close neighbors and confederates at the time. Both had stood shoulder to shoulder in their determination to drive Laurent away—even if it meant destroying his vineyard or hurting his wife.

One died bitter and unrepentant and the other became one of the dearest people in Laurent's life.

Suddenly, Laurent's ears caught the distinct whine of a wounded animal high on the cold breeze that whistled through the vines.

He froze and listened hard for the sound to repeat itself.

It came again. High and keening.

More bereft than wounded.

And not an animal.

46

The sound was coming from an old hand-dug well.

Created in the early eighteen hundreds, the well had been dry and useless for as long as Laurent had had the property. An annoyance more than anything, everyone knew the location of the well and the children knew better than anyone to stay clear of it.

As he moved swiftly toward the well and the source of the noise, Laurent's mind raced at the thought of who could be stupid enough to have fallen into it. He quickly corrected himself. The opening of the well was too narrow for anyone over the age of five to accidentally fall into. A person would have to deliberately lower himself into the space.

And what fool would do that?

He reached the well opening—just a crosshatch of two wooden planks on the ground—that were now pushed aside—and dropped to his knees. Immediately he heard the sound again. It was definitely an animal.

His first thought was Mila's missing goat. It was too dark to see but he could detect movement and hear the sound of water sloshing at the bottom.

"Help," a shaking voice called up to him.

"Stay there," Laurent commanded as he turned and walked with long strides to his car. Within moments he was back with a flashlight, rope and a rough wool blanket that he kept in his trunk.

Working wordlessly, Laurent made a knot in the rope and tossed one end of it down to Luc. Even from eight feet above him Laurent could hear the boy's teeth rattling with the cold.

"O-o-ok-k-k-kay," Luc stuttered when the rope was around his waist.

Laurent pulled him up, the frightened goat still in the boy's arms.

"I guess I was wrong about you," Laurent said as he jerked the rope off Luc and handed him the blanket. "I didn't think you'd be stupid enough to jump down an abandoned well to save a goat with no idea of how to get back up."

Luc sat with his arms around the goat, his shoulders shaking violently in the cold. His lips were blue and he was soaked to the bone.

Laurent tugged the blanket around the boy's shoulders. The goat was wet and filthy but as Laurent reached to pull it free from Luc's arms he hesitated.

He didn't know who was hanging on tighter, the goat or Luc, but clearly, they needed each other at the moment.

An hour later, the goat was dried off and sleeping soundly on one of the dog beds at Domaine St-Buvard and Luc was wearing a pair of Laurent's jeans with a worn sweatshirt—both oversized on him—after Laurent had tossed him into the shower. He sat now at the kitchen table at Domaine St-Buvard, his hand wrapped around a mug of steaming coffee, his hair wet from the shower, and his eyes dazed with disbelief.

The beating he'd taken from his incarceration last week had

faded to show only yellow and pale purple bruises on his cheek. But his right eye was swollen shut and his lip was split to indicate he'd been in another altercation since then.

"I couldn't stop them," Luc said softly. "I didn't know what to do."

"So you ran."

"I didn't know what to do. I...I..." He looked up at Laurent, agony stitched across his face.

"Say it."

Luc swallowed hard. "I'm sorry."

"That's a start."

Laurent spread mustard on one side of a sliced baguette and piled on a thick layer of cheese and ham before melting a knob of butter in a hot pan he had on the stove. Luc watched with fascination as Laurent slid the sandwich halves into the pan, the skillet sizzling as he did.

The dogs sat obediently, patiently at his feet waiting for scraps.

When Laurent slid the sandwich onto a plate and handed it to Luc, the boy never took his eyes off the food. He ate hungrily and then slowed and finished his meal self-consciously. Several times Laurent saw him turn to look at the little goat snoring peacefully on the bed.

"If I give you the goat, will you promise not to eat her?" Laurent said suddenly.

"Give...give me the...?" Luc looked at him as if Laurent had begun spouting Urdu.

"The goat. It belongs to my daughter but she is not old enough to be responsible for it. If you—"

"I promise I will take care of her!" Luc blurted, his eyes shining.

"You'd need to do it from my house," Laurent said. "Danielle's house is a mess now as you know."

A glimmer of shame invaded Luc's eye.

"You'll need to move in here," Laurent said.

"But, why do you want me? You already have a son."

Laurent couldn't help laughing.

"Well, it's true you can never have too many sons," Laurent said as if mulling the thought over. "But perhaps it's what *you* need that I think you should come to live here."

Luc had a core of decency in him that Gerard never did, Laurent realized. It wasn't just his sympathy or rapport for animals. There was something kindhearted about him. Even after everything he'd been through.

Luc looked at his empty sandwich plate.

"Why would you care what I need?"

"Because I once knew someone like you. Perhaps not as good with animals. But someone who needed more than he got. And died too soon as a result."

"What...what do I need to do for you?" Luc looked away, his eyes landing on the full pantry of food, the blazing fire in the hearth, the happy dogs dancing at Laurent's feet.

"First, I need you not to destroy my kitchen or throw a brick through my window."

"I didn't do that! But..." He looked down at his plate again. "But I let them in. So it's my fault."

Laurent realized Luc was trying to take responsibility without destroying his chance to live at Domaine St-Buvard.

"And," Laurent said. "I need you to respect my wife and get along with my children. Not just my dogs and the goat."

Luc looked at Laurent, his gaze sure and strong. "I can do that."

"I have work for you too," Laurent assured him. "Both my children have chores. I do not accept excuses unless there is bloodshed or trips to the emergency room involved."

"I can work hard."

"I remember that about you."

"I saw your son this summer," Luc said. "He looked smart."

"He is. But he is a kind boy. And I value that more than his brains."

"I understand."

"I know you do, Luc. I've noticed that you too are smart."

Tears jumped to Luc's eyes at Laurent's words. He was unused to praise.

"Can I really stay? I don't think your wife wants me here."

"My wife is a passionate, hard-headed woman," Laurent said, turning to submerge the now cooled pan into a sink of sudsy water. "She wants you. She just doesn't know it yet."

47

By the time Maggie had collected the kids and dropped them off at Grace's it was nearly five o'clock.

She texted Laurent to tell him the kids would have dinner at Grace's and then called Jean-Baptiste. His call went to voicemail but Maggie didn't leave a message. She turned off her phone. She knew this was getting to be a habit and she promised herself that as soon as she got some answers she would stop doing it.

Once she'd arrived in Arles she'd had to park even further away than usual. It gave her an uneasy feeling because it was already nearly dark and would be totally dark when she tried to make her way back to her car.

She kept to the main squares which were already bustling with diners. Even though most of the outdoor terraces were closed for the season, several of the *brasseries* and bistros had large plate-glass windows that looked onto the squares and sidewalks.

The failing afternoon light wove patterns through the gaps in the wicker-backed chairs and Maggie detected a faint fragrance of garlic and lemon in the air as the bistros prepared to satisfy their patrons with *paella*, *cassoulet* and *soupe de poisson.*

The weak winter sun disappeared behind a thick band of clouds, sending the temperatures plummeting. As she walked away from the busier intersections, she slowed her steps and then stopped.

The amphitheater was on her left. The Café Terrace was straight ahead.

And both were closed.

The sign on the café door read "*Closed for a death in the family.*"

An ominous tingle sidled up Maggie's spine.

Could it be the old lady?

Maggie stood with her back to the amphitheater. Of all the things she's anticipated, the possibility that the café across from the amphitheater might be closed was not one of them.

Frustrated, she turned away from the café to stare up at the forbidding artifice of the amphitheater. The creeping shadows of the coming evening made it look even more sinister.

With both the café and the arena closed, the street was deserted. Maggie could see from the foot of the wide stairs at the entrance of the amphitheater that the iron grill was already padlocked for the night.

But of course she knew now there was another way in.

She walked to the base of the stairs, hearing only the sounds of her own footfall and the distant burr of traffic on the other side of the arena.

Out of the corner of her eye Maggie saw a motion darting into the shadows and realized with a start that it was an animal. A cat.

They must be waiting for the old lady to feed them.

Maggie went to where she'd seen the flash of motion near the base of the stairs and moved closer to the wall, into the deep shadow cast by the amphitheater. The wall of the arena seemed to breathe as she touched it and she had to force herself not to snatch her hand away.

Was she looking for a hidden latch? A secret doorway?

She ran her hands over the rough stone of the wall but found nothing. She stood on tiptoe to see if there could be an egress where the side wall of the arena met the elevated stone walkway. But again, there was nothing.

She stood staring at the wall with her hands on her hips. What was she not seeing?

After a moment she turned to stare out onto the empty street behind her and felt an involuntary shiver as if she were being watched. The place had become deserted so quickly. That was clearly testimony to the popularity of the café but also because once the arena was closed to tourists there was no reason to be on this side of it.

A faint mewing sound made her turn and she saw a small black cat huddled by the wall, its eyes wide and cautious. When their eyes met, it dashed away into the darkness.

Feeling a shiver of excitement, Maggie dug out a flashlight from her jacket pocket and directed the beam back and forth around the base of the wall.

The light revealed a rusting grate at eyelevel no bigger than a paperback book, its bars spaced apart just wide enough to allow a cat inside. Maggie bent closer and shined her flashlight through the grate. She could see more stone on the inside which meant it was either an interior room or the wall of a hallway.

Suddenly her light beam picked out two plastic bowls on the stone floor inside, *proof that the old woman had indeed gotten in.*

Feeling a well of excitement building inside her, Maggie directed her flashlight beam at the wall around the grate. At first it looked to be no different from the first section she'd run her hands up and down but then she noticed there was a line between one section of stone that looked different from the others, like a seam or demarcation where there should have been grout or cement—but wasn't.

She stuck the flashlight in the waistband of her jeans and used both hands to push on the wall section beside the seam.

The wall panel gave way almost immediately. A creak of hinges accompanied the movement of the small panel of stone as it opened.

Maggie pushed the small stone door all the way open and pulled her flashlight back out to play the beam on the interior. She was looking at a narrow interior hallway.

She stepped through the door, careful not to close it behind her. Two cats sat watching her as she entered. By the light of her flashlight she saw several more plastic food bowls on the floor. All empty.

Madame Duvall must have taken ill before she'd had a chance to refill them, Maggie thought as she stepped past the cats, causing one to jump away. She moved silently away from the door.

What she was seeing looked much like the catacombs in Paris —without all the skulls and bones. Maggie shivered at the thought. This was a place of death, she reminded herself. Not just for poor Jean Barbeau but for all those gladiators and prisoners who'd been massacred here, torn apart by starving lions and bears.

At the thought of lions, Maggie glanced at a big tom cat who scrutinized her from an eye-level ledge. An image popped into her mind of his bigger, wilder counterpart prowling the interior of the arena, eager to devour some poor terrified soul.

Was this where Jemmy had been? He said he was following the cats. Ever since Maggie discovered that Barbeau wasn't a child molester she'd tried to take Jemmy out of the equation as any sort of reason for the man's death.

But something about that didn't gel.

Barbeau may not have been a child molester but it didn't mean Jemmy *wasn't* somehow a part of the puzzle.

It can't just be a coincidence that Jemmy happened to be in the amphitheater when the murder happened. Can it?

Coincidences connected to homicides were few and far between. In the past, every time Maggie had tried to attribute something to happenstance—*without exception*—she'd been wrong.

She shined her flashlight beam ahead in the narrow hall and moved forward, the sounds of her footsteps echoing in her ears as she walked. She felt a layer of sweat form on her palms and yet it was cold this deep inside the amphitheater.

Was her body trying to tell her something that her brain was too slow to register?

A small calico cat jumped in front of her and then turned away, its tail held high. Maggie followed it through an arched opening in the wall of the walkway.

Stepping through the archway, Maggie found herself in a small stone room with four more cats. They watched her with curiosity. It occurred to her as she scanned her beam around the room that there was no other way in or out of the room.

As Maggie watched the cats milling about, she tried yet again to capture the elusive idea that hovered at the edge of her mind.

And then it hit her.

What if it wasn't the *cats* being lured here with the food?

What if it was *a little boy* being lured here with the *cats*?

She thought about it for a moment and realized she *had* to put Jemmy back into the equation at least long enough to follow through with her theory.

And she hated doing that because she'd been so relieved the last two days by believing that with Barbeau no longer qualifying as a child molester it meant the murder had nothing to do with Jemmy.

It still might not, she reminded herself.

And then the thought that she hadn't wanted to face glared undeniably at her: Madame Duvall knew how to get into the amphitheater.

That meant her son Jacques knew too.

Had the police even bothered talking to Jacques? If they'd looked into his background, what would they have found? That he knew Jean Barbeau?

Maggie knew she needed to get in touch with Jean-Baptiste immediately. Only he could do the background check on Jacques Duvall that would show if he...

She heard a sound in the hallway.

Her heartbeat thundered in her ears as her brain tried to register if what she'd heard was connected to her own movements or the purring of the cats around her.

She was suddenly overwhelmed by the need to hide. She looked desperately around the room.

But there was nowhere.

She snapped off her flashlight and stood with her back to the wall. A light, dim at first but growing brighter by the second was coming from the hall and illuminating the entrance to the room.

And then suddenly, he was there, framed in the opening of the room where Maggie stood with her back pressed to the wall.

Maggie gasped when she saw him.

It was Thomas.

The waiter from the Café Terrace.

48

Thomas lifted the lantern in his hand.

For a moment, Maggie could only stare at him, her mouth open.

"Was I wrong about you, Madame? Had you not figured it out after all?"

"Thomas," Maggie said in shock, as one by one the puzzle pieces began to fall together in an ominous, stomach-clenching finality. "You killed Jean Barbeau."

Her skin felt clammy as she faced him in the gloom of the freezing cold room.

"I did the world a favor," Thomas said. "The bastard was preying on the little boy."

"No," Maggie said, swallowing hard, her mind racing. "He wasn't."

Thomas stared at her like he was trying to make up his mind. Then he smiled coldly.

"It doesn't really matter," he said.

"It was you, wasn't it? Who went after Jemmy?" Maggie said, not knowing how the idea had formed in her head, just knowing it was true. "How?"

Thomas shrugged. "When I knew he was going into the amphitheater, I knew the cats would interest him. All children love the cats. So I was ready."

Maggie's stomach lurched. She was seconds from vomiting onto the gravel and sand floor. Out of the corner of her eye, she saw the cats moving along the stone wall, the lantern transforming their shadows into elongated silhouettes.

Animals can tell the presence of evil.

"I watched him follow the cats into the second-tier hall. I knew he would have to walk past me to return to his group. So I waited."

"Jean Barbeau saw you, didn't he?" Maggie said.

Thomas snorted in derision. "The idiot yelled *What are you doing here*? I nearly jumped out of my skin."

Maggie saw in her mind's eye how it must have played out. Jemmy running after the cats, Barbeau confronting Thomas.

The struggle.

Thomas overpowering Jean Barbeau by strangling the life out of him.

"What choice did I have? The bastard saw me! What else could I do?"

"It must have thrilled you to think you could get away with his murder," Maggie said. "But you should know the police have a special loathing for people who prey on children. I'm told even the criminals you'll end up in prison with feel the same."

"I'm not worried," Thomas said as he set the lantern on the ground and pulled out a small handgun. "Because I am not going to prison."

Maggie's eyes were transfixed on the handgun. Unlike in the States guns were rare in Europe. To see one now, and pointed at her, filled her body with involuntary tremors.

How in the world did he get a gun?

"Oh, it's not mine," Thomas said, as if reading her thoughts. "It belongs to my boss, Jacques Duvall. It is an antique, belonging to his grandfather from the last war. Jacques reported it stolen a few weeks ago." He aimed the gun at Maggie's chest. "Once I kill you, I'll wipe it clean and leave it by your body." He shrugged. "The police will think it was a mugging. And since you've already established yourself as a pest with them..."

"By whom? Who told you that?"

He grinned. "You'd be surprised the things one overhears waiting tables. I heard it from both detectives."

Maggie's eyes darted to the lantern where it rested on the ground. Even if she were able to somehow get to it or knock it over, she'd still have to get past him and the doorway was too narrow. He'd easily be able to grab her even in pitch darkness if she tried to go out that way.

And there was no other way out.

"The fact that you broke into the amphitheater after hours," Thomas continued confidently, "will already place you in the category of *nuisance American tourist*. Most people will think you got what you deserved."

"I think you'll find the police will be a bit more interested in solving my murder than they were a child molester's," Maggie said bravely. "The American consulate will make sure of that."

A cat shot past Thomas and out of the room. Maggie felt a surge of desperate envy that it could escape so easily.

The waiter's body language was calm and loose, his weight on one hip as he leveled the gun at her chest.

"I'm not worried. I am the last person they would suspect."

When was her moment to act? Was there going to *be* a moment?

"If *I* figured out you were Barbeau's killer," Maggie said, forcing her voice to be steady, "the cops will too."

"Ah, but you *didn't* figure it out, did you?"

He was right. She'd thought *Jacques* was Barbeau's killer. The possibility that it might be Thomas hadn't even occurred to her. Not until she was looking down his gun barrel.

"But I would have eventually," Maggie said, her eyes glued to the end of his gun. "Once I knew there was a secret way into the amphitheater, I already started thinking of all the people who hadn't been on my radar before who might have killed Barbeau. People like Jacques and Bastien the tour guide and eventually I'd have come to you, too. So, I imagine at some point you followed Madame Duvall and that's how you discovered the secret door?"

"It wasn't hard," Thomas said with a shrug.

Maggie knew she couldn't dodge or run. If his gun held even a single round, he couldn't miss at this distance.

"So anyway," Maggie continued, wondering if stalling was going to help at all, "as soon as you look at all the people who might have known about the secret access and do a little digging into their background, well, it would be pretty easy to come up with a viable suspect. So tell me, Thomas, if someone were to dig into *your* background, would they find some interesting irregularities?"

Thomas's face clenched in anger and Maggie knew she'd struck a nerve.

"That's what I thought," she said. "There's no way you can go this long preying on children or whoever else you go after and not have had at least a complaint or two lodged against you over the years. Eventually, once I'd uncovered those you'd have jumped straight to the top of my prime suspect list."

"But unfortunately for you, you don't have *eventually*, do you? In fact, I believe you have no time at all."

As if to illustrate his point, he twisted the wrist on his free hand to mime looking at his watch.

It was the moment Maggie was looking for. It wasn't much. But it was all she was going to get.

Ducking, she snatched up a handful of sand at her feet and flung it into his face.

Thomas fired immediately. Maggie felt chips of rock fly against her cheek as the slug hit the ground.

"You die now!" Thomas screamed.

Desperately Maggie tried to grab for the lantern but only succeeded in pushing it further away as the ear-piercing explosion of another gunshot filled the small room accompanied by Thomas's cursing and screams of frustration.

Maggie scrambled to her knees, waiting for the next gunshot. Instead she heard Thomas's cursing ratchet up louder on top of the angry sounds of hissing and yowling cats.

When the gun dropped with a thud by her knee, at first Maggie just stared at it in the half-light.

Then frantically she scooped it up, feeling it hot and hard in her sweaty hand. Still on the ground, she pressed her back to the wall and looked up to see Thomas furiously batting the last screeching cat from his shoulders. His face was streaked with a track of blood down both cheeks from the cats' claws. His eyes were wild with insane fury.

He looked around on the ground.

For the gun.

And then he looked at Maggie.

She sat with her knees drawn up, her arms outstretched between them, and the gun held firmly with both hands.

Pointed at his crotch.

"Give it to me," Thomas said breathlessly, his hand outstretched. He moved toward her.

"Not another step," Maggie said hoarsely.

Thomas stopped and his hand dropped to his side. "You can't get out of here. I stand between you and the door."

"Not if you're lying on your back bleeding to death, you don't."

"You won't shoot me."

"Said every dead criminal ever."

Thomas smiled, his relaxed stance recovered in spite of the blood dripping from his chin. Maggie saw one of his ears was bleeding.

"I'm going to take it away from you," he said.

She tried to blot out his words. She fought to ignore the voice in her head that tried to rationally outline what was happening at this moment.

A flesh and blood living human being was standing in front of her.

The door to freedom beckoned beyond his shoulder.

She gripped the gun tighter in her sweaty hands.

Her arms began to tremble. And she knew he could see them shake.

"We need to do this now," Thomas said almost gently. "The gunshots might have been heard by someone. I can't take the risk they weren't. You can't kill me in cold blood. Just give me the gun or I'll take it from you."

If she told him to just go, could she trust he wouldn't wait in one of the darkened recesses ready to jump out at her?

Suddenly, in the midst of her terror Maggie saw a scene push to the fore of her panic, a scene that played out like a movie reel in her head, a scene that showed Jemmy, her sweet little boy, following the cats while this man was watching him, wanting him, ready to hurt him...

This man.

"You can't shoot me," Thomas said confidently, sneering now. "You don't have the nerve."

Maggie saw what he intended to do the second before he lunged at her.

She closed her eyes.

And pulled the trigger.

49

The moment after she pulled the trigger Maggie opened her eyes and saw the look of stark incredulity on Thomas's face as he clutched a blossoming, fountain of blood on his hip.

His words still echoed in the stone room and in her head.

"You can't shoot me. You don't have the nerve."

"Oh, sweetie," she whispered as Thomas sank to his knees. "I'm a mother. Nerve is all I have."

With the gun in her lap and Thomas gasping for breath on the ground beside her Maggie quickly turned her cellphone back on, in spite of the fact that the gunshot had robbed her of her ability to hear her own voice.

She forced her trembling fingers to text Laurent, Jean-Baptist and the Arles police before pulling off her jacket and pushing it against the wound in Thomas's hip.

After he lost consciousness, Maggie sat in the freezing room, the cats watching with twitching tails as she pushed on the wound and shook violently until she heard the police sirens and knew for a fact that it was all finally over.

Laurent made the sixty-minute drive from Domaine St-

Buvard in thirty minutes and arrived at the same time as the police and the ambulance. He rushed into the room and knelt by Maggie's side while the paramedics bundled Thomas up and took him away.

After that Laurent kept one arm firmly around Maggie throughout the long arduous questioning by the police, both at the amphitheater and later that night at police headquarters, before finally driving them both home a few hours after midnight.

If someone had told Maggie three weeks ago that everything would feel right with her world—even a world with her father no longer in it—and all she had to do was shoot a deranged waiter in the Arles amphitheater, she would have found it difficult to believe.

Now she sat with Danielle and Grace at the dining room table at Domaine St-Buvard, a mug of coffee in her hands and a plate of Danielle's *macarons* before her.

Through the French doors she watched Laurent, Luc and Jemmy standing at the end of the garden as they worked to repair a climbing rose arbor. Laughter drifted down from upstairs where Mila and Zouzou were looking through cooking magazines together.

"Are you sure you're okay, *chérie*?" Danielle asked.

Maggie tore her eyes from the sight of the three figures in the garden and looked at Danielle in surprise.

"What do you mean? The shooting was two weeks ago."

Grace reached for a cookie and gestured to the window. "I think she's referring to Luc moving in with you. God knows we're used to you blasting bad guys with guns at close range."

"Very funny," Maggie said.

"I'll bet Laurent blew a gasket, though," Grace said. "Didn't he?"

"He was just glad I was in one piece."

"Seems to me you depend on that reaction from him a lot," Grace said.

Maggie glanced out of the window. She saw Laurent pointing at something in the garden and then clap a hand on Luc's shoulder.

She still cringed when she remembered how unwelcoming she'd initially been to Luc.

But from the moment she knew who'd really killed Jean Barbeau *and why*, she'd felt a blanket of peace descend on her.

Suddenly all the wisdom that Danielle and even her mother had been trying to hammer into her through all the preceding days and weeks made sense.

Like an indelible message written in the stars, Maggie finally knew *in her bones* that no matter what she did, what provisions she made, what backup plans she concocted, she couldn't count on keeping Jemmy and Mila safe. She couldn't control what may or may not happen to them.

Or herself for that matter—as was pretty effectively illustrated by her confrontation with a child-molesting maniacal French waiter pointing an antique derringer at her in the Arles amphitheater.

But what she *could* control was her ability to accept what she could and couldn't control.

That, and her willingness to reach out to someone—like Luc—who needed her, *that* she could do. *That* she could in fact not fail to do.

Her phone chimed and she saw it was Jean-Baptiste.

"I need to take this," she told Grace and Danielle. "Don't eat all the *macarons*. I'll be back in a second."

Grabbing her jacket from the foyer peg, she hurried out the front door and accepted the call.

"Hey. What news do you have?" she said into the phone.

"*Bonjour*, Maggie. I will never get used to how you completely eliminate any social greeting or preface."

"It's the American in me. So? Did we get our confession?"

"I wish you would stop referring to it as *our confession*," Jean-Baptiste said, but Maggie could hear the smile in his voice. The fact that she'd called him so that he could be there the night it all went down had done a lot for his reputation and career.

"But yes, we did get it," he said. "Thomas was recalcitrant at first but after we'd re-interviewed Jacques Duvall and his mother and asked more pertinent questions, the café owner said he remembered seeing Thomas leave the café and go in the direction of the arena. At the time Jacques thought it was to take a smoke break. Then he remembered that Thomas doesn't smoke. Once Thomas knew it was hopeless he confessed. By the way the surgeons are confident he will make a full recovery."

"I'm relieved," Maggie said. She'd already found out that Jacques Duvall's mother was not the death in the family that the sign was referring to that night. It was a distant cousin.

"And Adelaide Barbeau? Did you talk to her?" she asked.

"Madame Barbeau has been informed that we have a suspect in custody for her husband's murder. I told her I would keep her informed so that she might be there at the trial."

"That had to make you feel good."

"You Americans say the oddest things."

"We make a good team, Jean-Baptiste."

"On our one and final joint effort."

"You never know, *mon ami*," Maggie said and laughed at the Gallic snort on the other end of the line.

When Maggie rejoined Danielle and Grace at the table, she could see through the window that both Jemmy and Luc were lifting a detached side of the lattice and attempting to position it in the ground where Laurent was directing them.

For the first time, it occurred to Maggie that adding another member of the family could actually serve as extra protection for all of them.

After all, isn't that partially what families are for? she thought as she watched. *To look out for one other?*

"Zouzou's already developed a crush on him," Grace said.

"Mila and Jemmy like him a lot, too," Maggie said. "And he works like a demon to please Laurent."

"Do you know anything about his past?" Danielle asked.

"A little. And more and more as the days go by." She turned to Danielle and put her hand on Danielle's hand. "Don't worry, Danielle. I trust Laurent's judgment. And I can tell he's a good kid." Then Maggie turned to Grace. "And speaking of Laurent's judgment, is it officially off between you and Brad?"

Grace shrugged. "It's for the best."

"As long as it was *you* who decided that," Maggie said, raising an eyebrow. "And not because you thought Laurent didn't like him. Because nobody gets to live your life but you, Grace."

"You are speaking in riddles, darling. Of course the decision was mine."

"Something a wise woman once taught me, although she never learned it for herself," Maggie said, is that we can't start the next chapter of our lives if we keep rereading the last one."

Grace looked at Maggie with surprise.

"Well, it's possible you might be onto something there," Grace said, smiling sadly.

"When are you leaving for Atlanta, *chérie*?" Danielle asked brightly, clearly ready to lighten the mood.

"We fly out in two days. I've been trying not to think of it. Thanks for taking Luc and the dogs while we're gone. I hope Luc doesn't feel like we're excluding him. Laurent thought it was too soon to bring him."

"I am sure he is glad just to have a roof over his head," Danielle said. "The boy was homeless, yes?"

"He was," Maggie said. "He lost his parents last year and was basically living on the streets since then."

"It is a wonderful thing what you are doing, *chérie*," Danielle said solemnly. "I heard he is wild but if there is anyone who can tame him it is Laurent."

"That's for sure," Maggie said. As she watched Luc outside she realized that while there was no way that Luc's coming into the family could ever replace her father, there was a sort of symmetry in the boy coming to live with them when he had.

"So, see, darling?" Grace said with a laugh. "You didn't lose Jemmy, you gained a full-blown teenager! If you need any advice, let me know. I'll see if I can find someone who knows something about them."

"You underrate yourself, Grace," Danielle said. "Zouzou is a wonderful girl."

"No thanks to me," Grace said with a shrug. "But in any event, girls are different from boys. I wouldn't have a clue as to what teenage boys need."

"I'm counting on Laurent to take the lead on that," Maggie said.

"I must admit he indeed looks like he is a hard worker," Danielle said and all three women looked out the window at Laurent and the boys in the garden.

"Funny," Grace said as she watched them. "Have you noticed? Luc looks enough like Jemmy to be his brother."

50

Jemmy helped Laurent in the kitchen with dinner that night while Luc and Mila groomed the goat.

Maggie was working on a project to help feed the amphitheater cats. At Jemmy's urging, she had created a Kickstarter campaign and was able to reach out with her newsletter to find donors.

Just in the last two weeks, she'd contacted a series of veterinarians in Arles who agreed to routinely round up the cats in order to give them shots and neuter them.

Laurent had weighed in with his opinion that the effort was a waste of time.

"Always there will be stray cats in France," he said.

Maggie knew Laurent was probably right. But that didn't mean the amphitheater cats had to go hungry. Or not enjoy the benefits of a flea and tick shampoo now and then.

Especially when she knew without a doubt that she wouldn't be alive today if not for them.

She stood now in the doorway between her office and the living room watching Mila and Luc brush the goat. Mila had readily accepted Luc into the family—as if he'd always been with them. Jemmy was much the same. It was only Luc who couldn't seem to believe his luck—or that all of this wouldn't be snatched away from him at any moment.

But it was early days. He'd relax in time.

"Mila, set the table," Laurent called from the kitchen. "Luc, have the dogs eaten? And put the goat outside where it belongs."

Mila jumped up and ran into the dining room while Luc carried the little goat outside. When he came back he rubbed his hands against his jeans as though he didn't know what to do with them.

He needn't worry that Laurent won't keep him busy, Maggie thought wryly. She went to him.

"Come sit with me, Luc," she said.

He looked at her like she'd asked him to strip naked.

Maggie sat on the couch facing the fire and patted the spot next to her. Luc sat down gingerly.

He looked remarkably less ragged than the first time she'd seen him. He was wearing new jeans and a sweatshirt and his hair had been trimmed. He fidgeted on the couch and stared at his hands which Maggie noted could use another scrubbing.

"I never thanked you for rescuing the goat," Maggie said. "So much happened that day that it all got lost in the shuffle."

A flush crept across Luc's cheeks. "It was nothing."

"Well, I know Mila was grateful and I know she's relieved to hand over ownership to you too."

Luc nodded. "She told me."

"Good."

They were quiet for a moment with only the sounds of Laurent and Jemmy clanging pots and pans in the kitchen, and the sound of Mila humming as she laid out the place settings in the dining room.

"I also meant to apologize to you for being so rude when you first came here," Maggie said.

He blushed darkly and clearly didn't know what to say.

"I know you and I haven't talked much since you came—"

"You have been very busy, Madame Dernier."

Yes, she had been very busy. Busy sorting out the fallout from being attacked in the amphitheater, busy forcing the police to reopen the Barbeau murder case, and busy working with Jean-Baptiste to make sure the case against Thomas Dubbet was as airtight as possible.

And there was still a newsletter to get out and preparations for a transatlantic trip.

And a final goodbye to say to a beloved father.

"I just want you to know, Luc," Maggie said reaching out to touch him and then stopping herself, thinking it might send him running for the hills, "that I'm really glad you're here. Okay?"

Luc stared at his hands and nodded. His neck was crimson.

"Laurent believes you are very special and now that I've gotten to know you a little, I see what he means."

Luc looked at her, an incredulous look on his face.

Maggie nearly laughed at his expression but she checked herself. This time she did reach over and pat his hand.

"So," she said brightly, "good talk!"

Released, Luc leapt up and hurried into the dining room where Maggie heard him ask Mila where they kept the dog food.

That night after the dogs had been out, the door locks all checked, all three children in their beds if not asleep, and Maggie in her nightgown, Laurent sat down on the bed to wind the mantle clock he kept over the fireplace in the bedroom.

Maggie watched him as she had so many times over the years.

Finally he turned to look over at her.

"*Ça va, chérie*?" he asked with a slight smile.

"When did you first suspect Luc was Gerard's son?"

Laurent put the clock back on the mantel. He pulled his sweater off over his head and got into bed beside her.

This time he didn't ask her to turn the light off.

"When did you guess?" he asked.

"When Grace pointed out to me today how much he looks like Jemmy. The dark hair, the blue eyes, the aquiline nose. My question is when did *you* know?"

"Not as soon as you might think. In fact I got the news from Roger about five seconds before I was pulling Luc out of the well in the north field."

"Roger Bedard?"

Laurent nodded. "I'd emailed him the day before to see what kind of information he could find on Luc's parents or the accident that killed them in Dijon."

"I thought you said Luc came from Alsace."

"No, that's what *Luc* said. Maybe he had been in Alsace at some point but that's not where he'd been living with his mother and stepfather at the time of the accident."

"How do you know he's Gerard's?" Maggie repeated.

"I don't, definitively," Laurent replied reaching out to pull her in close. "But everything fits. I don't need a DNA test to know."

"Tell me what you learned."

Laurent ran a hand across his face. Maggie knew he was tired. It had been a long day for him. He'd met with a new batch of potential workers for next year's harvest—all transients—and spent the morning at the monastery working on more housing options with *Frère* Jean. Maggie and Laurent had rendezvoused in Aix later that afternoon for a conference with Jemmy's teacher where they agreed that Jemmy would be advanced beyond his grade next year.

Maggie still wasn't entirely comfortable about the decision but she knew she couldn't hold Jemmy back. Not even if it meant he grew up a little faster and stepped away from her a little sooner.

"Even last summer I knew there was something about him that reminded me of Gerard," Laurent said. "I thought it was because they were both hoodlums. It didn't occur to me Luc might actually be related to him."

"Until it did occur to you."

Laurent sighed. "*Frère* Jean mentioned something in passing a few weeks ago. I thought little of it at the time—"

"What was it?"

"He said Luc's mother's name was Arielle. It is an unusual name."

"It's pretty."

"Gerard was seeing a woman in Dijon by that name."

"Wasn't he married to my sister at the time?"

"He was."

"So you put together the unusual name with the fact that Luc's mother died in Dijon with the fact that Luc sort of reminded you of Gerard and came up with a theory?"

He shrugged. "I cannot tell you how many times I doubted my own mind," he said, and then patted her bottom affectionately. "*This is madness*, I told myself. *I sound just like Maggie.*"

"Ha ha, very funny. And so you got Roger to double check the facts?"

"I did. The woman who died in the accident, Arielle Thayer, had a young son before she married Jean Thayer. Arielle *was* the woman Gerard had been involved with."

Luc is Gerard's son.

Maggie let the words simmer unspoken in the air between them. While Gerard was not guilty of murdering Maggie's sister Elise, he'd definitely contributed to her death.

And yet.

He was also Laurent's younger brother. Maggie knew Laurent had never made peace with the life that Gerard had led, the pain he'd put Maggie's family through, nor in the end the gruesome death Gerard had suffered.

"When will you tell Luc?" she asked.

Laurent had obviously given the question some thought because he answered immediately.

"When he knows without doubt that I would have taken him in even if we weren't blood related."

"You're a good man, Laurent Dernier," Maggie said and kissed him.

"And you, *chérie*, are more trouble than any man should ever expect to handle in a lifetime." He kissed her deeply and brushed the hair from her eyes. "But I am of course grateful beyond measure every day for you."

"And me, too, you big lug," Maggie said, returning his kiss and sinking into his embrace.

Just before sleep claimed her the realization came to Maggie that all the surprises life tended to dole out—the good and the bad—somehow only served to show her how truly and completely blessed her life was.

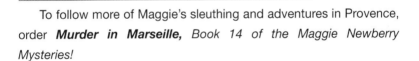

To follow more of Maggie's sleuthing and adventures in Provence, order ***Murder in Marseille,*** *Book 14 of the Maggie Newberry Mysteries!*

RECIPE FOR LAURENT'S PAELLA

Laurent's Paella

Laurent makes *paella Carmarguaise*, distinctive for its use of rice grown in the Camargue, the Rhône delta just south of Arles. But you can substitute any medium-grain rice.

You'll need:

1 large chicken breast, skinned and boned
6 oz Chorizo sausage, cut into ½ inch slices
1 lb. medium prawns (shrimp) peeled
1 cup squid, cut into bitesize rings (optional)
12 ounces Monkfish fillet cut into bitesize pieces
12 fresh mussels
1 large onion coarsely chopped
1 red pepper, cut into ½ inch dice
3 cloves garlic, minced
1 14-oz can diced tomatoes
12 threads saffron
1 tsp paprika
½ tsp ground coriander

1 tsp fresh thyme minced
salt and black pepper
1 cup dry white wine
4 or 5 cups of chicken broth
2 cups of rice
2 cups baby green peas
3 TB capers
½ cup fresh pitted olives, black or green
1 bunch of parsley
2 lemons cut in quarters lengthwise
Extra virgin olive oil

1. Cook mussels in a little water in a covered pot until they open. (Discard any that don't open.) Set mussels aside.

2. Cut chicken into bite-sized pieces. With 2 TB olive oil in a paella pan or any deep sauté pan, sauté the chicken until done. Set aside on plate.

3. Add chorizo to the pan and sauté for several minutes until done. Set aside with chicken.

4. Add 2 TB olive oil and sauté onions, pepper and garlic until tender. Add the tomatoes, seasonings, white wine, and 4 cups chicken broth.

5. Bring the liquid to a simmer. Add the rice and stir in paprika, coriander, thyme and saffron. Push rice under the liquid and simmer without stirring for 10 minutes. Add prawns, squid, fish and peas, pushing the ingredients under the unabsorbed liquid.

6. Simmer all for another 10 minutes or until rice is tender. If the rice seems too dry, add a small amount of warm broth to keep paella somewhat juicy.

7. Stir in chicken, mussels and chorizo.

8. Remove from heat and sprinkle with capers and olives. Garnish with parsley and lemon wedges.

ABOUT THE AUTHOR

USA TODAY Bestselling Author Susan Kiernan-Lewis is the author of *The Maggie Newberry Mysteries,* the post-apocalyptic thriller series *The Irish End Games, The Mia Kazmaroff Mysteries, The Stranded in Provence Mysteries,* and *An American in Paris Mysteries.* If you enjoyed *Murder in Arles,* please leave a review saying so on your purchase site.

Visit my website at www.susankiernanlewis.com or follow me at Author Susan Kiernan-Lewis on Facebook.

Made in the USA
Middletown, DE
09 January 2022

58278761R00163